Heartbeat Harmony

ALEXA ASTON

OLIVER-HEBER BOOKS

Prologue

Autumn Sutherland reached into her pocket and popped a few peanut M&Ms into her mouth. It seemed she lived on them, especially since she had just finished working another double shift at the hospital. Well, chocolate was supposed to be good for your health, as well as your soul. The peanuts were simply an added bonus.

She pushed open the door to the restroom and went inside, not recalling the last time she'd had a chance to empty her bladder. Or eat a real meal. Or even talk with her husband.

Flint told her it would all be worth it. He was in his second year of residency and had three more to go in his program. Sometimes, though, Autumn didn't know if she could keep up the pace she'd maintained for several years. They had married after graduation, just before Flint's first year in medical school. She was madly in love and found it hard to believe someone as handsome and charming as Flint Ferris loved her in return. Med school ate up two things, however. Money and time. Flint didn't want to have massive

1

debt when he finished his residency, so most of Autumn's nursing salary had gone to pay for med school. That meant using what little was left over to live in a cramped apartment in the sketchy neighborhood surrounding the hospital. Driving a shared car that was eleven years old. Living like college students, subsisting on ramen noodles and energy bars.

She could do all that. After all, it was an investment in their future. It was the time she didn't have with Flint that was finally adding up. Now that he was a resident and earned a fairly decent salary, she had become a charge nurse for a short while. It was more money. More responsibility. And she thrived at it. Charge nurses, though, weren't allowed to pull doubles at this particular hospital. Flint had finally asked Autumn to leave her new position and go back to regular staff nurse work so that she could work some double shifts each week, telling her now that they had finished paying off his med school loans, it was time to build their nest egg, putting away savings for a house. As usual, she did whatever Flint wanted.

And now she found she was resentful.

Med school was behind him. So were the hellacious intern years. He was a respected resident, on track to complete his residency in general surgery. His hours were still long, but if she weren't working so much, they could actually spend some time together. She couldn't recall the last time they'd gone to a movie, much less watched one on streaming. They didn't eat out because Flint said it was too expensive, and they needed to save their money for a house.

The only time he had made an effort to be with her was two weeks ago, when her brother's team had played in the Super Bowl in New Orleans. West was a star player for the Dallas Cowboys and had wanted his family at the game. Even at that, Flint barely talked to her, spending most of his time on his phone, ignoring both her and her family.

At this point, she would call them little more than roommates. They were ships passing in the night, never sharing a meal or even a conversation.

Autumn was trusting. Patient. Always putting everyone ahead of herself. This time, though, *she* needed to be first. With Flint. With herself. He should be home when she got there, getting ready to report to the hospital. They would have maybe a forty-minute overlap, more if she walked home faster.

She intended to say a lot in those forty minutes. She would tell Flint she was going back to a charge nurse position. That would be easy to arrange since nurses were quitting left and right. Autumn had a proven track record. She would also ask Flint—no, demand—that they *do* something together. Even if it were just ordering takeout and watching something on TV. Though most of her days were filled with work, she still felt the gnawing pain of loneliness. She wanted her husband's company and didn't think that was too much to ask.

Most importantly, she wanted to schedule a time to make love. Flint would balk at that. He hated being told what to do and when to do it. The fact that he'd gotten this far in his residency with only being disciplined twice surprised her. But she wanted more of her husband than she was getting. It might be pushing the conversation, with the limited time they would have, to talk about a baby. Flint had put her off about that, saying she couldn't be a great nurse and a great mother because she was working so many hours. If she went back to being a charge nurse, though, she could get pregnant. The hospital had a wonderful daycare facility for employees. It would allow her to pop in and see their baby during her brief breaks.

Determination filled her as she washed her hands and then splashed water on her face. Looking into the mirror, the reflection showed a pretty but tired woman of twenty-nine looking back at her. It was time to get some sleep. Have sex with her husband. Get pregnant. Have a true marriage.

She went to the locker room and claimed her purse and raincoat. It had been raining when she'd left the apartment yesterday. She'd walked the six blocks in the rain, arriving drenched. Flint had taken the car, and she never knew whether he had it or if he had left it because it wouldn't start. The sedan needed a new transmission, but those were pricey. Maybe she'd work a few more doubles this month in order to pay for it. Or just trade it in. But that would mean a car payment.

Feeling overwhelmed, Autumn decided to think about it tomorrow.

Gathering the still damp clothes from her locker, she shoved them into a backpack and slung it over her shoulder, deciding it would be better to simply wear her scrubs home. She also grabbed a pack of peanut butter crackers from her stash and opened them, eating them as she rode the elevator downstairs.

She emerged from the employees' entrance to a quiet morning. It was just after seven.

"Autumn!"

Turning, she saw Jeannie Barlett had pulled up to the curb. "Hey, Jeannie."

"Want a lift?"

Relief swept through her. "You're a lifesaver."

She got into the car. Jeannie had given her a ride home before, so she didn't bother with directions.

"I heard Gloria is leaving at the end of the week."

"Seriously? I was thinking about talking to HR about a charge nurse position. If she's leaving, that would be perfect timing for me."

Jeannie smiled. "Well, go for it. You're the best charge nurse I've ever seen. You know how to calm people. Patients, as well as staff. You're fair when creating a schedule. And you stay on top of things. HR would be happy to have you back in that role." Jeannie paused. "What does Dr. Ferris say about it?"

"I'm going to tell Dr. Ferris about the opening when I get home. We overlap for less than an hour this morning. It'll be the first time I'll have seen him in three days."

Her friend's mouth tightened. "I hope he'll let you do it," Jeannie said quietly.

"*Let* me? I make my own decisions," she defended. "Yes, I run them by Flint, but—"

"You're coming off another double, Autumn. You look really tired. It's not as if your husband is in med school anymore. He's pulling a decent salary as a resident, and yet you work yourself to the bone."

"We're saving for a house," she said abruptly. Then regretting her tone, she sighed. "I'm sorry. I sound ungrateful. Here you are, giving me a ride, and I'm spoiling for a fight."

"I just don't want you to be taken advantage of," Jeannie said. "You're a terrific nurse. A wonderful person. Dr. Ferris needs to realize what a gem he has in you."

They reached her apartment complex, and Jeannie turned in, winding around to her building near the rear. She stopped the car.

"Thanks for the ride." Autumn leaned over and hugged her friend.

She got out and hurried up the stairs. With Jeannie

giving her a ride, that had saved a good half-hour. Anticipation filled her. Maybe she and Flint could even sit and have a quick breakfast together as they talked.

Unlocking the door, she slipped off her backpack, setting it on the rickety coffee table before unzipping it and removing her clothes. She heard the shower going as she went to the kitchen, draping her clothes over a chair. She couldn't wait for the day she had a washer and dryer instead of schlepping her laundry to a Laundromat or washing it in the sink by hand.

Autumn had a wild thought as she slipped out of her shoes and set her cell phone on the charger. She pulled her scrub shirt over her head, placing it on the table. The pink scrub pants went next, followed by her bra and underwear. Naked, she left the kitchen, ready to surprise her husband in the shower. Maybe a talk could wait. Instead, spontaneous sex sounded really good right now.

She stepped into the darkened bedroom. The bathroom door was open, and the light was on. As she crossed the threshold, Flint turned the water off. Disappointed, she was still ready to surprise him and slid the shower curtain back quietly. Dumbfounded, she stood there, her jaw dropping.

Her husband was kissing another woman. Another wet, naked woman.

He barely broke the kiss, his lips hovering above hers, both their eyes still closed.

"Gotta hurry. She'll be here in about fifteen minutes."

Flint's mouth returned to someone she now recognized. Gloria, the charge nurse who was leaving.

"*She* is already home."

Autumn watched them spring apart, their heads whipping toward her voice. Panic filled Gloria's eyes, and she started babbling.

"Get out of *my* shower and *my* apartment," Autumn ordered, her voice tight.

Gloria stepped over the edge of the tub, squeezing past Autumn, who had planted her feet and didn't intend to go anywhere. She glared silently at Flint, even as she heard Gloria still jabbering apologies, gathering her clothes.

For a full sixty seconds, she locked eyes with her cheating husband. Autumn knew how long because she counted the seconds off in her head. She heard footsteps. The apartment door opening and closing.

Then she slammed her fist into Flint's nose.

Her knuckles hurt like hell, but the crunch she'd heard was very satisfying. Her brother would be very proud she had made contact with the punch.

"Autumn!" he shouted, his hands flying to his face, blood spurting.

While Flint was busy cradling his nose, she swung her foot back, bringing it up and kicking him hard in the balls.

His shriek was even more satisfying.

Turning, she left the tiny bathroom and returned to the kitchen, redressing in her work scrubs. She was shaking, but she didn't want to give her husband the satisfaction of seeing it. Taking a seat at the kitchen table, a wedding gift from her parents, she crossed her arms and her legs.

And waited.

Less than five minutes later, Flint appeared. Instead of looking contrite, anger sparked in his eyes. He was dressed haphazardly, toilet paper stuffed up his nose.

"What the hell was that, Autumn?"

"That was me tired of being a doormat, Flint," she said. "Finding out my husband is cheating on me seems to have shaken me out of the haze."

A sudden calmness blanketed her. She took a deep breath and expelled it.

"I want an uncontested divorce," she told her husband of seven years.

"Autumn, listen. I—"

"No! I have done all the listening I'm going to do. It's your turn to pay attention to me for once. I want an uncontested divorce. I could ask for fault grounds, which means my spouse engaged in misconduct. Like banging a colleague of mine. I won't do that and embarrass you or me. No-fault divorce means neither of us will accuse the other of wrongdoing."

Flint looked as if he were about to speak, and she held her hand up to stop him.

"We have no children. No real estate to divide. I've played ATM for you for years, so we have no debt." She shook her head. "I cannot believe I've wasted my entire twenties, living like a pauper, paying entirely for your medical school, doing everything for a man I rarely even saw."

She shook her head. "You owe me, Flint. I will file for divorce today. You will accept the papers without objection. We'll have to wait sixty days and then ask the court to schedule the divorce hearing."

He looked at her, completely perplexed by the new Autumn she had suddenly become. "How do you know so much about all this?"

"Because a fellow nurse at work recently went through this," she explained curtly. "When you come home after your shift, you will sign any document I have waiting for you. You will give me your key and then pack and go somewhere for those sixty days. I don't care where. You will not talk about our divorce to anyone at work. If you do, I will drag this out and make you sorry."

He looked at her, a stubborn look in her eyes. "You wouldn't dare."

"Just try me." Autumn stood. Not just physically, but she wanted him to know she was standing her ground. "I've been such a fool," she said, an overwhelming sadness rushing through her, the sudden death of her marriage hitting her as her adrenaline wore off.

Flint snorted. "You certainly were. You were a way for me to get me through med school for free, Autumn. You're a lousy lay. And you are so dumb. Blind to everything."

She felt herself begin to crumble, digging her fingernails into her palms. "Obviously, Gloria wasn't the first," she stated, thinking back to all the times Flint had said he needed to work late. To stay by the side of a patient he was worried wouldn't pull through or one who needed his support. Now, she knew those patients had been few. If they had existed at all.

He laughed easily and then winced. "You can have your divorce, Nancy Nightingale. Always swooping in to help everyone else. You should've looked after yourself. I was going to divorce you anyway. You've served your purpose. Just be glad I don't file assault charges against you."

Autumn glared at him until the cocky look left his face. "If you do, I'll tell the medical director and the hospital's board my side of the story," she said crisply. "You still have the rest of your residency to get through. Hospital boards don't like gossip. Or besmirched reputations. They want their surgeons to have a pristine reputation. Keep quiet, Flint, and I'll do the same."

He stormed from the kitchen. Seconds later, the door slammed.

Autumn sat again, numbness overwhelming her. She thought she might cry, but she supposed she was in shock.

She didn't want to live here anymore. Shower where Flint and Gloria had. Sleep in a bed where countless other women had lain. But she couldn't afford to break the lease and pay for another apartment. She would tough it out. Fortunately, their lease was up in two months. If the court date went too far beyond that, she'd go to one of those residence hotels and stay. At least there, they had hot meals and happy hours.

She changed clothes and looked up no-fault, uncontested divorce in Texas. She found a website which had all the forms and simple directions. Within an hour, she had used the electronic filing system to send in the completed documents, saving her a trip to the Harris County's district clerk's office.

Still dry-eyed, she decided to get some sleep. She didn't think she could eat. The idea of food made her nauseous.

Just before she closed her eyes, her cell rang. She picked it up from the charger and saw Summer's name. Swallowing, she answered.

"Hey."

"I know something's wrong," her twin said from Manhattan. "Tell me."

Autumn let out a long wail. The tears which had not come now arrived like a monsoon. She held the cell to her ear, crying, listening as Summer spoke soothingly to her, telling her it was all right. That they could do anything together.

Finally, she managed to get herself under control and said, "I just asked Flint for a divorce. No, I didn't ask. I told him I wanted one."

"I thought that was going to be what you said."

In times of trouble, no matter how far apart they were, she and Summer had some kind of sixth sense that the other one was hurting, even knowing what might be wrong before being told.

"I came home and caught him with another woman. A nurse I'm friendly with."

"That sucks."

"I know."

They were quiet a few moments, and then Summer asked, "Should I fly to Houston?"

"Not now. I just submitted the papers online. Did you know you can file for divorce in Texas on the internet?"

"No, but maybe I can use it in a book," her sister joked. "When do you want me to come?"

"Give me some time. If Flint doesn't contest it, we can ask for a court date in sixty days." Autumn wiped away a tear. "That's when I'll need you. Stay in New York for now."

"Will you keep your job at the hospital? It might be hard because he will still be there."

"I know. I need to think about things. A lot of things," she said quietly.

"I have an idea, Autumn. I was talking to Mom last night. Just about stuff. You know, she's always wanting her ducklings to come home. Anyway, she mentioned a new community hospital and medical offices that are opening just outside Hawthorne. She didn't say when, but I gathered it would be pretty soon. What do you think?"

Nodding to herself, Autumn said, "Yeah. She brought it up to me before. I brushed it off. Now? It's a real possibility, Summer."

Her twin cursed under her breath. "Listen, I've got to go. Dragon Lady is giving me the evil eye. Can I call you tonight? After work?"

"I'll be here. I'm going to try and get some sleep now. I just finished working a double shift."

"Love you."

She sighed. "I love you, too."

Autumn ended the connection and placed her phone back on the charger. She closed her eyes.

This chapter in her life was ending. Messy as hell, but it meant she had the opportunity to make a fresh start somewhere else.

And somewhere else just might be back home in Hawthorne.

CHAPTER
One

E li awoke with a start, fearing he'd overslept for the most important interview of his life. He grabbed his phone, seeing it was only five-thirty. He fell back against the pillow, cell in hand, his heart racing. Taking a few slow, deep breaths, he regained his equilibrium.

He wanted this job. More importantly, he *needed* this job. After seven years in the ER, he knew if he didn't change things up soon, he was headed for an early grave. That was a sad thought, seeing as how he was only thirty-four. Not that he was afraid of hard work. He had been an overachiever his entire life, putting in more hours than anyone around him. Heading up an emergency room, though, was tough on the man or woman who did so. Eli never did anything halfway. Because of it, he was facing a serious case of burnout.

The position at the newest Hogan Health facility was a light at the end of his very dark tunnel.

His heart rate back to normal now, he rose and dressed quickly in a T-shirt and sweatpants, going through some stretches before grabbing his room key and heading out the door. As he jogged through the streets of Hawthorne, he got a feel for the town. It had a population of just under thirty thousand and a mix of Mom-and-Pop stores, with a few franchise places thrown in.

He ran through downtown, passing a few eating establishments and shops. A bank. Post office. Real estate office. Dentist and orthodontist. Dry cleaners. Donut shop. Two gas stations. Seeing the map of the town in his mind, he continued, passing residential streets, until he arrived at the high school. He had read everything he could about Hawthorne, wanting to familiarize himself with the small town, and that included stories about the Hawthorne Hawks.

The high school had quite the football program, led by its coach of several decades. One of the current Dallas Cowboys had played here before winning a scholarship to Texas A&M University. He knew the Cowboys had recently won the Super Bowl only because people at work talked about it. Eli rarely had time to listen to the news and had never watched a single game of any sport. He had run cross country in high school, though, and continued to run as an adult, believing it was the best exercise to keep him in shape for long days on his feet in the ER.

It would be nice to watch a game on TV. Even go to a sporting event in person. Eli had zero hobbies, other than his morning run. His life had been work, work, work. And then more work. But if he landed the job as medical director of Hogan Health's new Hawthorne Community Hospital, he would have time for a life. Hobbies.

And hopefully a family.

Not that he'd ever had a serious relationship. He'd only gone on a handful of dates over the years. His life trajectory had thrown him a lot of curves, and dating hadn't been in the picture, considering that he had graduated from high school at fourteen. He had barely been shaving by then and didn't even have a driver's license. Girls hadn't given him a second glance back then. If they did now, he was too swamped with work to notice and too socially awkward to pick up on any cues anyway.

Eli returned to the small inn where he had spent the night, showering and shaving, then dressing in the only suit he owned. He lived in his scrubs and only had a handful of street clothes, including this suit and its accompanying dress shirt and tie. He'd actually stopped at Target on his way to Hawthorne to buy a belt and pair of dress shoes since he owned neither.

His belly yowled, letting him know he better fuel up or be embarrassed during his interview. He had seen a diner on his run and drove there now, parking on the square and entering. It was a little past seven on a weekday, and the diner was about three-quarters full.

A spry-looking man with abundant white hair and merry blue eyes greeted him.

"You look hungry, young man. Well, you've come to the right place. I'm Dizzy Baker. Welcome to Dizzy's Diner, my place for the last fifty years. Let me show you to a booth."

Eli followed, thinking Dizzy was an unusual nickname.

"Here you go," Dizzy said, indicating a booth and handing Eli a menu once he slid into it. "Can I get you some coffee?"

"Yes, please."

"Passing through town?"

He was taken aback by the question but decided the old man didn't mean any harm by it. His gut told him small towns were different from the large cities he'd lived in.

"I have a job interview today."

Before he could say more, the owner said, "Must be something to do with Hogan Health. Boy, are we glad to be getting a hospital here in Hawthorne. It's a good half-hour or more drive to the nearest hospital now. We have a couple of doctors in town, but any specialist, you gotta drive. I've had cataract surgery. Had to drive. Knee replacement. Had to drive. Thank goodness I haven't had something serious like a heart attack or stroke. I'd probably be DOA." Dizzy laughed at his own joke. "Be right back with the coffee, son."

For a moment, Eli's throat tightened. He hadn't been anyone's son in a long time. Because of his mom's drug addiction, her parental rights had been terminated, and he had gone into foster care when he was five. He could barely recall what she had even looked like. No dad had been in the picture.

Who he did remember was his little brother, who liked playing with trucks and kicking a ball. Eli had taken care of them both because his mom never seemed to be able to do so. He could remember making them peanut butter sandwiches. Washing his brother's face with a washcloth. Playing with him and teasing him.

But he couldn't for the life of him recall his brother's name.

When the case worker came and took Eli away, he remembered crying, asking for his baby brother to come with them. She had patiently told him that his brother would be going somewhere else. He had watched another adult take his brother's hand and pull him in the opposite direction. Both brothers had started shouting, crying out for one another, as they were escorted to different cars.

All his life, Eli had been lonely, wondering what had happened to his little brother. If he had been adopted. Where he was now. He promised himself that if he got this job in Hawthorne, he would hire a private investigator and try to locate what felt like his missing half.

Dizzy returned with the coffee and placed it on the table. "What can I get for you?"

He hadn't even looked at the menu and glanced down quickly, asking for the number two, which had both eggs and pancakes and came with a choice of meat and biscuits and gravy.

"Eggs over easy. Bacon crisp."

Dizzy waved, catching the eye of the short order cook. "A two for here." Then he slid into the booth opposite Eli.

"I was named after Dizzy Dean, the famous baseball player. My daddy was a baseball fan. Had two girls before me. Ruth was named after Babe Ruth and Mary Lou for Lou Gehrig. I'm actually Delbert. Mama insisted I have a proper name, but everyone's always called me Dizzy."

Dizzy told Eli about Hawthorne during the five minutes it took for his order to be ready. He enjoyed hearing the old man's stories and knew he would be a regular at the diner. Or hoped he would be.

"I'll leave you to eat. Good luck with your interview. What's it for?"

"Medical Director for the hospital."

"Oh, you're a fancy doctor." Dizzy thrust out a hand. "Never did get your name."

"Eli. Dr. Eli Carson."

"Well, I hope it goes well for you, Dr. Carson."

He smiled shyly. "We're old friends now, Dizzy. Make it Eli."

Dizzy grinned. "Eli, it is."

He ate his meal in silence after that, watching people at

other tables wondering if he would get to know any of them. Dizzy never brought him his check, so he went to the front where the old man stood by the cash register.

"I need to pay my bill and get going," he explained.

"No charge today, Eli."

He started to protest, but the owner cut him off. "My place. My rules."

"Then thank you for a delicious breakfast. The bacon was perfect, and I haven't had gravy that good in a long time."

"You're welcome. Let me know if you get the job."

"Will do."

Eli left the diner, feeling good about himself. He had always been withdrawn, not speaking to others unless spoken to. As an adult, most of his conversations were one-sided, giving orders to other doctors, residents, or nurses regarding a patient's care. He had never had the luxury of having friends. And yet he'd found it incredibly easy to converse with the friendly Dizzy, who seemed to have never met a stranger.

Maybe small-town life would be conducive to making friends *and* finding someone to marry.

He stopped by the inn again, wanting to brush his teeth and use the restroom before his interview. He also checked out, placing his suitcase in the trunk of the car he'd rented to make the drive from Houston to Hawthorne. The interview would take place at the public library, which he had also passed on his run. Eli parked and ran his fingers through his hair before exiting the car and heading toward the building.

Unfortunately, the door was locked. Panic swept through him, and he questioned if he had the right day. The right place and time.

Then an attractive, older woman of about sixty unlocked the door. She had unique turquoise eyes and auburn hair.

"You must be Dr. Carson," she said, giving him a friendly

smile. "I'm Meg Sutherland, the head librarian. Come on in. We're not open to the public just yet, but Dr. Richards is expecting you."

He breathed a sigh of relief. Peter Richards was the name of the man who was supposed to interview him. Eli had already done a phone interview, as well as one on Zoom. This third interview was for the finalists for the position.

"Thank you," he said, following her inside.

"You'll be in a conference room," she told him as they walked through a large, empty room, an employee shelving books on the far side. "Can I get you some water? Coffee?"

"No, thanks. I'd probably knock it over onto Dr. Richards' notes and be out of the running before the race even started."

She laughed, and he wondered at the change in him. He was never funny. He never volunteered information, especially that he could be a real klutz if medicine wasn't involved.

What was Hawthorne doing to him?

"It's right in here. Have a seat. Dr. Richards must have stepped out for a moment."

"Thank you."

She left, and Eli took the chair opposite one where a laptop was, along with a pad and pen. He saw a few lines scrawled on the pad and looked away, not wanting to invade his interviewer's privacy.

"Ah, good. You're here. Peter Richards. VP of HR for Hogan Health."

The doctor who entered offered his hand and shook Eli's briskly before taking a seat. He opened the laptop and typed for a minute, obviously setting up for the interview. Eli swallowed, his mouth dry, wishing now he had taken Meg Sutherland up on the offer of water.

"Okay, we can get started."

Eli felt himself sitting up a little straighter. He wanted this job. He could taste it.

"You've done very well in your previous two interviews, Dr. Carson. Tell me about yourself."

He hadn't expected such a casual question, which was actually a loaded one. How far back should he go? How detailed should he get? He decided to swing for the fences. Go big—or go home.

"I don't have the background most medical doctors do. Yes, I graduated from Rice University and did my medical training at UT Southwestern Medical Center in Dallas. Both, as you know, are exceptional places of learning. It was my path to them that varies from others."

He paused, taking a calming breath, and told his story.

"I grew up in foster care. No known father. An addicted mother who lost custody of her two sons. My brother and I went into the system when I was five and he was three. We never saw one another again."

He let that sit for a minute, seeing he had the VP's attention now and that this was no run of the mill interview where accolades and degrees would be trotted out.

"Even at five, I was considered too old to adopt by most couples. That meant living in a series of foster care homes. They are every bit as terrible as books and movies say they are, filled with violence and a pecking order among the children who live there. While I did live with one family for two years who proved to be exceptional caregivers and had a heart for children, I found most foster parents took in kids for the extra money. They paid very little attention to those in their care, and they turned a blind eye for what went on behind closed doors."

Dr. Richards straightened his tie. "You come from a seriously disadvantaged background, Dr. Carson."

"Yes. I wanted to escape it and make something of myself. Help others—because no one at any of those houses ever helped me. Fortunately, I had several wonderful teachers who recognized my potential. They are the ones who deserve all the credit for challenging me. Encouraging me. Making me the physician I am today."

Eli went on, elaborating on how he had skipped two grades in elementary school one year and jumped another a year later.

"I graduated high school at fourteen and college at seventeen. I completed med school by the time I was twenty. I was one of the few who finished my education with no debt. Because of my high IQ and perfect SAT score, one of my teachers hooked me up with a foundation which funds the education of disadvantaged students. Between the foundation's help and the scholarships I earned, I had no loans to pay back."

He met Dr. Richards' eyes. "I feel I'm in a unique position, able to understand people on a different level than most of my peers. I'm only thirty-four and have seven years in the ER under my belt, two as an ER physician and five more as its head. I work at the largest ER in Houston, and I've seen everything from gunshot wounds to Ebola. I know how to manage budgets. Staff. Patients. I'm detail-oriented, yet I can make quick, life-saving decisions in a split second.

"I'm up for the challenge of opening a new hospital, Dr. Richards. I've studied other hospitals Hogan Health has opened in its system over the past five years. Hogan Health is the fastest-growing healthcare provider in the South and Southwest. I think I'd be a perfect fit for a Hogan Health facility. I've also spent a little time in Hawthorne, getting to know it. I had a wonderful conversation just this morning with the owner of Dizzy's Diner. I know how eager this community is to have a care facility operating here."

Eli paused, clearing his throat. "I want to help the residents of Hawthorne by providing them with cutting-edge, quality, affordable healthcare."

He fell silent, worried that he had said too much, and his answer had been too radical. The medical community, for all its talk of bells and whistles and innovation, was still conservative in many of its approaches, and that included those hired in positions such as the one he hoped to obtain today.

Dr. Richards studied him for a long moment, then he seemed to come to some decision.

"Give me a moment."

He fiddled with the laptop again, typing rapidly, and then took a moment to smooth his hair.

"Good morning, Herbert."

"Peter. How are the interviews going this morning? You're in Hawthorne, right?"

The physician smiled. "Yes, sir. I'd like you to meet Dr. Eli Carson."

Richards spun the laptop around, and Eli saw a familiar man in his mid-fifties, with gold-framed glasses and a fatherly smile.

"Ah, Dr. Carson. Herbert Hogan here."

Eli tried to relax and smiled. "I recognize you from your commercials and billboards, Mr. Hogan. You—and Hogan Health—seem to be everywhere."

"We try, Dr. Carson. Hogan Health has been growing by leaps and bounds. Not too fast, though. We have the big picture in mind. We're trying to move into communities now in Texas, Oklahoma, and Arkansas, ones which are smaller and need a local healthcare facility."

"The citizens of Hawthorne are tired of driving for thirty

minutes or longer to reach a hospital or see a healthcare specialist," he replied. "I think locating one of your hospitals here will be a popular choice."

"Only if we do it right, Dr. Carson," Herbert Hogan said, smiling. "We need professionals who are organized. Efficient. Caring. That means from the medical director to the janitor." Pausing, the CEO then asked, "Do you believe you're a good fit for Hogan Health?"

"Absolutely," Eli replied without hesitation.

"Then I would like to offer you a two-year contract as medical director. Peter will give you the specifics. Salary. Benefits. Responsibilities. You'll be in charge of hiring the staff and overseeing the last bit of construction. How soon can you come onboard?"

"I can put in my two-week notice when we get off this call," he said, tempering his enthusiasm. "I think I can talk the head of my hospital into letting me leave in a week, however."

"Do whatever it takes, but I want you in Hawthorne as soon as possible," Hogan said. "Let me see Peter now."

Eli turned the laptop's screen so that it faced Dr. Richards.

"Go over the works, Peter. The particulars in the contract. The signing bonus. Let Dr. Carson know that a company car and house are included in the package. Good work."

"Thank you, Herbert."

Richards tapped a few keys, ending the call, and closed the laptop. He reached for a briefcase, extracting several different documents, and took his time going over each with Eli. His head began to spin, seeing what his salary would be, as well as all the duties he would be assuming. It was frightening and thrilling at the same time.

When Richards finished, he asked, "Any more questions?"

"None. Where do I sign?"

Eli placed his signature several different places, with Richards assuring him that he would receive copies of everything.

"I think we should go over and see the facility now. It's really coming together."

"When will it open?" he asked.

"We're aiming for June first. That gives us three months."

They left the library, with Meg giving him a wave. When Richards stepped in front of Eli, he turned around and gave her a thumbs up to indicate he'd gotten the job. She returned it, beaming at him.

He rode with Richards, who asked that Eli call him Peter. They reached the construction site in a little over ten minutes and parked.

"The outside is completely finished," Peter told him. "The inside is being worked on now, from painting to flooring to electricity, heating, and air. Once that's all completed, equipment will be arriving. You'll be supervising all that, as well as interviewing for numerous positions."

They saw every inch of the facility, and Eli was impressed by the thought which had gone into each decision. They ended the tour at what would be his new office.

"You'll get to pick out your own furnishings. A perk of the job. I'll ask the construction manager for them to finish up in here so that you'll have a place to work out of when you return to Hawthorne."

Peter offered Eli his hand. "Glad to have you as a part of the Hogan Health team."

He took it. "Glad to be a part of the system."

When he reached his rental, he began the drive to Dallas-

Fort Worth airport, where he had a six o'clock flight back to Houston. As the plane took off and he looked out the window, a calm settled over him.

Eli had a new job. It would be a fresh, new chapter in his life. The best one yet.

Because he had found a place where he felt he finally belonged.

CHAPTER
Two

"I can't thank you enough for letting me store my things in your garage, Jeannie," Autumn said.

Her friend laughed. "It's not as if you have a ton of stuff."

She glanced at the small stack in the corner which held all her worldly possessions. Two of the boxes contained clothes. She didn't have many because she worked in scrubs and even wore them when she was home or out running errands. One box contained a few books and framed pictures. The other was a hodgepodge.

"Ready to go?" Jeannie asked.

Autumn nodded. She rolled her suitcase to Jeannie's car and placed it in the trunk before getting into the passenger's seat.

"I appreciate you taking me to the airport. I could've called a rideshare."

"No reason to. Besides, this will give us a little time to talk." Jeannie glanced over. "How are you doing? You've certainly kept things quiet at work."

"In another life, I would probably make for a good serial killer. I'm organized and don't leave a trace of myself behind."

The day she had caught Flint cheating, Autumn had gone to the bank, where she had removed half of what was in their savings account and half of the amount in their checking account. The savings account was substantial since she had finished paying off Flint's medical school bills several years ago. She opened a new savings and checking account in her name only and asked the bank clerk to remove her from the other joint accounts she had shared with her husband.

She had also gone to HR the next day, filling out paperwork to send her direct deposit check to the new account. Autumn didn't tell HR about her separation from her husband, nor did she mention it to anyone at work other than Jeannie. Since she never wore her wedding band at work, no one realized that she had stopped wearing it altogether. She did tell the head of HR that she was interested in interviewing for the charge nurse opening with Gloria leaving. Since she had served in that capacity previously, no interview was necessary. She had simply taken on Gloria's schedule the following week.

Gloria, who hadn't been a friend but was more than an acquaintance, wrote Autumn an apology. She started reading it and couldn't stomach the whiny tone. Tearing it into tiny pieces and tossing them in the trash made her feel slightly better.

Knowing it would be impossible to avoid running into Flint, she had prepared herself. Autumn had seen him three times at work in the past two months. Once, she was getting off the elevator and he was getting on. She gave him a cool "Hi." The second time had been in the hospital cafeteria. He was with another doctor, their discussion looking serious. Flint hadn't even seen her. The final time had been at a staff meeting. They had sat on opposite sides of the room, which no one would find unusual since nurses usually sat with other nurses and doctors with doctors in these types of meetings.

Outside of work, they had met twice. The first time was the day she had caught him cheating. He came home after his shift. Flint looked around, as if he had expected her to pack for him.

She hadn't.

He took his precious coffeemaker, the TV, and the cable box. She didn't care. He was welcome to them. Last night, he had stopped by again, when she told him that she was leaving what little furniture was there since their lease ended this coming Saturday. Autumn had already told the apartment's leasing agent that she was leaving and if her soon-to-be ex-husband wanted to renew this lease, only his name was going to go on it. With the apartment so close to the hospital, she thought Flint might keep it as a little love nest for all the stupid women who fell for his lines, the same as she had.

Well, she wasn't that naïve, starry-eyed young woman anymore. She was an adult who didn't plan on entering a relationship for a long, long time. If ever.

"I did turn in my resignation letter two weeks ago and asked them to keep that quiet until I left," she now shared with Jeannie. "Today was my last day."

"Oh, we would've given you a party," Jeannie protested.

"That's exactly why I didn't want word leaking out. Once I'm gone, gossip will spread quickly about Flint and me. I didn't want to be around to suffer the sympathetic glances or hear the vicious rumors being spread. As it is, he admitted Gloria wasn't the first. Who knows who else at work he's slept with? Other nurses or doctors. Administrative staff. The cafeteria manager. I couldn't stay. I need a fresh start."

Jeannie had been the only person Autumn shared

anything with, other than Summer. Her twin knew everything and had promised to keep quiet, especially with West's wedding this weekend.

"Have you at least told your family?" her friend asked, as if she read Autumn's mind.

"My sister knows. That's it."

"Will it hurt going to West's wedding and seeing all that happiness when you're feeling miserable?"

"I don't think it will at all. First, I'm happy for West and Kelby. They dated briefly in high school years ago. I think the idea of a second chance romance is pretty cool. Summer does, too. She's threatening to write about their whirlwind romance, just changing the names and some of the details."

"Does she even know any details? You've always said West is so private."

"She'll make it all up. And yes, as an NFL player, West has been in the spotlight a good decade now. He's dated casually for years, but those were barely romances. This is the real deal with Kelby. I'm happy for them."

"I knew you would be resigning, but you haven't mentioned where you've applied. With your sterling reputation and skills, you can go pretty much anywhere you choose. Let's face it. Houston has more than its fair share of hospitals."

"I have something else in mind."

Briefly, she told Jeannie about the new hospital opening in her hometown.

"It's part of the Hogan Health network of hospitals. I've got an interview tomorrow morning with its medical director. If I don't get the job, then I may look for a position in Ft. Worth or Dallas."

"You won't need to look for other opportunities. You'll

ace this interview." Jeannie paused. "Will it be weird being back where you grew up?"

"I don't think so. I've always loved Hawthorne. I've actually missed small-town life. I rarely went home because I was working so much, and Flint didn't like Hawthorne. He said there was nothing to do there." She paused. "I haven't told my family I'm coming in early. I'm going to stay at a motel in Decatur and then drive in for the interview tomorrow. After it, I'll change clothes and head back to DFW to pick up Summer. Her flight is coming in late tomorrow afternoon. Then we'll ride up together to Hawthorne."

"Staying at your folks' house?"

She nodded. "The drive will give Summer and me time to talk. She's always been great about helping me process things."

They turned into the airport, and Jeannie asked what terminal Autumn was flying out of. She told her, and minutes later, they pulled up to the curb.

Her friend popped the trunk and got out with Autumn.

"I guess this is goodbye?" Jeannie asked, her eyes misting with tears.

"Hey, we'll always be friends," Autumn said, hugging her. "In fact, I have to fly back early next week for my court date for the divorce. We can get together then. You can even help me find a car, and I'll take my boxes off your hands."

Flint had taken their ancient vehicle. It was fine with her. It wouldn't have made the trip from one end of Texas to the other for this weekend's wedding.

"New or used?"

"Slightly used, if I can find that. Three, four years old. In good condition."

"Let me talk with my cousin. She mentioned that her

husband was wanting a new car. He likes to trade his in every few years for something newer and shinier."

"Thanks, I really appreciate that."

They hugged, with Autumn retrieving her suitcase and rolling it into the terminal. She checked her bag, having brought enough clothes for the interview, the wedding activities, and the next couple of days she would be in Hawthorne before returning to Houston. She hated having to come back, but she needed to appear in court in order for the divorce to be finalized.

The actual flight was only about forty-five minutes, but the wheels up, wheels down, and taxiing to the gate took an extra fifteen minutes. She went to the car rental counter and found only two other customers ahead of her in line. Within thirty minutes, she had the key fob in hand and was on the road to Decatur, where she'd be staying overnight at a chain motel.

As Autumn drove on the highway, she felt herself loosening up. For the first time in her adult life, she was free. No job. Nowhere to live. No husband. No responsibility.

It was liberating.

She had always been the quiet, studious girl, never causing trouble in her classes. Grades were important to her, and she was diligent in her studies. She had spent two years in Waco at Baylor University and then transferred to their nursing program, finishing her last two years at the Baylor campus in Dallas. At work, she was known for keeping impeccable charts and for knowing every patient's name and their current status. While she could never think of herself as a wild thing, she wanted to live a little. Learn more about herself and become who she was truly meant to be, not an extension of Flint. For too long, Autumn had kept all her thoughts and opinions to herself when around her husband, wanting to please him and not rock the boat.

Her gut told her she was ready to be Autumn Sutherland again. She would take back her maiden name when the divorce was finalized next week. The thought of that made her almost giddy. It would also be nice never to have to think about being a Ferris again. Flint's family hadn't taken to her, and she'd never truly felt a part of the Ferris family. Satisfied with her decision, she flipped on the radio and found an oldies station to sing along to.

Ironically, an iconic piano riff began, and she recognized the opening notes of *Don't Stop Believin,'* the most famous song by the band, Journey. As she sang at the top of her lungs, she knew she was ready to begin believing in herself again.

Would it be nice if she landed the job at the new hospital in her hometown? Absolutely. She would get to see more of her parents, as well as West and Kelby. If she didn't, she would easily have other opportunities, given her background and the severe shortage of nurses in the state. No decisions needed to be made yet. Everything would hinge on the outcome of tomorrow's interview.

She pulled into a Sonic, desperate for something to eat. Even though it was lunchtime, she ordered a sausage breakfast burrito and tater tots, accompanied by a diet limeade and her favorite thing in the world, Sonic's crushed ice. The carhop brought her order, and Autumn ate in the car, letting her thoughts drift as she satisfied her hunger.

Back on the highway, she reached Decatur. It was only half past one, so it was too early to check in to her hotel. She decided to swing by the regional hospital in town, which had been bought by Hogan Health last year. She knew the network was focusing on purchasing existing hospitals in smaller towns and building new ones in several adjoining states. It might be nice to go inside one of their healthcare facilities and see what they were all about before her interview took place.

She pulled into the entrance, following the signs to the parking lot. She reached a point where employees turned right into one lot, and visitors were to head straight to a different lot. Autumn stopped at the stop sign and started to go when a car came barreling out of the employees' lot. It struck the front of her rental, causing her to scream as the airbag deployed. She threw her hands up instinctively to block the bag, grateful she did so, or else she thought the force of the bag might have broken her nose or at least bruised her face badly.

Immediately, she swung open her door, ready to give the reckless driver who smashed into her a piece of her mind. He, too, was getting out, hurrying toward her.

"Are you all right?" he asked.

"Why weren't you paying more attention to what you were doing? Coming from the employees' parking lot, you must work here. If you're a doctor or nurse, I hope you exercise more care with your patients than you did with your car. Cars are lethal weapons—they can kill!"

He placed a hand on her shoulder, and she angrily shrugged it off, her anger exploding. "I don't need you touching me. I'm fine."

"You need to go inside and get checked out."

"I'm a nurse," she spat out. "I know an injury when I see one, and I'm not hurt. Just this rental car is, and I'm sure you've brought a world of headaches to me now which I'll have to deal with. And my insurance will probably go up due to your stupid negligence."

"Your current insurance should cover the damage to your rental car," he said.

"You don't know that," Autumn said, beginning to shake like a leaf. "I've been driving an eleven-year-old car that wasn't worth the cost of a Starbucks Mocha Grande, so I've gone with the minimal amount of coverage. And I gave it up two months ago. I kicked out my cheating husband and he took that vehicle. I've been walking to work."

She turned, finding the curb, and went to sit on it. Hanging her head in her lap, she burst into tears.

Autumn felt the stranger come and sit next to her. The first thing she thought was that he smelled good. Something citrusy. She hadn't really looked him in the face because she had suddenly turned so angry.

"Your credit card company should be liable for it if you used one to rent the vehicle," he said softly. "And if not, I'll pay for any damage. Let's exchange information."

Glancing up, tears in her eyes, she said, "I need to apologize. I've blurted out a lot of personal information, and I'm really sorry for that. I want you to know I'm a rational person. I walked in on my husband cheating, and we're getting a divorce. It'll be finalized next week. I've been keeping my head down, living my life, working, trying to put one foot in front of the other. I didn't realize I had so much anger bottled up inside me."

She smiled ruefully. "And I seem to have taken it out on you."

Autumn saw his face relax. It was a nice face. Even a handsome one. He had medium brown hair and deep brown eyes which looked at her with sympathy now. He smiled at her in return as he reached into his pocket.

Handing her a card, he said, "Thanks for sharing. And yes, I was distracted. It's totally unlike me. I just have a thousand and one things I need to get done and not enough time to complete everything. The accident is completely my fault.

I didn't yield to you as I should have. I crashed into you. I'll make certain my insurance agent understands that."

Wiping the backs of her hands against her cheek, she nodded. "Thank you. I suppose I should have recorded your statement of culpability in case you change your mind," she teased.

The man chuckled. "Pull out your cell. I'll talk directly into the mic."

"No, I trust you. You have a very trustworthy face."

"So do you," he replied. Then he said, "I'm sorry about your husband. I don't understand why anyone who loves someone would cheat on the person they love."

Autumn shook her head. "It took a long time to learn that he only loved himself. Never me."

Her words hung in the air a moment, and she couldn't believe she had shared such an intimate part of her life with this stranger. She had told him more than anyone in Houston. The only person who had truly heard the entire sad story was Summer.

"Why don't I call my insurance agent now and see how to proceed?" he asked. "Maybe you can call your credit card company at the same time and check on their policy regarding automobile rentals. And you'll need to notify the company where you picked up your rental." He looked around. "We should actually move our cars out of the way before we do so." Pointing, he said, "Over there. I think they're both drivable."

"Okay."

The stranger came to his feet and offered Autumn his hand. She took it, an odd feeling washing over her as she did so.

"Thanks."

His gaze met hers. "I still think we should get you checked out. For my peace of mind."

"Let's get business taken care of first," she said, putting him off because she knew nothing was wrong with her. Plus, at the moment, she had no insurance coverage. The fees racked up for an ER visit would be astronomical.

Walking back to her car, Autumn sighed. This whole mess would take up the rest of today, and she had wanted to prepare for her interview. Study the Hogan Health website, as well as the one for the hospital in Hawthorne. Just thinking of what lay ahead in the next several hours made her head start to ache.

She opened the driver's door and pushed aside as much of the exploded airbag as she could and got behind the wheel, realizing she held the card he had given her in her hand. When she read it, an expletive was the first thing that came out of her mouth, a very un-Autumn-like thing to do. Many nurses F-bombed all over the place, but Autumn couldn't remember the last time she had cursed. She stared at the name on the card. The man who had hit her was Dr. Eli Carson.

And she was supposed to interview with him tomorrow morning.

CHAPTER

Three

E li ran his fingers through his hair as he explained the situation to his new insurance agent.

"You *never* admit guilt, Dr. Carson," the agent said harshly. "Never."

"But it was clearly my fault. I can send you a diagram if you'd like. I was the one who made the mistake. Thank goodness the other driver doesn't seem to be hurt. I will encourage her to go inside the hospital once we have things settled and have someone take a look at her."

He listened as the agent continued to chew him out, thinking that this wasn't very good customer service. He had only been with the agency a couple of months, but he wasn't pleased at this turn of events. Then again, the insurance—and car—came through his position at Hogan Health. A company car and accompanying insurance had been provided to him, as well as other benefits.

Eli answered a few more questions and then hung up. The agent had provided the number of a body shop to call, and he did so now, explaining about the accident.

"Need a tow for it, Doc?"

"Yes."

Although he had been able to drive the car a short distance to clear the intersection, he didn't think he could make it very far in it.

"The person whom I hit may also need a tow. She's driving a rental car and is on the phone now about that."

"I can send another truck if she's told to take care of it," the voice on the phone assured him. "You can let the tow truck driver know when he gets there, and he can text me the info. For now, it'll be about forty-five minutes to an hour before I can get someone there for your car."

"Thank you. I'll be waiting."

Eli hung up and walked toward the woman, who looked to be in her late twenties. She was very pretty, about five-four, with a beautiful mane of auburn hair. What had drawn him in were her exquisite turquoise eyes, a blend of blue and green tones that mesmerized him. They were reminiscent of the librarian whom he had met a few months ago when his interview had taken place at the city's library.

This woman only wore a soft shade of lipstick, no other makeup. Even in the world of the ER, female nurses always came to work with perfect makeup, even if they did pull their hair back in a ponytail or bun. It was nice to see a woman let her natural beauty shine.

If he weren't so occupied with other things just now, he would ask her out, but Eli hadn't been on a date in years. The fact that she drove a rented car meant she wasn't even from the area, most likely. And why would she agree to have dinner with a stranger who had slammed into her car?

It pleased him that he had even thought of asking her out. The idea of dating someone, even marrying them, really appealed to him. Now that he had a job which paid extremely well, along with normal work hours, it would be nice to find someone to spend the rest of his life with. Just because this woman would probably decline if he asked her to go to dinner with him didn't mean others back in Hawthorne would do the same. It had been easier to deal with his loneliness during the years he'd worked in Houston because running the ER was so all-consuming. Here in Hawthorne, though, even though he was incredibly busy, he was putting down roots.

And roots meant a family to him, something he yearned for.

Eli moved toward the woman, realizing he had yet to ask her what her name was. He stood several feet from her car, though, trying to give her privacy as she spoke on the phone. She nodded to herself a few times and then jotted something down. He could see her conversation was coming to an end.

She glanced up and opened the car's door, stepping out. Though she probably didn't realize it, her clothing was still covered in dust from the airbag being deployed. He noticed her eyes were quite red now, and she rubbed one as she coughed.

"Don't do that," he cautioned, stepping toward her and taking her chin in his hand, studying her.

"What are you *doing*?" she demanded, jerking her head away and stepping back.

"Is your throat irritated?" he asked quickly. "Your eyes are itchy and watery, right?"

When she nodded, Eli took her elbow and began pulling her toward the ER entrance, saying, "The effects of airbag dust vary from person to person. It can cause irritation to mucus membranes and clog your air passage, which can seriously impact your breathing."

"I blocked the airbag when it erupted," she told him as

they went through the doors of the building. "I didn't swallow anything." She glanced down. "I see I'm covered in dust, though. That's probably why my throat feels sore."

"We need to flush this away."

Keeping his hand on her elbow, he hurried toward someone holding a tablet.

"Dr. Mitchell, this woman was in an auto accident outside the hospital. I think the sodium azide from the air bag device is causing some serious irritation. Her eyes are itching, and her throat is sore. Her breathing hasn't slowed and doesn't seem shallow, but we need to move fast."

Eli looked to her. "Even a small amount ingested can cause your body to shut down."

"Sami," Mitchell said. "Air bag deployed. Help Dr. Carson take care of this young woman."

The nurse took the woman's free elbow, and they rushed her to a room. Quickly, the pair stripped off her shirt and jeans, along with her shoes. Eli had done this a thousand times when a patient had come into his ER in Houston, always in an impersonal, professional manner. This time seemed different, however.

"Come with me, ma'am," the nurse said. "We're going to stick you in a shower and wash all this residue away. Stay here, Dr. Carson. I've got this under control."

Sami took the woman's phone and set it on the table, leading her away. Eli paced the small room, afraid he had not only caused an accident but worrying he might have seriously hurt the pretty stranger. It wasn't helping any that he couldn't forget about the swell of her breasts and the curve of her hips.

Ten minutes later, they returned. The woman's hair was wet and dripping. She wore a pair of hospital scrubs. Her face was flushed, but her breathing still seemed normal.

"May I?"

Eli borrowed Sami's stethoscope and asked the woman to sit on the table. He listened to her heart. Checked her pulse. Borrowed Sami's flashlight and looked into both eyes and her mouth. In the meantime, Sami took the woman's blood pressure and checked her oxygen levels.

"All good on my end, Dr. Carson," Sami said.

"Same here." He looked at the woman. "It seems you're going to live. I haven't killed you after all."

"I told you that I was all right," she said, sounding irritated. "What about your tow truck? Didn't your insurance agent arrange for that?"

"Damn," he said. "I need to get back outside."

The woman smiled at Sami as she slipped her phone into her pocket. "I'll get your scrubs back to you. Thanks for letting me borrow them and not making me wear that dreaded hospital gown."

"Not a problem. I'm sorry that we needed to dispose of your jeans and shirt. The shirt was really cute on you."

"Thank you."

"I'll buy you new ones," Eli said. "Right now, you and I need to get back outside."

"I need to see someone about payment. ER visits don't come cheap."

"I know people," he mumbled, glancing to Sami, who nodded in return. "Let's go."

He took her elbow again, leading her back outside.

"I can walk on my own," she declared, pulling from his grasp. "And there's your tow truck turning in now."

"Stay here," Eli ordered, meeting the driver and speaking briefly with him and another man who accompanied him.

As they began hooking his car up, he returned to the woman. "What did you find out regarding your rental?"

"Thankfully, my credit card does have a waiver to cover the situation since I rented the vehicle with it. I called the car rental company, and they said to have it towed to a place here in Decatur. They'll take it from there." She frowned. "I just have to find a way back to DFW, where I rented it, because I need to pick up another car."

"What about renting another car here in Decatur?" he asked.

She shook her head. "I flew in from Houston and will be in the area until early next week. I need to fly back. If I rented a car here and returned it, I'd still need to find a way back to the airport. I'd rather rent at the airport."

"Then I'll take you to DFW to rent one," he said. "It's the least I can do."

She looked at the tow truck, which now had his wrecked car attached to it. "Your car is about to leave the premises. Where are you going to get another one?"

"I'll rent one here in Decatur and drive you to DFW now. That is, if you feel comfortable getting in the car with me."

Laughing, she said, "Maybe I should be the one to drive back to the airport." She paused. "Oh, wait. This guy is from the company I'm supposed to use to have the rental towed."

Racing to the driver, who had just climbed inside the truck, she waved and spoke to him a moment while Eli admired her backside.

After a brief conversation, she returned to him and said, "They'll come back for my car. He said to call a rideshare to take us to a rental place. I need to get my suitcase and backpack out of the trunk, though."

He accompanied her across the street and lifted the suitcase from the vehicle, while she slung the backpack over her shoulder.

"Are you sure you want to take me all the way to the airport?" she asked. "That's really going out of your way."

"It's the least I can do," he replied. "My screwup. I need to make things right with you."

"Then I'll spring for the ride," she said, pulling her cell from her pocket and requesting a car.

"Less than three minutes," she informed him.

They stood in awkward silence now, two people who had shared an experience, yet ones who knew nothing about the other. The driver arrived, and she hurried to him, speaking a moment and then waving Eli over. He rolled her suitcase to the car, and the driver popped the trunk so Eli could place the luggage inside.

When they arrived at the car rental company, she said, "You can rent what you need. I asked our driver if he'd be willing to take me all the way to DFW, and he's got the time. I don't want to put you out any more than I already have."

Disappointment flooded him. Eli had hoped to get to know her a bit on the drive down to Dallas. Now, he doubted he would ever see her and those amazing turquoise eyes again. It made sense, though. She didn't know anything about him. She would feel safer with the driver in the front seat than a stranger who had carelessly crashed into her car.

"If you're sure," he said, leaving the door open, hoping she would change her mind.

"I am. Thank you for having me go into ER. I could have gotten really sick if I hadn't cleaned the dust off me. My brother is getting married on Saturday, and I would have hated to miss his wedding."

"Well, good luck to you. And your brother," he said, masking the hurt he felt at being cut loose so quickly.

Eli exited the car and entered the car agency without a backward glance. The insurance agent had said his policy would allow him to rent a car for up to two weeks. If the repairs to his own car weren't through by then, he could apply for an extension. He liked the Genesis SUV Hogan Health had provided for him, so he rented a Nissan Rogue SUV. The one car he had owned for a few short months had been a four-door sedan, and he preferred sitting higher up and seeing more of the road behind the wheel of an SUV.

The return trip to Hawthorne only took half an hour. The entire time, Eli couldn't help but wonder why he hadn't gotten the woman's name. If she had found another car to rent. And why she had been at the hospital. If she were in town for a wedding, it made no sense for her to be at the hospital. Maybe she was killing two birds with one stone and had some relative who had been recently hospitalized. As long as she was in town, she was able to stop by and offer a little sympathy.

He returned to the office, telling Nancy, his executive assistant, she could leave for the day. Eli then typed up a few notes regarding his visit to Hogan Health Decatur Hospital. He had seen a few things he would like to incorporate here in Hawthorne, as well as a couple of items he wished to avoid. He wanted Triple H—Hogan Health Hawthorne—to run as efficiently and smoothly as possible.

Eli left the office at half-past six, stopping to have dinner at the diner. Dizzy joined him, talking his ear off as usual, but Eli didn't mind. He liked the old man's stories, and he had learned a lot about the town during his visits to the diner.

The next morning, he met with the construction manager. They went to view the operating theaters. When he returned to his office, Nancy said, "Your nine o'clock interview is waiting in the conference room, Dr. Carson. I've placed her folder on the table for you."

He didn't need it. Eli already knew everything about

Autumn Ferris that he needed to know. Her employment history was steady, with her only having worked at one hospital in the eight years since she graduated from nursing school. The nurse's supervisor had raved about Autumn, saying she was an excellent nurse and charge nurse, one of the best she had ever worked with, and how sorry they were to be losing her. The supervisor didn't mention why her employee was leaving, and Eli knew not to ask. Perhaps it might come up in today's interview.

As he approached the conference room, he decided he would ask a handful of questions and then offer Autumn Ferris the job on the spot. She was more than qualified. Eli needed positions filled quickly, and if Autumn accepted the job offer he had in mind, she could help ease his burden and interview potential nurses for the staff he was building.

Opening the door, he breezed into the room—and stopped dead in his tracks.

Autumn Ferris sat at the conference table, wearing light makeup and a navy suit.

And she was the woman he had crashed into yesterday.

CHAPTER
Four

A utumn swallowed nervously as the door opened. It wouldn't be Nancy Nichols, the administrative assistant who had greeted her and given her a bottled water, seating her in this conference room not five minutes ago. No, it would be Dr. Eli Carson, the man she had spent time with yesterday after their auto accident.

The man who would decide if she lived and worked in Hawthorne. Or not.

He paused in the doorway a second, maintaining his composure. She would have expected nothing less.

After their encounter yesterday, Autumn had Googled Dr. Carson and learned that he had run the largest ER in Houston for several years. No one did that kind of job and became rattled, even with the odd situation they found themselves in.

She rose and extended her hand. "Dr. Carson. We meet again."

He took it. Once more, Autumn felt her heart flutter at the contact, angry that it did so. She couldn't be attracted to the man who potentially would be her new boss. She wasn't even divorced yet and had no intention or interest in seeing anyone after it was finalized, casually or otherwise.

And definitely not her boss.

"I'm sorry I didn't get your name yesterday," he said lightly, shaking and releasing her hand, then taking a seat at the head of the table. She had thought that would be where he would sit because a file folder had been placed in front of the chair, along with a bottle of water. She had taken the seat to the left of his chair and took it again.

"I apologize for not offering it. I think I was more rattled by the wreck and the airbag releasing than I first thought. We both were concerned about our cars and how to proceed. If you recall, you didn't introduce yourself either." She paused. "You did give me your card. When I saw the familiar name, I should have said something right away. Things moved quickly, though. I made my calls. You made yours. Then you figured out I was having trouble with the dust released from the airbag and rushed me into the ER."

Autumn hesitated. "By then, it almost seemed too late to tell you who I was and that we had an appointment scheduled together this morning."

"Is that why you didn't let me drive you down to DFW to pick up a new rental?"

"Yes. I wanted everything to remain professional between us. Frankly, I didn't want to be beholden to you for such a huge favor, even though it was incredibly kind of you to offer to do so. I'm sorry the accident happened, and I'd like to put it behind us so that we can proceed with this interview."

She gazed directly into his eyes. "I am very interested in the position, Dr. Carson. Usually, I am excellent in a crisis. I supplied the names of three references when I applied for the job, and they will tell you that I handle situations in a professional manner and think quickly on my feet, pivoting when I need to." She hesitated. "I'm sorry you saw a very bad side of me yesterday. I raised my voice to you. I didn't treat you with the kindness I normally do others. That was wrong of me. I want you to know that's not who I am, the out-of-control woman you saw yesterday. I hope we can start fresh now."

Autumn watched him processing what she had to say. Obviously, this man already knew too much about her, and it wasn't from her resumé. She had admitted to him her husband had cheated on her, something she was terribly embarrassed about. She'd also lost her temper, something she rarely did. Other than yesterday, she couldn't recall the last time she had raised her voice, much less reacted in anger.

"I think we can do that, Ms. Ferris." He opened the folder and began skimming it.

"Would you please address me as Ms. Sutherland? Or even Autumn?" She felt the blush heat her cheeks. "You already know I'll be granted a divorce next week. I plan to petition the court and go back to using my maiden name. I want to be known as Autumn Sutherland at my next job, whether it's with Hogan Health or at another hospital."

"I see."

He continued to look through the file, and she recognized her resumé and transcripts, as well as recommendation letters she had requested be emailed to Dr. Carson when she had applied for the job. She was afraid to look directly at him, so she surreptitiously studied his long, tanned fingers as he turned the pages. He remained silent as he perused everything, and she wondered how many others had applied for this particular job.

Then he closed the file and gazed directly at her. "Tell me why you would be a good fit a Triple H."

She frowned a moment, and he added, "That's what I'm

calling the place. Hogan Health Hawthorne seems like a mouthful. It's my little nickname."

Autumn smiled at the admission. "I like it. It's catchy. People in Hawthorne will like it, too. They are more than ready to have a medical facility in town. I know because I'm originally from Hawthorne. I graduated from Hawthorne High School—Go, Hawks—and my parents still live here. Mom is the head librarian at the public library, and Dad is the superintendent of Hawthorne ISD, so my roots run deep within the community."

She paused, taking a deep breath. "I've been on the Hogan Health site to familiarize myself with the corporation's policies and how they run their healthcare network." Autumn smiled ruefully. "That's why I was in the parking lot yesterday when we literally ran into each other. I wanted to go inside and check out one of Hogan's hospitals in person. Little did I know I would experience it from the ER as a patient."

Dr. Carson looked perplexed for a moment, and then he burst out in laughter. She joined in, feeling much more at ease now.

"I'll be honest, Ms. Sutherland. I've been going through a lot of applications in the two months since I was hired on as the medical director. I'm trying to put a top-notch staff into place, and yours stood out. I had already decided to offer you a position before you walked through that door. Your credentials are exceptional, and when I made a few phone calls to confirm my opinion of you, I was a little envious of how your past co-workers showered you with praise."

He paused a moment. "But I want to go by the book. Why should I hire you? What's not in this paperwork that I don't know about you?"

Confidence filled her now. "First, I've held the position of charge nurse at a large hospital in Houston. I would need no training in that regard. I know how to manage a nursing staff and coordinate patient care and oversee the day-to-day operations of a department so that both workers and patients are in a safe environment. I'm excellent when it comes to delegating, and I read people well, so I can evaluate a person's strengths and weaknesses. Based upon my impressions and experience, I know how to get the best work performance out of a fellow professional."

Now, she was on a roll. "I like employing a personal touch—a hallmark of Hogan Health—so not only do I oversee admissions and discharges of patients, but I make certain I rotate with other nursing staff to provide bedside care and get to know our patients and help guide their progress. Many charge nurses are more about the paperwork. I'm efficient and organized and can do that while also seeing to direct patient care."

By now, she had his full attention, and he studied her with interest. "Keep going."

"Because of my people skills, I am able to make critical decisions on everything from resource allocation to patient assignments. I have an innate sense for how a unit should operate. I'm the point person, so I collaborate with physicians, first and foremost, but also with other department leaders and staff. I fight for my staff, making certain there's adequate staffing in my unit and a good nurse-to-patient ratio —another hallmark of Hogan Health. I'm familiar with designing a schedule and rotate it so no one gets stuck with multiple shifts they don't enjoy."

"Hogan Health looks for employees, especially in this type of leadership position, who are flexible," he said.

"That describes me," she said enthusiastically. "I've been in the trenches long enough to know how fast-paced a hospital environment is, Dr. Carson. As a charge nurse, I have to be a problem solver and have excellent decision-making skills. A situation can turn critical in seconds, whether it's a patient's health taking a turn for the worse or a conflict between staff members. I exercise good judgment and stay on top of things."

She smiled. "And despite flying off the handle yesterday, I can keep my composure in a crisis. I believe I'm open and fair-minded and staff members will come to me if they need something or see a need that I can do something about. Hogan Health is known for implementing evidence-based protocols to ensure the best patient outcomes. They also promote a culture which values collaboration and communication. They value proactive employees. I would be a valuable, contributing member to the Triple H team, and I hope you will give me your full consideration."

Dr. Carson had already told Autumn he wanted to hire her. With everything she had just related to him, her gut told her that she was guaranteed to land this charge nurse position. She wondered if she might be given a choice as to the unit she would work with.

He set down the pen he'd been holding, one which he hadn't used to take a single note. Having read about him and learned how quickly he had finished his schooling and medical training, she wondered if he had an eidetic memory.

"You have your heart set on being a charge nurse?" he asked.

"I do. For me, it would be a step backward in my career to simply be hired on as a staff nurse. While I've done that job, I'm looking for more of a challenge in this next phase in my life. I'm happy to work in whatever unit you might specify, though my experience is on the cardiac and obstetric wards.

If either of those positions are open, I would be more valuable there."

His gaze met hers. "I'm not going to be offering you a charge nurse position today, Ms. Sutherland."

Autumn heard what he said, feeling like a deflated balloon as it slowly lost air. She had no idea where she had gone wrong in the interview, unless he was holding her behavior after yesterday's accident against her. Some physicians had what was termed a "God complex," believing they were superior to others. She hadn't picked up on this regarding Dr. Carson, but the medical director might have those inflated feelings of ability and privilege. He might not have liked the way she had challenged him yesterday.

As disappointment filled her, she rose, saying, "Thank you for your time, Dr. Carson. I hope you find the people you are looking for to staff Triple H."

He frowned. "Sit back down, Ms. Sutherland." His tone held authority in it, and she complied.

"I told you I was ready to hire you before having ever met you. Now that I have spoken with you in person, I believe you've applied for the wrong position."

"Wrong?" she questioned. "I'm not following you."

"I wish to offer you the position as Triple H's Director of Nursing."

"*Director* of Nursing?" she echoed, floored by his suggestion.

"Exactly," Dr. Carson said, smiling enthusiastically at her. "You would work alongside me, helping to hire the nursing staff, as well as create a business plan and budget. You would implement all Hogan Health policies and procedures and work with each department's nurses to establish their particular goals."

"I could impact every nurse in the hospital," Autumn said, hearing the wonder in her voice.

"You would have the final say in each department's nursing budget, which would mean acting as liaison between the different departments, as well as with Hogan Health's corporate office. You would be the voice—the spokesperson— of the entire nursing staff at Triple H. It would be your responsibility to make certain all standards are maintained and your staff's voice is heard."

Her head was spinning from what he said. "I would be able to impact every aspect for nurses and patients at Triple H."

"Exactly," he agreed. "I know it's a big career trajectory jump for you. I'm almost certain Hogan Health would want you to earn your CDONA."

Dr. Carson referred to the Certified Director of Nursing Exam.

"I had thought about a position such as this being down the line for me," she admitted. "It was in the back of my mind when I earned my masters in nursing several years ago. I know to sit for CDONA, you need a year's experience at a director of nursing level."

"That's right." He sat back in his chair. "I can't think of a better candidate for this position, Ms. Sutherland. You have the drive, the personality, and the people skills. You're articulate and knowledgeable. Is this position something you would consider taking on? If not, you'd be the first charge nurse I hire, so you would have your pick of which unit you would prefer to be over."

Adrenaline rushed through her. "I'm ready for a new chapter in my professional and personal life, Dr. Carson. I would be thrilled to accept your offer to be Triple H's Director of Nursing."

He gave her an admiring glance. "I was hoping you would say that, Ms. Sutherland. You're exactly the kind of person who would fit well into the Hogan Health team, as well as the team I'm wishing to create here at Triple H. I'll admit that I've been focusing on filling out my staff of doctors first. You could start by filling the open positions for charge and staff nurses. It would take a huge chunk off my plate and free up time to complete other responsibilities."

She was elated. Overwhelmed. And very eager to begin.

"How soon can you start?" he asked.

Autumn beamed at him. "Is next Wednesday good?"

"If that's the soonest I can get you here, that's fine, Ms. Sutherland."

"I only have one request. Would you please call me Autumn?"

"In private, yes. In public, I would prefer to maintain a high level of professionalism."

"I understand, Dr. Carson."

He cocked his head. "Since we're in private, you should call me Eli."

"I can do that, Eli." She grinned.

"Then let's go tell Nancy you're on board. I'll have her pull the architect's master plans of the hospital, so you can become familiar with the layout. Are you free the rest of the day?"

"I need to leave Hawthorne by two this afternoon to pick up my sister at the airport. She's flying in from New York for our brother's wedding."

"Then we'll quickly review the plans before I walk you around the facility. I'll make sure Nancy provides you with a list of your job responsibilities, and you can see the number of nursing positions which need to be filled and start setting up interviews. Nancy will have the applications you can peruse.

Phone interviews—or even Zoom—for most of them, simply because time is critical, and we need to move fast."

They left the conference room and returned to Nancy. Eli told her that Autumn would be the new Director of Nursing. If Nancy was surprised by this decision, she hid it well. She joined them on the tour of the facilities and filled in the gaps for things Eli didn't know the details about. Once they finished, Nancy pulled together materials and placed them in notebooks, telling Autumn she'd have everything ready and in her office by Wednesday morning when she reported for work.

"I'll also have the corporate office send over your contract for you to sign when you arrive," the assistant said. "We're so happy to have you here at Triple H, Ms. Ferris."

"It's Sutherland," Eli announced. "Ms. Sutherland."

"Of course, Dr. Carson," Nancy said smoothly. "I'll make a note so that we get the right name and spelling on the door."

She confirmed with Autumn how to spell her last name, who said, "I hope you'll call me Autumn. In the future."

Nancy smiled. "I'd be happy to do that."

Eli escorted her back to the conference room, instructing Nancy to bring them copies of the proposed budgets. The two of them went over these for the next hour. Nancy popped in and asked if she could order lunch for them.

No, I need to get out of the office. Do you have time to grab a bite at Dizzy's Diner?" Eli asked Autumn.

"That's one of my favorite places to eat. I haven't seen Dizzy in forever."

"He hasn't changed," Eli said, causing her to laugh.

He walked her downstairs, and they decided to drive separately. By the time they finished their late lunch, it would be time to drive south to pick up Summer.

Dizzy greeted her warmly, giving her a bear hug. "Been too long, Autumn."

"I know. Hopefully, I'll be in more often now," she told him. Then leaning in, she quietly said, "I'm moving back to Hawthorne to work at the hospital. I just got the job, so not even Mom and Dad know. Keep it under your hat until Monday, okay?"

His eyes full of mischief, the old man said, "It's under lock and key." He mimicked locking his lips and tossing away the imaginary key.

Autumn enjoyed her lunch with Eli Carson. He seemed a little aloof, but she didn't mind. He asked her questions about growing up in Hawthorne and her family.

"My sister and I are twins," she shared. "Summer is a book editor in Manhattan, but she's always wanted to write novels. She's hoping to be published soon. Even leave her editing job if that's feasible. My brother played for the Dallas Cowboys this past decade, but he'll be coaching at Hawthorne High School this coming fall."

"I guess your parents will be happy to have two of their children coming back to the roost," Eli said.

"Where is your family?" she asked.

A shadow crossed his face. "I don't have any," he said softly. "I've always been on my own. Grew up in foster care. Never stayed with any one family for too long."

Without thinking, she took one of his hands and squeezed it. "I'm sorry to hear that, Eli. Hawthorne is a wonderful, friendly town. I think you'll find a home here. And the Triple H staff will become family to you."

Then she realized her hand was over his, and she quickly removed it. "I'm sorry," she apologized.

"Don't be," he said. "It felt nice."

She felt the heat flood her cheeks. "I wasn't being forward."

"I know you weren't. I didn't take it that way."

"I don't want to get involved with anyone," she blurted out. "Especially my boss. I'll be flying back to Houston on Sunday to finalize my divorce. Dating isn't in my future, Eli."

"I understand, Autumn." He dipped a fry into his ketchup and ate it, his face expressionless.

She was glad she had been upfront about things. She didn't believe any good came out of hospital romances. Working for Hogan Health in such a high-level position would be what she considered a dream job, and she didn't want anything to ruin it for her.

Not even a shy, handsome doctor. Eli Carson would be off-limits. Autumn just needed to keep telling herself that over and over.

Until she believed it.

CHAPTER
Five

A utumn said goodbye to Eli after lunch ended. She had insisted upon paying for her portion even though he told her it could be written off since they had spent a good amount of it discussing various things regarding Triple H.

She got into the car she had rented yesterday and drove back to DFW. Summer had texted when she got on her flight at LaGuardia, saying she was on time. Autumn checked the American Airlines app and saw that was still the case. She made a mental note of the terminal and baggage claim and parked, going inside to wait for her twin.

Minutes later, Summer breezed through the glass doors, spotting Autumn, and rushing toward her. They hugged long and hard, and she had to blink rapidly to keep tears from spilling down her cheeks.

"Oh, why did we have to wait for a wedding to see one another?" Summer asked. "You know, now that you're between jobs, you should come to New York. I can play tour guide for you. You've never visited me or the city. I have so much to show you."

Autumn had always wanted to travel but never had the chance to do so. Marrying straight out of college and going to work to put Flint through med school hadn't left any money for extras. She couldn't afford a cup of Starbucks, much less a flight to Manhattan. That would change with her new job. Her salary would increase dramatically, but she would have to work a year or more before she could put in for vacation time. Still, she would plan a trip to visit her twin and see all the places Summer talked about.

Summer hugged her again spontaneously. "Oh, I'm so glad you're going to be on your own now. Flint stifled you, Twinnie. You've been married your entire adult life. You'll finally get to live a little."

"Like you, Ms. Workaholic?" she teased.

"Okay, maybe I do work a lot, but I love what I do. At least most of the time. Oh, there's my bag already. Boy, that never happens. I think it's the first one coming down the carousel."

Summer collected a suitcase large enough to have been taken on a two-week trip to Europe. She rolled it to where Autumn stood. "Where to?"

"Follow me."

She led them to the rental, and Summer placed her suitcase inside the trunk, dwarfing the one already in there. They got into the car and went through the tollbooth, getting on the highway.

"All right, I waited to ask until we were on the road. Tell me about your interview."

"Well, I didn't get the charge nurse position," she began.

"What? That's criminal. I know you had to be the best candidate for it," Summer insisted. "You have experience. Great references. Just let me know the name of the jerk who interviewed you, and I'll kick his ass."

And Summer would. She had always been the more outgoing of them. The one who spoke up when Autumn was quiet. The one who never put up with bullying or nonsense and would protect Autumn with everything she had.

"His name is Dr. Eli Carson, and no ass kicking is necessary. In fact, you might want to do a little ass kissing. He thought I was better qualified for a different position." She waited a beat. "Director of Nursing."

Summer absorbed this information. "That sounds as if you'll be in charge of all the nurses at the hospital." She let out a huge squeal. "That's awesome, Twinnie! Tell me everything."

She cleared her throat. "The story starts the day before the interview. When Eli drove his car smack into my rental."

Summer gasped. "What?"

Autumn walked Summer through the story, with many interruptions from her twin. Her sister had never been one to let an entire story go by before she asked questions. Instead, Summer wanted details throughout Autumn's retelling of the events.

"That's like a meet cute out of a romance novel," her sister said.

She could feel her cheeks heating and focused on the road ahead.

"You're too quiet," Summer noted. "Spill. Wait. It *was* a meet cute! You *like* this guy. What does he look like? Hot as hell or just really cute? Tall or short? Dark hair or—"

"Stop," she insisted. "He's very nice-looking, but he's my new boss, Summer. Besides, I'm not even divorced yet. And when that happens on Monday, I need the ink to be more than dry on the papers before I jump into a relationship."

Summer shook her head. "I'm not saying leap into an

affair with your hot boss." She paused. "But you could think about it."

"Summer!"

"What are you going to do, Autumn? Do you have some timetable in your head about how long you suffer in silence and be alone—and lonely—before you'll allow yourself to date again?"

"No," she said brusquely. "I just think I should give myself some time before I even think about dating. And when I do dip my toe into that pool, it most certainly will not be with Eli."

"See? You're already calling him Eli and not Dr. Carson. That's a sign, Autumn."

"You're impossible," she told her twin, exasperated and yet loving Summer at the same time.

"Okay. So, no dating the Hot Doc. But I do hope you will not impose some arbitrary timeframe and stay locked away from the world. You might not feel like dating for a long while, and that's okay. But you might meet someone interesting, and if you do, you should go out with him. Autumn, it's been years since I think you had fun, much less great sex."

She gave her twin the side eye.

"All I'm saying is be open. Don't have some list of imaginary rules you must abide by. Go with the flow."

"Frankly, I can't see myself dating anyone anytime soon. I'm hurting, Summer. My marriage of eight years is ending. Yes, it hasn't been good for the last several years, and I didn't see much of Flint. We'd become more like roommates than spouses. It probably helped that I caught him naked with another woman. My love for him had been hanging on by a thread, and that snapped it. But I'm emotionally raw."

She didn't speak for a few minutes before saying, "I'm eager to start over. Get to know myself. I appreciate that I'll be living in Hawthorne again, and I know I'll be really busy, learning the new job and meeting new people."

"Mom said there'll be lots of new people moving to town. Doctors. Nurses. Support staff. I hope you'll find a few friends among them. And maybe go out with those friends and have some fun."

"That would be nice." Autumn sighed. "Honestly, I've worked so many hours over the last several years, I didn't have time for friends. Or me. Any free time was sucked up taking clothes to the Laundromat or shopping for groceries. I'd love to simply read a book after work or watch something on TV. Have dinner with a girlfriend. Work out."

"Well, I'm thrilled for you." Summer paused. "Where are you going to live?"

"I'm going to hit Mom and Dad up about that. I'd like to stay with them a couple of months while I look around. Mom has said there's not much available in housing, though there are new apartments and houses being built because of the influx of people coming to Hawthorne."

"They'll love having you home. Mom will spoil you rotten with her cooking. You'll also get to see West and Kelby."

"Isn't that crazy that he's the new head coach at our alma mater?" she asked.

West had played in the Super Bowl only a few months ago. He had retired from football and come back to their hometown, landing a position on the high school's coaching staff. A week ago, however, Coach Markham, West's mentor, had suffered a heart attack and had decided to retire from coaching and education. Since he was the school district's athletic director, he had asked West to take over as AD and head coach of the Hawthorne Hawks.

"I'm sure it'll be strange to him, being on the sidelines

and not out on the field, but if anyone can be successful at coaching, it's West," Summer said.

"I always liked Kelby," she said. "I can't believe they've gotten back together after all these years."

"Second chance romances are a big trope in romance," her twin said. "I think a lot of people out there wish they could have a do-over with an old flame. West and Kelby are simply proving that given a second chance, they are making a go of it. I'm happy for her, especially since she's had a rough go of things."

"Like what?" she asked.

Her twin laughed. "You really don't watch any news or read anything online, do you?"

"I told you that I haven't had two minutes to myself in what seems like years. What's up with Kelby? Obviously, I know she got divorced. I remember she married that UT quarterback, but I don't know how long that lasted."

"To make the proverbial long story short—and I'm getting this from social media—I haven't talked to Kelby or West about any of this. She married Bax. He got injured his first year in the NFL. Turned to alcohol and then drugs, so Kelby dumped him."

"That's awful."

"Oh, it gets worse. Bax was arrested several months ago for murdering someone. I think his bookie, but don't quote me on that. And he got shanked by one or more inmates while incarcerated and died. It was all over the news. Naturally, Kelby came up. Pictures of her and Bax were all over the internet."

"I'm sorry to hear that. Kelby has such a good heart. She didn't deserve a loser jerk like that."

"At least she's free now, and West is taking advantage of

that. Ooh, I see Sonic. Pull in now. I've got to have some Sonic ice."

Sonic Drive-ins peppered Texas, and the twins thought they had the best crushed ice. They both ordered large Dr Peppers and sipped on them as they drew closer to Hawthorne.

When they arrived, they claimed their luggage from the car. By then, their parents had rushed outside, eager to see their daughters. Hugs were exchanged, and Dad rolled their suitcases into the house.

"I'll take these up to Autumn's old room," he told them. She knew her mother had turned Summer's bedroom into a craft room after the twins had flown from the nest, while her room had become a guestroom.

"Mine's a little heavy," Summer warned.

Dad grinned. "This old man's been working out, I'll have you know." He picked up the larger suitcase and grunted. "I see I'm going to get an additional workout carrying these up the stairs."

"Don't complain," Mom said. "Our girls are home. I'm just so happy to see you both together. Oh, when you pulled up, I called in an order to Pizza Palace." She looked at Summer. "And I don't want to hear how New York pizza is the best in the world."

"It is really good, Mom," Summer said. "But since Mario and Mischa are from New York, their pizza is pretty darn amazing as it is. Now trying to get a good bagel in Hawthorne?" she sniffed. "That's another story."

Mom laughed. "I have to agree with you on that. That bagel place you took us to on our last visit was wonderful." She looked to Autumn. "I brought a dozen home with us on the plane. They say it's something in the water in New York that affects the bagels. I believe it."

Dad returned downstairs, opening a bottle of wine and pouring everyone a glass. The pizza arrived, and they gathered in the kitchen.

"I have some good news," Autumn began. "First, I'll return to Houston on Sunday because my divorce petition will be heard Monday. Basically, it'll be a rubber stamp kind of thing."

"I know you're hurting, honey," Mom said, sympathy in her eyes. "But you're still young. You have a lot of living ahead of you."

"I agree. Because of that, I'm going to be leaving Houston. I'm also going back to my maiden name."

"Sutherland is a good one," Dad agreed. "I think simply not having to introduce yourself as Ferris will help put distance between you and that boy."

"He's not a boy, Dad. He's a grown man. A doctor and a cheater. I'm better off without him. I know that."

"Where do you plan on moving?" Mom asked. "I know you probably have your pick of places. Everywhere seems to be short of nurses and teachers here in Texas."

"I had an interview today and have accepted a job at the new Hogan Health hospital opening soon here in Hawthorne."

Her parents looked stunned. Then Mom squealed with joy, jumping up to hug her. They both congratulated her. Dad poured more wine and made a toast. "To a new chapter and new start for our sweet Autumn."

They clinked their glasses together, and Mom said, "I'm thrilled for you, honey. Was it for a staff nurse or charge nurse position?"

"I interviewed for charge nurse, but Dr. Carson decided I would suit better in the position of Director of Nursing. I'm going to be in charge of all the nurses at the facility," she said, her excitement obvious to her family.

"That's remarkable, Autumn," Dad said. "A great deal of responsibility. Tell us what you'll be doing."

She walked them through what Eli had told her regarding the job description, and Dad likened it to many things he did as a school superintendent.

"We couldn't be more proud of you," he said.

"When do you start?" Mom asked eagerly.

"Next Wednesday."

"Oh, you'll need to live here for a while then," Mom said matter-of-factly. "That will give you time to find something. Rentals are scarce now. Even if you want to buy a home, not much is on the market."

"I don't want the commitment of buying just yet," she said. "I am tired of apartment living, though, after all these years. Maybe I can find a small house to rent and take some time before I buy a home."

"Meanwhile, I'll be living in my miniscule Brooklyn apartment," Summer bemoaned. "I can practically touch all four walls if I stand in the center of it."

"She's not joking," Dad confirmed. "I cannot believe what they charge in rent there. It's outrageous."

"My publisher is thinking about letting more people work from home," Summer said. "If I get the chance to do so, I will. I could work from anywhere." Her gaze met Autumn's. "Maybe even Texas."

She threw her arms around her twin. "I hope that's the case. Maybe we could be roommates."

"You always said I was too messy, Autumn, but living in a couple hundred square feet, I've had to change my ways. I'll keep you posted on what happens."

After dinner, they continued to sit at the table, helping

their mother make some table decorations for the upcoming wedding. Mom told them that BBQ Bliss would be catering the small affair, and Autumn couldn't wait to sink her teeth into some good brisket. Flint hadn't liked barbeque of any kind, and so she had rarely eaten it.

Summer began yawning, and Mom said, "You're on New York time, so you should go to bed. You, too, Autumn. You've been working around the clock. You need to be rested up for the wedding and then your new job."

"I don't want to talk about that this weekend," she said. "It's West and Kelby's time to shine. I'll tell them about the divorce and new job after the wedding."

She went up the stairs, arms linked with Summer. They got ready for bed and then climbed into the queen-sized bed. Summer linked her fingers through Autumn's.

"I'm so glad you're gaining your freedom," her twin said. "And coming home to Hawthorne."

"Me, too," she said softly, drifting off to sleep, feeling safe and happy for the first time in years.

CHAPTER
Six

The past six weeks had been some of the most satisfying of Eli's life. He had dabbled in everything from recruiting and hiring staff to working with the new board of trustees for Triple H. The hospital would officially open in two weeks, and Hogan Health would hold a large party to launch its newest facility, inviting the entire community of Hawthorne.

In the meantime, though, Nancy thought it would be a good idea if he held something at his house to welcome all his new department heads and build camaraderie. He had reluctantly agreed to do so this morning, having only been to two other parties his entire life.

Both had proved to be disastrous.

He now wrapped up the first meeting he had held with all his department heads, saying, "I hope you are beginning to settle into life in Hawthorne and here at work. To welcome you, I'm having a party at my house a week from this coming Saturday. Nancy will be sending you an evite. I hope you'll be able to join in."

Eli knew he was one of the few—if not the only person seated at this table—to have permanent housing. Hogan Health was paying for the doctors seated at this table to receive a housing allowance until they could find lodging of their own. Some were staying at Hawthorne's only motel, while others were renting rooms at local B&Bs. Construction was booming in the city and on its outskirts, with so many professionals associated with the hospital coming to the area.

"If you don't have any more concerns, I'll turn you loose to do whatever you need to be doing," he said genially.

People rose and began chatting, striking up conversations with others as they walked out the door.

"Could I see you a moment, Ms. Sutherland?" Eli asked, and she turned to head back in his direction.

"Have a seat," he invited, and she took a chair to his left, opening her notebook again and clicking her pen, poised to take notes.

He admitted to himself that the best part of the past few weeks had been getting to work with Autumn. She was not only knowledgeable and efficient but nurturing, as well. She had done an excellent job putting together a nursing staff Triple H could be proud of. A few of her hires were a bit unusual, but he knew it took all kinds of people to complete a hospital's staff. He himself had made a few unique hires with the doctors he had chosen to become his colleagues. Many of them skewed on the younger side, in their thirties, with a few in their early forties. He wanted a young staff, hoping to mold it not only in the philosophy of Hogan Health but also the vision he had for his new hospital.

And Eli definitely thought of Triple H as his.

Addressing Autumn now, he said, "This is on the personal side, not the professional one. I need some advice. I didn't want Nancy to know how socially inept I am." He paused. "You and I have become friends, and I feel I can show my true self to you."

"First, Nancy adores you, Eli. She tells everyone how brilliant you are. But thank you for trusting me. What can I help you with?"

"It's this damn party I mentioned at the end of our staff meeting," he said, sounding disgruntled. "Nancy thought I should hold something at my house. Something informal to bring the leadership of the hospital together in a more casual setting, so the department heads could get to know one another better. They've all been working long hours, trying to prepare for our opening, and they haven't had much time to create bonds with one another."

"I'm not quite sure where I come in," she said, frowning.

Eli sighed, straightening his tie. "I don't know the first thing about how to hold a party. I've only been to a couple and have never hosted one."

"That's easy enough," she told him. "Do you want to center it around a meal? Or just serve appetizers and drinks?"

He shrugged. "I have absolutely zero idea where to begin, Autumn."

She thought a moment. "Some of the department heads are new to Texas, so we should make it centered around Texas. I think you should have BBQ Bliss cater the food. They're the best barbeque joint within miles, and it would give people an introduction to Texas food. Shorty can not only prepare everything, but he can also serve. That'll free you up to host your guests."

He felt his face reddening and sheepishly admitted, "I don't have any furniture for guests to sit on."

Autumn frowned. "You live in a house with no furniture?"

Eli got up and closed the door, not wanting Nancy or anyone else to overhear what he was about to share.

"You may have noticed I'm a little awkward around people. Not good at the small talk thing. If it involves anything in the world of medicine, I'm fine. I can also hone in on a problem. Quickly find a solution. But anything beyond work-related stuff, I'm hopeless."

"I have noticed you're a bit reserved, but you seem personable enough when you're talking to others. Are you one of those introverts who performs as an extrovert at work?"

"That about sums me up," he admitted. "I know there's the whole philosophy of nature versus nurture. Well, I got absolutely zero nurturing growing up. I guess it's in my nature to be clueless outside of work situations."

He fell silent and appreciated that Autumn didn't push him. She had a good sense of people and simply waited for him to open up to her now. He had told her a little bit before, but he decided to put all his cards on the table with her now.

"I grew up in the foster care system. My mother was an addict who was forced to relinquish her parental rights. No father was in the picture. I went into foster care when I was five. By the time you're five or six, you're considered unadoptable. That too many bad patterns are already set, and you can't be saved from whatever forced you into foster care in the first place. I left my last placement home when I went away to college. I didn't age out in the system, Autumn. My IQ was off the charts. I skipped several grades and graduated from high school when I was fourteen. While those around me were getting their driver's license and starting to date, I was this oddity who sat on the periphery of each class. The young, pint-sized kid who always broke the curve and ruined things for everyone. I had no family at home and no friends at school because everyone was so much older than I was."

"That must have been difficult, being so alone."

"At the time, it didn't bother me. I was a loner and lost myself in a world of books. I won a combination of scholarships which paid for my undergraduate at Rice. I lived with two married professors my first couple of years, but they were childless and didn't interact much with me, which I preferred. The wife took a visiting professor's job in Oslo for a year, and so I moved to the dorm for my final year. Again, I was the fish out of water. Students in my classes were getting drunk and getting laid. I did neither. I earned my bachelor's degree at seventeen and headed straight to med school."

Eli shrugged. "Same song, next verse. I focused on my studies and learning everything I could so I'd be the best doctor. A few others reached out. Tried to befriend me, but we mostly wound up as acquaintances, trading notes and talking medicine. I had nothing in common with the other students in med school, other than the fact that we were in med school together. By then, some of my classmates were already married. A few of them even had kids, and I still wasn't old enough to vote. I'm socially awkward because I never had the shared experiences of others my own age. Playing video games with someone. Being on a sports team and competing together. That kind of thing."

She looked at him with empathy. Thank goodness he saw no pity in her amazing turquoise eyes. He wouldn't have been able to stand that.

"Do you not know how to choose furniture for yourself, Eli? If that's the case, I can help guide you through that process."

"Would you?" he asked eagerly. "I spent my residency and then seven years after that as a physician in the ER. I lived in an apartment close to the hospital and merely biked to work each day. I did get my driver's license along the way, more to use as identification than anything else, but I haven't had a whole lot of driving experience." He shrugged. "You know that."

She laughed, and Eli thought her laughter sounded musical. Hearing it made a glow fill him, as though his insides warmed with happiness.

"Hopefully, you're getting some practice driving around Hawthorne, from your house to the hospital and back. On errands. That kind of thing."

Nodding, he confirmed, "Yes, I am feeling more comfortable behind the wheel of a car these days. Would you mind coming to my house after work now? If you see it, you may be able to give me a better idea as to how I should furnish it. At least have something for people to sit on."

Autumn glanced at her watch. "It's close to quitting time now. Why don't we head to your place? Text me your address, and I'll meet you there."

Relief swept through him. "Thank you. You don't know how much I appreciate this." He texted her the address.

"See you in about fifteen minutes," she told him, leaving the conference room.

His step light, Eli returned to his office, where Nancy told him that she was ready to send out the evites.

"You have a time in mind, Dr. Carson?"

With confidence, he said, "I'm going to have barbeque catered in. People can eat and then mingle afterward."

"That's a wonderful idea. Shall we say seven next Saturday?"

He assumed that would be an acceptable time since she suggested it, so he merely nodded. "Sure, Nancy. Run with it."

"I already have the template in place. I'll simply fill in the time and send the evites out now."

Eli thanked her and went into his office, skimming to see if he had any emails which couldn't wait. Thankfully, he didn't, so he collected his briefcase and left his office, telling Nancy he would see her in the morning.

As he drove to his house, he felt the excitement building within him. He told himself not to make too much of Autumn coming over to help him. It was simply in her nature to help others. Still, he was eager to be in her company, away from work.

He pulled into the driveway, seeing a car sitting at the curb. As he got out, she did the same, heading up the sidewalk.

"Are you still driving a rental car?" he asked.

"No, this is the first new car I've ever bought. The size of the monthly payment makes me wince, but thanks to my new salary, I'm comfortable with it."

"Glad to hear that."

"Your house is beautiful. I love a Colonial. They're so traditional."

He had been drawn to the red brick house the moment he saw it. Thankfully, the people at Hogan Health had hired a good architect. The layout of the home was functional, and it was quite spacious. Not that he ever went to its many rooms, but it was nice knowing that he lived in such a beautiful place.

As he inserted his key into the lock, he told her, "Prepare yourself."

Opening the door, Eli ushered Autumn inside and closed it behind them. He tried to see the house through her eyes as he placed his briefcase on the floor.

The foyer was large. Off to the left was a home office,

shut off with French doors. To the right was a dining room. Both stood empty. They walked straight ahead into what he'd seen on the plans was called the great room. It held a lawn chair, a card table, and a folding chair. His laptop sat on the card table. The rest of the room was empty.

Her eyes swept over the room. "You weren't kidding. No furniture, other than this?"

"Nope. I have a sleeping bag in the primary bedroom. I did bring a few towels with me. A couple of plates and coffee mugs are in the kitchen. And I bought a decent coffeemaker for the first time so I could brew a cup before I went into work each day. Other than that, it's a blank slate."

"Do you mind if I walk through the house?" she asked.

"Be my guest."

Eli followed Autumn around as she familiarized herself with the floor plan. They went upstairs. It held three bedrooms and a media room, along with two bathrooms. Back downstairs, they stepped outside onto the large, covered patio.

"Eli, you have an outdoor kitchen!" she said, wonder in her voice. "And a pool! This will be a terrific place to host parties, including the one next Saturday. Of course, you'll need to fill the pool with water and hire a pool company to maintain it."

"I haven't gotten around to doing that yet."

"You need to," she insisted. "This is a lovely backyard. The landscaping is beautifully done. I know the house is new, but they did a wonderful job incorporating the trees which were already here."

He did like the mature trees on the property which shaded the large backyard and the lone oak tree that did the same in the front.

Autumn bristled with palpable excitement. "Let's sit and

make a list of all we need to do. There's no way you can have an entirely furnished house by next weekend, but you can have several of the rooms completed if we work fast. Let's start in the great room."

"Start how? I guess I need chairs. A sofa. What else?"

She took a seat in the folding chair, pushing his laptop aside. She placed the spiral notebook which seemed to accompany her everywhere onto the table and opened it, drawing a large square. She began sketching furniture in the room, creating different areas for conversation, and he saw her vision for the room coming to life.

"This is just a rough drawing. We can get online where they have great tools to do this very thing. You can simply type in dimensions of a room and sizes of different furniture and drop and drag the furniture around, putting it different places, until you hit upon what works for you. You definitely want this great room furnished in time for next weekend's party."

She paused. "Would you want a TV in here?"

"I don't watch TV," he said. "I've never had time for it."

"Things are different now. You're not in the ER eighteen hours a day. TV will be a way you can relax. No sense right now schlepping all the way upstairs to the media room. We'll put one in this room. I'm going to give you a list of TV shows to stream." She hesitated. "You do know what streaming is?"

He laughed. "I've heard of it. You'll need to tell me where to get it and what to ask for, though."

Autumn talked about having the dining room and kitchen furnished in the next ten days. The kitchen had a large eat-in nook which would seat a table of six easily.

She lifted the lid to his laptop, asking him to sign in. "We can see better here than on my cell phone."

After he logged in, she called up a few different furniture

sites, skimming through them, trying to get an idea of his tastes.

"Honestly, Autumn, I have no taste. The foster homes I grew up in were furnished with stuff from Goodwill or garage sales. Pieces which had seen better days. I've lived with this card table, chair, and sleeping bag for more years than I can count. You seem to have good taste. Could you just pick out things for me?"

Frowning, she said, "I'm happy to do so, Eli. I don't want to overstep, though."

"You're not. You're doing me a huge favor."

"You should definitely furnish your bedroom while we're at it. I would leave your entire upstairs empty for now. Of course, being the workaholic you are, we should also get your home office completed sometime in the near future."

He grinned. "I'm going to appoint you my fairy godmother. Just wave your wand, Autumn. For the first time in my life, I can say that money is no object. Hogan Health is paying me extremely well to run their new hospital. I have a beautiful house, and I need the proper furniture to fill it."

She nodded thoughtfully. "I'm going to pull some different things together online and share them with you. We may be able to order directly, or we could take a trip to a larger city so we could see a showroom. Sometimes, it's better to see things in person and get an idea of the size before making a purchase."

"I can't thank you enough for taking the time to do this. Can I buy you dinner?"

"Why don't we order pizza now? Have you had anything from Pizza Palace yet?"

Eli broke out in a huge grin. "You're talking about one of my favorite places in Hawthorne. I love that thin, New York crust they make."

"Then order something for us now, and I'll get started. And no pepperoni," she added. "While I like the taste of it, my stomach and pepperoni simply do not get along. Anything else is fine."

"All right."

He called in his usual order of sausage, mushrooms, and onions, and they told him it would be delivered in half an hour. Eli included two unsweetened teas with his order, having noticed Autumn seemed partial to the drink.

Pulling up the lawn chair close to the card table, he watched her zip through various sites, flagging different links. By the time their pizza arrived, he had a good idea what his great room and dining room would look like when furnished.

As they ate the pizza, she brought up different sites with bedroom furniture. He thought her taste excellent, things he would have chosen for himself.

They finished the pizza and sat back, with Autumn saying, "I'm so full. I think the best thing of coming back to Hawthorne, besides being close to family, is getting pizza from Pizza Palace."

Eli said, "I envy you. Having family here. Your parents. Your brother."

"And my new sister-in-law. Kelby was a couple of years ahead of me in high school, and she was always very nice. Her brother and mine were best friends growing up and are still close. West and Kelby kind of dated in high school, but it's nice to see them come together all these years later and be so happy."

She laughed. "They are so in love. I've teased them about how many times I've caught them kissing."

He had never kissed a woman. He had been on a handful of dates, but they had led nowhere. He'd thought the women boring and dating a waste of time.

But not Autumn Sutherland. She was never boring. It seemed they always had things to talk about. He looked at her mouth now, and something stirred within him. He wondered what it would be like to kiss her. Taste her. Make love to her.

That wasn't going to happen. Her divorce was in her recent past. She had specifically said that she did not want to date anyone.

Especially her boss.

Eli shoved all fantasies of beginning a relationship with her to the far corners of his mind.

"Are you free this coming Saturday, Eli? I really think you should see some pieces in person before committing such a huge chunk of change to furnish your house."

He had a conference call with Peter at ten-thirty, but he would find a way to move it to another time. Instead, he looked at her brightly.

"I'd be happy to accompany you to as many showrooms as you think are necessary."

Spending an entire day in Autumn's company would be his idea of heaven.

CHAPTER
Seven

Autumn checked her appearance in the mirror and muttered under her breath, "This is not a date. It's not even close to a date."

Then why did she have that butterfly feeling in her belly? The one where excitement was mixed with nervousness and you couldn't wait to see a person. The idea of spending time with them caused everything else to fall by the wayside.

Looking herself squarely in the eye, she said, "This is not happening. Eli Carson is your boss. This is the best job you've ever had. Don't blow it."

She still couldn't believe she had been hired to supervise the entire nursing program at Triple H. Hogan Health had spared no expense in putting together this hospital. She'd learned they had a standard floor plan, which they used throughout most of their healthcare facilities, simply tweaking it if needed to fit the community they built in. Triple H sat on fifty acres just outside Hawthorne, and the landscaping was top-notch. Inside, it had a clean, modern feel, from the lobby and cafeteria to the hospital rooms and operating suites. Autumn had to almost pinch herself to realize she worked there.

Her former hospital in Houston had been ten times as large, but it was older. While the technology was updated regularly, the place had a tired feeling about it. Every time she entered Triple H, she felt energized.

Or was that because of Eli?

She admitted to herself that she was attracted to the handsome medical director. They had become close during her time at the facility. Of course, he had known from the start, before she even knew who he was, that her rotten husband had cheated on her. That she was broken and an emotional wreck because of it. Thank goodness Eli had been able to see past all that and focus on her good qualities. Her knowledge and skills. Her compassion and empathy. The experience she brought. Autumn had always had a strong work ethic, and that had not changed with her coming to a new job. If anything, she worked harder, wanting to prove that she was qualified for the lofty position Eli had placed her in. His faith in her ability to oversee the entire nursing operation gave her great confidence.

Still, he was so sexy. Nothing like Flint, but everything that seemed to appeal to her, from his lean, hard runner's body to his dark brown hair which he constantly ran his fingers through. It was sometimes hard to stay focused in a meeting because she wondered what it would be like to kiss him. Autumn liked that he was a little offbeat, occasionally even klutzy. Somehow, it made him all the more attractive to her.

She couldn't imagine experiencing the childhood he had. Eli was forced to grow up fast, being thrust into the foster care system as a small boy. He had poured all his energy into school. Being so intelligent and skipping grades must have baffled his foster parents. They would have had no idea how to help him thrive when they couldn't even manage their own expectations about the boy whom they had taken in. Autumn was glad Eli had shared his past with her. She appreciated their growing friendship. She felt the trust flow between them. It was a long time since she had trusted someone, and it felt good.

Now, if she could only keep everything between them as just friendship in her head and not act impulsively. That was more Summer, who was outgoing and sometimes leaped before she bothered to look. Of the twins, Autumn had always been the more cautious and discerning. And look where that had gotten her, married to a man who used her to pay his way through medical school and beyond. A man who had thought her a simple fool and had broken his vow to be faithful time and again.

She picked up a tube of lipstick and applied a coat, rubbing her lips together and blotting them lightly with a tissue. Spritzing on a tad of perfume, she viewed her image one more time. She'd kept everything very casual today, wearing jeans and a striped blue and white T-shirt with slip-on sneakers. In no way was this a date. Eli was merely asking a friend to help him out in an area in which he had no experience.

Going downstairs, she saw a note on the kitchen table. Picking it up, she saw her parents had already left for a winery today. They wouldn't be home until after dinner tonight. Autumn smiled, feeling good that her parents were still very much in love and tried to do dates together, away from Hawthorne. Mom and Dad loved this town, but they always had eyes of its citizens on them when they were in public because of the positions they held within the community. Sometimes, they just needed to get away and be themselves without prying eyes on them.

She went to the laundry room and found a small cooler, placing a few bottled waters and soft drink cans in it and covering them in ice. Although they wouldn't be going far, she always liked to be prepared. She slipped a couple of protein bars in her purse, as well.

The doorbell rang, startling her. Taking the cooler and tossing her purse over her shoulder, she went to answer it and found Eli standing on the porch. His brown hair was getting a little shaggy, and he would need a haircut soon. She couldn't see his warm, brown eyes because they were hidden behind a pair of dark sunglasses. He wore a short-sleeved navy T-shirt and a faded pair of jeans. The shirt wasn't tight, but it sure wasn't loose. It nicely showed off his biceps and broad chest. He looked lean and mean and hot as hell.

"Hey," she said, handing the cooler to him so she could dig in her purse for her keys.

"Did I do something wrong?" he asked. "I can hear it in your tone."

She inserted the key in the lock and turned it. "Most people just text when they pull up. I would've come out and met you."

"Oh." He sounded puzzled. "I thought coming to the front door was the right thing to do."

"Maybe in 1975," she teased. "Don't worry about it. Let's go."

As they walked to his car, he asked, "What's in the cooler?"

"Just a few drinks. I never go on the road without drinks and snacks."

"Are we driving to Dallas or Ft. Worth?" he asked.

"No. The variety would be better, but delivery all the

way out to Hawthorne might be a problem. Remember, we want this furniture on hand before next Saturday. That's a week away."

He opened her door for her and then the one behind it, placing the cooler on the floorboard before going around and sliding behind the wheel. "Where to?"

"Two places in opposite directions. Since Hawthorne is halfway between Gainesville and Decatur, we're going both places. Decatur has a little more choice, so let's hit it first."

Her words caused her to start laughing, and Eli looked at her as he pulled away from the curb. "Did I miss something?"

"I guess since you never watch TV, you also don't go to the movies often."

"Never. Why?"

"My dad is a movie buff. Growing up, he made us watch old black and white classics such as *Casablanca* and *The Thin Man*. But he also liked other classic movies, such as comedies. One he and West watched over and over was *The Blues Brothers*. There's a line where Elwood says to his brother Jake, 'It's 106 miles to Chicago, we've got a full tank of gas, half a pack of cigarettes, it's dark and we're wearing sunglasses.' Jake replies, 'Hit it,' and off they go. I guess I'm hoping you have a full tank, and we have good luck today."

Eli pulled his sunglasses down on his nose. "Got the full tank and the glasses, Jake. We can stop for cigarettes if you'd like."

Autumn laughed again. "I like it when you loosen up, Eli."

He pushed the sunglasses back into place. "I think you're helping me do that very thing, Autumn."

On the way to Decatur, he asked about the TV list she was drawing up for him.

"I'm going to limit it to ten shows," she told him. "The

good thing is that they have multiple seasons. The bad thing is they have multiple seasons. It'll be time consuming to watch, but you can watch one every day when you get home. Unwind. Cook dinner. Have a glass a wine and watch some *Breaking Bad* or *The Sopranos* or *Game of Thrones*."

"I've heard of *Game of Thrones*. A few years back, that's all the residents were talking about. And I think I saw about five minutes of *Breaking Bad* once. The teacher who sold drugs?"

"Oh, it was so much more than that. The three I mentioned can all be pretty dark. I'll put a few lighter things on the list. A few quirky comedies like *The Office* or *The Good Place*." She sighed. "You've missed out culturally, Eli. We'll need to make up time."

"I do like to read," he said. "I don't sleep much. I never did, even as a kid. I'd come home from sixteen, eighteen hours in the ER and instead of crashing, I'd pick up some Chinese takeout and read for an hour before going to bed."

"What do you like to read?" she asked.

"Mostly thrillers. I like a ticking time bomb plot, where somebody has to save the world from something. David Baldacci. Lee Child. Michael Connelly. Brad Thor. Those are some of my favorite authors. Do you read?"

"Like you, I worked long hours in Houston. I pulled a lot of double shifts. I really didn't have time to read. I look forward to doing so again. While I think my new job will be challenging, the hours will be a lot more regular, especially once the hospital opens. Yours should be, too, except when a crisis hits."

They looked at one another and said in unison, "And there's always a crisis."

Both laughed, and Autumn said, "When I do read, I like the classics. Hawthorne. Hardy. Dickens. And Summer, my sister, turned me on to Jane Austen. I can never get enough Austen. Her dialogue is so witty. The people are so charming. Well, at least some of them are. I was very into *Downton Abbey*."

Eli gave her a blank look.

"Another cultural touchpoint you missed. It's the life in an English country house. Starts at the time the *Titanic* sank and moves forward over the next few decades. You get to see life above stairs, as well as glimpse life below stairs. That means the rich people versus the servants."

"That sounds interesting."

"I'll put it on the list," she said, taking out her phone and adding it to the growing list for him. She would need to pare this down, else it would be overwhelming. "You'll love *Downton Abbey*. It may be about a different era, but it's the story of people. I think that's what we see in a hospital, you especially with your ER experience. You get a slice of someone's life. A lot of times it's a bad slice, and we have to do our best to help a patient and their family through the trauma and help the healing to begin. At least, if that's possible. I know not all outcomes are good ones."

"Enough talk about work," Eli declared. "Let's talk the virtues of a queen-sized versus a king-sized bed."

Autumn giggled. "My parents started with a queen, but they upgraded quickly to a king. They had a dog and two cats sleeping with them, and they didn't have room for all five of them in their bed."

"They slept with their pets?" he asked, sounding perplexed.

"Lots of people do that. I guess you've never had a pet."

"Nope. Foster care is not conducive to owning possessions, much less having pets."

"Why? Did you have stuff taken?"

"All. The. Time. Kids who have nothing long to have something to call their own. Consequently, if you got something, you were the envy of everyone else in your home. Most places I stayed in were like a group home. They had five or six kids. Petty jealousy was the emotion of every day. That's why I learned not to focus on material possessions because they were fleeting. I invested in myself instead."

Hearing him talk about his experiences hurt her heart. Though he had given her no details, she could imagine at one point he had some prized possession which had been stolen from him. She wondered if he had ever celebrated a single Christmas or gotten a gift for his birthday and decided that those were things which were overlooked. His life had been one of survival, not the little luxuries in life.

They arrived in Decatur, shopping at a couple of different furniture stores. Eli sat on sofas and in chairs. He lay on top of mattresses, getting a feel for the bed. She had him look at coffee tables and lamps. In the end, they were able to find everything they needed in both stores. Delivery was no problem in the first store, but the second balked, saying they needed an extra fee to deliver before next Saturday. Autumn felt they were trying to take advantage of them.

"Maybe you should cancel that order right now," she told the salesman. "Dr. Carson needs these items in a hurry. He's the new head of Hawthorne's Hogan Hospital. Did you know the hospital is bringing almost three hundred people to the area? And that all those doctors and nurses and accountants and cafeteria workers and parking lot attendants are going to need furniture? Why, Dr. Carson would gladly share where he's buying his. Then again, he may not be buying anything at all here if he can't get it delivered in time."

She looked pointedly at the salesman, who blushed. "I

think we can arrange a timely delivery for Dr. Carson, Mrs. Carson."

Autumn didn't bother correcting the salesman's mistake. Instead, she asked, "When will we be receiving everything?"

He tapped a few keys on his computer. "Wednesday after four."

"That works for us," she said sweetly. "Thank you." She glanced to Eli. "Darling, give them your credit card."

He stifled a smile. "Of course, sweetheart," he replied, handing it over.

Ten minutes later, they walked out, laughing.

"You're good. Scary good," he told her. "You had that salesman dancing to your tune."

She shrugged. "He was just being difficult, trying to tack on extra fees. I knew he'd rather have the sale than lose it, so I pushed a little."

"If I ever had any doubt you could manage the entire nursing staff, that has been dispelled."

They reached his car and got inside. "We never took a break for lunch," he said. "And that protein bar you gave me didn't count."

"But we got a lot done," she protested. "Everything will be delivered by midweek. Now, you'll need to shop for things such as bed linens. Sheets. A duvet or comforter."

"Great. Another world I'm unfamiliar with," he grumbled good-naturedly.

"Tell you what. You can trust me with that. I'll handle the linens, including hand towels and soaps for your bathrooms. And toilet paper. You have to have rolls and rolls of toilet paper. That's the sign of a prepared house."

"Want to grab a very late lunch? Or should I call it an early dinner? It's almost four."

"I am hungry. Let's eat here in town before heading back to Hawthorne."

"We passed a steakhouse on our way here."

"Steak is always good with me," she happily agreed.

They entered the restaurant, and Autumn saw they were the only customers there. She supposed they were even earlier than the old people who liked to come for early bird specials.

The hostess seated them, and they both ordered Caesar salads, New York strips, and decided to share a few sides. Eli told her to choose, so she ordered mushrooms, lobster mac and cheese, and zucchini. They also ordered a glass of cabernet each.

The meal was pleasant. They weren't rushed, and the food was delicious. They passed on dessert, though, both saying they were too full.

Inside the car, she felt blanketed by sadness suddenly, knowing this day was coming to an end. As they drove along the highway, she wanted to tell Eli how much she had enjoyed his company today but was afraid to do so.

"Autumn, I had a really nice time with you today," he said as they drew close to the Hawthorne limits. "I've never really had a friend before. You're a really good one."

Her throat grew thick. Before she could reply, Eli suddenly swerved, and the car slid off the road into the gravel.

"What in the world?" she demanded, sounding like her grandmother.

"A dog. I swerved so I wouldn't hit him," Eli revealed.

He opened his door, and she did the same. That was when Autumn saw the pup limping along the side of the road.

"He's hurt," she said, and they both headed to the animal.

"Be careful," Eli warned. "He might bite."

They got about a dozen feet from the dog, and she dropped to her knees. "Hey, boy," she said softly. "Hey. Want to come see me?"

The dog, which might have been a golden color except for the dried mud covering him, turned. She judged him to be about four months old and ached at how scrawny the pup was. She saw a mixture of fear and hope in his eyes.

"Come here, boy," Eli encouraged. "That's right. Come see us. This is Autumn. She's a very nice lady. And I'm Eli."

As the pup slowly limped toward them, Eli also knelt beside her. "I want to keep him. I don't see a collar."

The dog reached them, and they both held out their hands, letting him sniff them. Gradually, they began petting the animal, whose fur was matted. She had no idea what kind of dog he was.

Eli scooped up the pup, holding him close to his chest. "I see me in him. Lost. Lonely. Needing someone." He grinned at her. "And I did go with the king-sized bed. There would be plenty of room. He's got no collar. No tags."

"He could have a chip," she warned. "But I doubt it, with him being so young. I'm afraid this is a case of dumping him on the side of the road, hoping someone would drive by and pick him up."

Eli's big palm began petting the dog's head. "You've got a home now. A home with me. I won't let anything happen to you."

Hearing that was when Autumn lost her heart to Dr. Eli Carson.

CHAPTER
Eight

E li had never thought about getting a pet. For years, his life had been consumed by work. He had only come home to his apartment to sleep and shower before returning to his ER. It would have been cruel to leave an animal on its own with him rarely at home. Things were different now, though. He had a stable job with regular hours. Having a dog would make for a good companion.

And this little pup needed him as much as he needed it.

"Are you really serious about wanting to keep him?" Autumn asked.

He nodded. "He needs a home, and I have one to offer him. If you're right and someone merely dumped him on the road because they didn't want him, I want this little fellow to know that he is wanted."

He scratched between the dog's ears, and the pup closed his eyes, a blissful look on his face.

"Well, if you're serious about this, Eli, you're going to need to name him. Or her. That's the first thing we need to find out. May I?"

Autumn leaned close and lifted the dog's tale for a moment. "Definitely a boy," she declared. "Now, you'll need to name him. He needs to hear it regularly so he can learn to answer to it."

"Atticus," Eli said immediately. "*To Kill a Mockingbird* is my favorite book. Atticus Finch was a real hero to me. I wanted to grow up and be a role model for others, just as he was. To make a difference, just as Atticus did in Maycomb."

She smiled. "I like that name." Glancing down, she stroked the pup. "Atticus, do you like your name? Yes, you do. You're such a good boy."

The dog's trembling had subsided, and Eli felt calmer simply for holding the dog. He decided their relationship would benefit the both of them.

"Let me drive the rest of the way," Autumn told him. "You need to continue to bond with Atticus. He already trusts you. Let's build on that."

"Good idea," he replied.

They returned to his car, with Autumn opening the passenger door so he could keep his arms around his new furry friend. She even leaned over and buckled Eli's seatbelt for him, giving him a whiff of her floral shampoo and the subtle scent of vanilla which clung to her skin.

Autumn got behind the wheel and started the car, making a few adjustments with the seat and mirrors.

As she pulled back onto the highway, she said, "There's not a twenty-four-hour emergency vet clinic in Hawthorne that I'm aware of. We can Google it, but I think you'll have to wait until Monday to have Atticus seen by a vet. He's going to need a physical and shots. Also, the vet will need to check to see why he's limping. You'll also want to have him neutered."

"We can examine him when we get back to my house,"

Eli said. "After all, we are medical professionals. We might be able to figure out what's wrong with him."

"You're going to need several things. Food. Bowls. A doggy bed."

"I thought you said that pets slept with their owners." He stroked Atticus soft fur.

"You can do that when you sleep at night, but you might keep a doggy bed in your great room. A lot of people crate their dogs during the day while they're gone for work. We don't know if he's housebroken or not, so you'll also need some pee pads. A few toys, too."

"I'm glad you know something about this. I've never been around a dog before."

"We had both dogs and cats when I was growing up. My parents lost their last cat a year ago. Dad said that they'd had pets for forty years of marriage and that he was ready for a break. I think he's beginning to eye retirement and do some traveling. I think he doesn't want to worry about boarding pets while they're gone. That's something you need to think about, Eli. Having a pet is a big responsibility. It's almost like having a child. You have to put their welfare above yours. They're helpless and dependent upon you. You're their protector. Are you up for that kind of responsibility?"

He glanced down at Atticus and already couldn't imagine life without the pup.

Looking back to Autumn, he said, "I think it was love at first sight. On both our parts. Yes, I'm up for being a dog dad. My hours are regular now. Once the hospital opens, I'll even have weekends to myself, for the most part. I'm ready to take on pet ownership."

"Then we'll stop at Walmart. I can pick up everything Atticus will need there. Besides what I mentioned before, he'll need a collar and leash. You'll want to walk him regularly."

"I'm a runner," he shared. "It's really my only hobby outside of work. Do you think he might be able to run with me?"

"We'll need to see what the vet says about his injury. If it's not too serious, I'm sure he'll be able to accompany you on your runs once he's healed, but you'll need to build up to them over time."

She pulled into the Walmart parking lot and rolled down the windows before cutting the engine.

"You two stay here. I know what Atticus will need, and this will give you more time together."

Eli sat contentedly with his new dog, holding an entire conversation with Atticus, telling the dog about his new home and what his life would be like. He had heard people talking about their pets before, thinking it a bit strange that they seemed so gaga over them. Now that he had a dog of his own, he was beginning to understand those feelings.

Autumn returned twenty minutes later, pushing a shopping cart.

"Stay in the car. I'll just put these things in the back seat."

She placed two sacks on the floorboard and lifted a large crate, resting it on the back seat. Digging through one of the sacks, she pulled out something.

"This is a collapsible bowl for travel," she told him as she opened it up and took a bottle of water from the cooler, pouring water into it.

Handing it to Eli, he placed it under Atticus' snout. Immediately, the dog began lapping at the water.

"This is good to keep in the car in case you take Atticus on a road trip with you. Or even if you drive somewhere and then go for a run, you can have water waiting for him in the car."

He handed the bowl back to her, and she filled it again. Eli let Atticus drink the rest of it.

"That's enough for now," Autumn warned. "We don't want him to drink too much too fast and get sick. Who knows the last time he ate or drank?"

As she drove to his house, she gave him advice on what to do with Atticus. How often to feed him. When to take him out to pee or poop. Told him she'd bought bags so he could scoop the poop.

"You're right," she said. "He's going to make a wonderful companion to you. Dogs are extremely loyal. Atticus will know that you saved him, and he will give his undying affection to you."

"Do you know of a vet in town?" he asked.

"Mom and Dad used the same vet for years, but he retired about three years ago. I think Dr. Bridges bought that practice."

He carried Atticus inside the house while Autumn collected the purchases from Walmart. She placed the crate and doggy bed in the great room and then brought the sacks into the kitchen, emptying them and placing the items on the counter.

"I only bought a small bag of food. The vet may have a recommendation for a line he carries at his practice. This will get you through the rest of the weekend, however."

She reached out and petted Atticus' head, and he woofed softly.

"I also bought some doggy shampoo and a brush. I think we should give him a bath now. He's not going to like it at all, but he needs to be cleaned up."

"Would you stay and help supervise? I'm not really sure how to go about it."

"I'm happy to help out, Eli."

They took Atticus to the primary bathroom, where Autumn filled the large soaking tub with a couple of inches of warm water. She had brought the collapsible bowl with her.

"This is what we'll use to rinse him for now. You might want to buy a plastic pitcher for in the future."

He placed the pup into the tub and saw how the dog began to tremble again.

"Just talk to him soothingly," she encouraged. "He already trusts you."

"This is for your own good, Atticus," he said gently. "We don't know how long you were out there or what's in your coat, so you get to have this nice bath."

He held the dog while Autumn poured warm water over the animal, wetting his coat. She poured shampoo into her hands and rubbed it across the dog's back, chest, and legs. Atticus seemed to understand that this was for his benefit, and his shaking subsided.

Autumn rinsed him, both continuing to talk softly to the dog.

"I didn't think to purchase a towel for him. We'll need to use one of yours."

"In the linen closet," he said, wincing as she opened it. He only owned two towels, and one hung from a hook on the back of the bathroom door now.

"I hate to use your last towel, but Atticus needs it," she said. "Do you think when I shop for your bedding that I might need to purchase a few bath towels?"

"Get whatever you need. I'll reimburse you for that and whatever you spent today on Atticus."

They dried the dog together and noticed that he favored

his right paw. Autumn held it up to her, inspecting it. She pulled out her cell phone from her pocket and turned on the flashlight.

"It looks as if he has a thorn jammed pretty deeply. That must be the cause of his limp."

Eli directed her to the medicine cabinet, where she removed tweezers, alcohol, ointment, and some gauze pads. He held Atticus steady as she removed the thorn and rubbed alcohol and the ointment on it. The dog whimpered slightly but stayed still otherwise.

"I'm going to cover his paw with one of the larger gauze pads," she explained.

She did so and retrieved a coated rubber band from her purse, placing it around the pup's leg. "This should hold it in place until he can see the vet."

Eli carried Atticus to the kitchen. Autumn poured half a cup of food into one of the pet bowls she'd purchased, and the dog enthusiastically gobbled it up.

"This should be it for now," she said. "He may not have eaten much for a good while, so we don't want him to overeat and be sick. I would feed him a third of a cup three or four times tomorrow at scattered intervals. Dr. Bridges will be able to give you more of a schedule once you see him."

Atticus looked as if he were about to drop from exhaustion, so Eli scooped up the pup and placed him in the dog bed in the great room. Within seconds, the dog closed his eyes and fell asleep.

He moved to sit in the lawn chair since Autumn had taken the folding chair.

"You've certainly had a full day, Eli. From buying furniture to claiming your first pet. I'm glad you decided to bring him home with you. I think rescuing an animal is one of the most noble things a person can do. I know people will pay hundreds—sometimes, thousands—to buy a purebred, but I believe rescue dogs make for the best pets."

"Should I leave a message at this Dr. Bridge's clinic?" he asked.

"That's a good idea. You want to get Atticus in to see him as soon as you can." She pulled her phone from her pocket and searched, giving him the vet's phone number.

He input it into his contact list and then dialed the number.

"You have reached the voicemail of Hawthorne Animal Clinic. Please leave your name, number, and a detailed message of what your pet needs. We'll get back to you as soon as possible."

After the beep sounded, Eli said, "This is Dr. Eli Carson. I'm the new medical director at the hospital about to open. I just found a dog abandoned on the side of the road when I was out today and want to adopt him if he doesn't have a microchip. I need to bring Atticus in for an examination and whatever shots he needs."

"Register," whispered Autumn.

"And register him with the city," he added. Eli left his cell number and said he looked forward to hearing from them.

"It'll probably be Monday before you get a call back. I do know they board pets, however, so someone will be in this weekend to care for those animals. Whether or not they listen to the messages and jot them down is another thing."

"I'm set to go for now. I can't thank you enough for all your help, Autumn. I wouldn't have known the first thing to do for Atticus. I appreciate your guidance, with him and the furniture shopping spree."

"I know the background you came from would be considered a disadvantaged one, Eli, but you've made so much of yourself. You have landed a wonderful position at a prestigious hospital. You're now a homeowner who's about to have furniture he can sit on and sleep in. And you've decided to join the ranks of pet owners. I think you're doing quite well for yourself."

"And I've made a friend in you," he said. "I've told you that I've never really had friends before, just acquaintances or work colleagues. I've never gone out for drinks with a group from work or gone to a movie or dinner with people. I value the friendship that we are building."

"I do, too," she said softly, looking at him in a strange way.

Then Autumn shot to her feet. "I need to go," she said brusquely. "I have things to do at home. I'm glad we were able to furnish most of your downstairs, Eli, as well as finding Atticus."

He accompanied her to the door, wondering if he had overstepped by sharing how much their new friendship meant to him.

"Thank you for everything today, Autumn."

She bit her lip as if she were thinking something over and then said, "I was glad to be of assistance, Eli. See you at work on Monday. Enjoy Atticus."

He watched as she hurried down the sidewalk. She got into her new car, which she seemed very proud of, and he watched her drive away, feeling a hole in his heart with her departure.

Autumn may have felt as if he were the one at a disadvantage growing up, but she'd gone from what probably had been an idyllic childhood in Hawthorne to a messy adult life. A bad marriage. A cheating husband. Years of pulling long hours of double shifts. Just as he was starting a new chapter in his own life, he realized that Autumn was doing the same.

And much as Eli wanted to take things beyond friendship with Autumn, if he tried to do so, it would likely cost him the friendship they had already established. That would mean working together and always being uncomfortable around one another. He couldn't risk that.

He went to his bedroom, bringing his ancient sleeping bag with him, putting it next to Atticus' dog bed. Slipping inside it, he rested one hand on his new pet's flank. He would have to direct all his affection to his new furry friend.

And not Autumn Sutherland.

CHAPTER
Nine

Autumn got out of the shower. She wrapped her wet hair in a towel and dressed before doing her makeup. Her hand trembled slightly, so she gripped her wrist with her fingers so that her smoky eye wouldn't turn into a mess.

Tonight was the party Eli was throwing for the department heads and their spouses or significant others, which would include about fifteen employees. She was eager to get to know this upper management staff better, especially because she was working on assigning all her nurses to their different departments.

But more importantly, she was eager to be in Eli's company again.

Foolishly, she had dashed out of his house last Saturday after spending a wonderful day with him. He had a dry sense of humor and an array of experiences well beyond what she had gone through. Just listening to his stories about patients who had come into his ER in Houston had been eye-opening. Autumn had never worked in the emergency room, so she was glad she hadn't after hearing about some of his more unusual patients.

They had shared a nice early dinner, and she found herself relaxed in his company. Eli wasn't a man who wanted her to impress him. Autumn had already done so, which was why he had hired her. Instead, it was pleasant spending time with him.

Not to mention how easy he was on the eye.

When he had almost wrecked his car a second time just to keep from hitting a stray dog, she began to understand him even more. It was easy to see how Eli related to a thin pup who had been thrown away. No one had wanted the dog, and no one had wanted Eli. Even if his mother had, her addiction had cost her a life of watching her son grow up. Autumn was glad Eli had found Atticus. It had endeared him to her.

And that could be a dangerous thing.

The more she was around Eli, the more she admired him. Respected him. And was attracted to him. She hoped she had hidden her feelings. With him not being able to read social cues well, most likely he had no idea of her growing feelings for him. They were why she had left so abruptly last week. Suddenly, Autumn had thought if she didn't kiss Eli Carson, she would go crazy. Since kissing your boss was a recipe for disaster, much less becoming involved with him, she had hightailed it out of his house without an explanation, hurting his feelings in the process. He had just told her how he valued her friendship, and she had been ready to lock lips with him. Putting distance between them was the only thing she could think to do.

At least she hadn't left him totally alone. He'd had Atticus.

Trying to keep things as normal as possible between them, she had stopped by his office late Monday afternoon, asking if Dr. Bridges had seen Atticus. The vet had, telling Eli that his dog was most likely a mix of a golden retriever and cocker spaniel.

That's when Atticus had popped out from behind Eli's desk, loping toward her. Autumn had bent, ruffling the dog's fur, giving her attention to the dog instead of hot doc.

Eli explained that Dr. Bridges had told him that Atticus was a hybrid which was intelligent, good as a family dog because he could be calm, and yet energetic and playful. He would need lots of attention and exercise. Eli had decided to bring Atticus to work with him this first week. His crate was in the corner of Eli's office, but for the most part, the dog would accompany his owner on a leash as he made his way about the hospital and have free rein within Eli's office.

It surprised her how quickly he had taken to Atticus, seeing that he had never had a dog or any kind of pet before, but it pleased Autumn. She saw the pair was happy with one another.

Of course, Atticus would be at tonight's party. She figured the dog would be the ultimate icebreaker. Already, he was proving popular with the staff because she had several people mention Atticus to her. He would likely be popular with patients, too, if Eli continued bringing the dog to work with him.

She turned her focus back to her appearance, blowing her hair dry. It fell past her shoulders and was board straight, unlike Summer's which always dried in soft waves. She spritzed on some perfume and then found a pair of sandals. Her sundress was new, a pale tangerine which went well with her auburn hair. She had even FaceTimed with Summer in the Target dressing room, trying on this dress and another one before her twin had encouraged her to go with the tangerine. She liked that it had pockets, always a plus to her.

Going downstairs, she found her parents sitting on the sofa, an open bottle of wine in front of them, along with a platter of cheese, crackers, and grapes.

"What are you up to this evening?" Dad asked, pausing the program they were watching. "We're bingeing ..." His voice trailed off as he looked at his wife. "What's this girl's name again?"

"Emily, dear. We're watching *Emily in Paris*."

"Well, she wears a lot of crazy clothes, but she's pretty charming," Dad said. "And she seems to fall in love with every good-looking guy that crosses her path. There's been a French chef. An English businessman. Now, she looks like she'll hook up with this Italian fellow."

"Don't say hook up, Dad," Autumn said.

"Well, that's what she's doing," he insisted.

"You do need to try this show, Autumn," Mom urged. "It's really cute."

"When I have time," she said. "I'm heading out now. Dr. Carson is holding a barbeque for department heads and admin staff at his house, hoping that everyone will click."

"Hawthorne can't wait for this hospital to open," Mom said.

"You'll get your wish next Wednesday. I hope you're both coming to the launch party for Triple H."

"You bet we'll be there," Dad said. "Everyone in the community can't wait to see it."

"Six o'clock, right, dear?" Mom asked.

"Yes. There's a reception in the lobby starting at six, then tours of the facility will be offered by various staff members. We officially open our doors at seven the next morning."

"We're getting old," her father said. "It'll be nice to have specialists closer to home instead of having to go up to Gainesville or down to Decatur."

"Besides the medical office building which has already opened, Hogan Health has broken ground on a second medical office," she told her parents. "I imagine there'll be every kind of doctor you would need to see in those two buildings."

"Glad to know just as we're falling apart, we have good medical care nearby," Mom said cheerfully.

Autumn went and kissed her mother's cheek. "You're not falling apart, Mom. You just had plantar fasciitis in your foot. I know it's painful, but it's not the end of the world."

"Your father's shoulder has been bothering him. His right knee, as well. I'm hoping to get him in to see someone now that school has let out. If he needs surgery, it can be done right here in Hawthorne."

"Don't rush me, woman. I'll go get things checked out when I want to."

Mom's brows shot up. "You'll go when I make the appointment, Joe. Because I know *you* won't make one."

"Dad, you'll never win this argument. Just go the yes, dear route."

"Good advice, Autumn. Enjoy your barbeque."

He hit play, and the TV show began again. Looking at the screen at the young woman, her dad was right. Emily did dress outlandishly. She had a kind face, though, and she was glad her parents still enjoyed watching programs together after over forty years of marriage.

That was what she wanted. A man like her dad, one who would be steady as a rock. Love her and their children. Enjoy doing simple things together, from sharing a glass of wine to reading in the same room. Flint had never made time for her, much less prioritized their marriage. Though it hurt to admit it, he hadn't loved her and had only used her.

Eli would never use anyone that way. He would never hurt anyone because he had been hurt so badly himself.

As she went out to her car and unlocked it, she tried to push thoughts of her boss away. The more she was around him, though, the more she wanted to know about him.

And the more she wanted more than the friendship he had offered to her.

Autumn arrived at Eli's house. She had stopped by once this week to deliver the purchases she had made for him, including bedding and linens for his en suite bathroom and the powder room. She had also picked up a few kitchen towels and even a mat for Atticus' food and water bowls.

She had not volunteered to be present when the two furniture deliveries had been scheduled. Eli had the printed diagrams of where his new furniture should be placed, and she hadn't wanted to insert herself into his personal life more than she already had. She saw Shorty's catering truck sitting in the driveway. The thought of brisket caused her mouth to water. No other vehicles had arrived yet although it was a few minutes past seven. She hoped all the department heads had RSVP'd and would be here soon, wanting Eli's first time hosting a party to be successful.

Autumn rang the doorbell, and it was quickly answered by Eli himself, who gave her a big smile.

"Come in," he said enthusiastically. "I just had my first bite of brisket. It's amazing!"

He sounded like a schoolboy as she entered the foyer, and she asked, "You've never had brisket before?"

"Barbeque is expensive. It's not something you feed a foster kid. Most of my meals from college until now have been eaten in cafeterias, either at school or a hospital, and they don't serve barbeque either."

Her heart went out to this man. She realized she had

taken so much for granted in her life. Her middle-class upbringing had been, in her own eyes, average. She now saw that it had been full of so many wonderful things Eli had never experienced, as well abundant love within her family.

Worry suddenly crossed his face. "You're the first here. I thought everyone would be here by now."

"Did you have a good response to your evite?"

Nodding, he said, "Nancy said everyone said they would be here." He paused. "Maybe they changed their minds."

"Don't fret," she told him. "A lot of people like to be what is termed fashionably late."

He seemed to relax hearing that. "Shorty and Marge have been setting up in the kitchen."

"You need to have a place for women to put their purses," she said. "Since your bedroom is off the great room, it would be convenient for purses to be left on the bed for easy access."

"Sure. But come look at everything."

He led her into the dining room, where she admired the large mahogany table. It seated ten and had a matching buffet. Autumn opted not to purchase a china cabinet for him since those seemed to be no longer important, and Eli had no china to display anyway. He took her to the great room, and she studied it with a critical eye. A large sectional and rocker were the focal point and placed in the center of the room, but there were also a few other conversational stations within the room where others could gather, as well as a reading nook by the window.

Glancing above the fireplace, she commented, "I see you also have a new big screen TV in place."

"I talked to Bill Bennett about that. He seems to be the resident sports authority and had several suggestions for what I should buy and what viewing package to purchase. My assistant's brother is a handyman, and he hung the screen. He also got the router set up, so my internet is on. I think the next room I want to work on furnishing will be my office."

"Everything looks really good in here, Eli. I hope you're happy with how the room turned out."

He shrugged. "I simply followed the floor plan you created. You have an excellent eye, Autumn. For color. Fabrics. Placement. Even the area rug in here and the dining room really pulls everything together. I couldn't have done that on my own." He paused. "My house is starting to feel like a home now. All because of you."

She felt heat rise in her cheeks and said, "Let's see how the bedroom looks," heading that way, Eli following.

The clean, masculine lines of the room, along with the palate of slate blue and grays, reflected Eli's personality. She hadn't gone overboard with too many decorative pillows on the bed, knowing he would find that too fussy. She had chosen a wall unit in cherry wood, which had storage beneath the bed, and an accompanying dresser and armoire. The bedroom suite fit well in the room. Autumn set her purse on top of the comforter.

"Have you been letting Atticus sleep with you? Where is he?"

"Begging in the kitchen. His nose perked up the minute Shorty brought in the first tray."

As they left the bedroom, she asked, "How is Atticus adjusting to his new life?"

Eli chuckled. "He acts as if he owns the house. Thank you for the recommendation of Dr. Bridges. I liked him the moment I met him."

"Is he housebroken?"

"He is. No accidents, so far."

"He may become excited with a lot of people in the house this evening," she warned. "Keep your eye on that. Cockers have a tendency to tinkle when they get overexcited. There also might be a guest or two who don't really feel comfortable around dogs, so you may need to lock him upstairs with a few of his toys."

She tried hard to keep from laughing at the stricken look appearing on Eli's face. "But you can wait and see. He might get along with everyone just fine."

They moved into the kitchen, and Shorty and Marge greeted her.

"It's great to have you back in town, Autumn," Marge said. "Now Meg has two of her birds who have returned to the nest. We'll just have to see if Summer sees the light and makes her way back to Hawthorne."

"I should've moved back a long time ago, for your barbeque and the pizza at Pizza Palace alone," she teased.

"Dr. Carson said you were the one who suggested we cater tonight," Shorty said. "Thank you for that, Autumn. I hear you'll be working at the new hospital."

"Yes, I'm going to be in charge of all the nurses on staff."

"We told Dr. Carson what a hardworking family the Sutherlands are and that he's got a real gem in you," Marge added.

The doorbell rang, and Eli said, "I'll get it," looking relieved that more guests had finally arrived.

"Thank you for agreeing to cater this evening," she told the couple. "Some of these new doctors will have never tasted barbeque. Eating something from BBQ Bliss will be a great introduction to Hawthorne for them."

In the next twenty minutes, every department head showed up, most bringing their spouses. Barbara Bennett, who was head of women's services, pulled Autumn aside.

"I'm so glad to see you here tonight. I don't want to talk

business, but I do have a few things I want to run by you regarding the scheduling of nurses in my department."

"Happy to listen and see if we can work things out," she replied.

They were still discussing Barbara's nursing staff needs when Bill, her husband and the new head of oncology, interrupted.

"Enough shop talk, you two," he said. "People are going through the buffet line now. Come grab yourselves a plate."

She accompanied the couple to the kitchen, where Shorty and Marge were dishing up plates for everyone. Autumn asked for brisket, a link of spicy sausage, and two jalapeño poppers, one chicken and one shrimp. She also took sides of coleslaw and baked beans and saw the kitchen table already filled with guests. She glanced into the dining room and saw it, too, had a full house.

"Guess we should make our way outside," she said, leading the Bennetts through the French doors.

Autumn had told Eli that he needed to pick out some patio furniture, saying that he should trust himself to do so. She told him both Walmart and the local Home Depot had a good selection this time of year and saw that he had done an excellent job. On the patio was a long table which seated eight. Colorful cushions adorned the chairs. By the pool, she spied four lounge chairs with tables between them, guests sitting on them, as well.

Taking a seat, the Bennetts joined her, and they greeted Dr. Paul Gentry, who was head of radiology. His wife Tilda would be in charge of imaging at Triple H. Dr. Steven Landry also greeted them. He was in his mid-forties, the oldest of Eli's department head hires, and the head of heart and vascular health. Steven introduced Autumn to his wife.

Eli joined them, Atticus shadowing him.

"I'm glad everyone found a place to sit," he told the group. "My only request is don't feed my dog. No matter how sad his eyes are."

Barbara said, "We're getting used to seeing Atticus around Triple H. Will he accompany you to work once the hospital opens?"

"I haven't decided yet," Eli told them. "He was dumped on the side of a road, and I knew I had to bring him home. This is my first week with him, and I didn't want him left alone in an empty house. He's not a service dog, obviously, so once the hospital opens, I can't have him wandering the halls with me. He's a good boy, though, so he may simply come to work with me each day and stay in my office."

Looking sheepish, Eli added, "He already has a doggy bed in my office, along with a few chew toys."

Bill laughed. "Barbara and I have two German shepherds, and they pretty much rule our roost. It was hard finding a house to rent which had enough backyard for them. We did meet with that architect you recommended, Autumn. If fact, we just bought a lot down the street from Eli and will break ground this next week."

Autumn said, "I'm glad the architect worked out for you. I knew about him because he drew up the plans for my brother's new house, and it's being built as we speak. West and Kelby bought five acres, so they'll have plenty of elbow room."

Bill asked, "West? As in West Sutherland?"

"That's my brother," she said proudly. "West is the head football coach for the Hawthorne Hawks."

Barbara laughed. "You won't find a bigger football fan than Bill. The Cowboys have always been his favorite team, even if he is from Pittsburgh originally."

"If you promise you won't drool all over him, I'll introduce you to West," Autumn promised. "He and Kelby are planning to come to the hospital's reception next week."

"I'll be on my best behavior. Scout's honor," Bill said, holding up the Boy Scout salute.

"West actually was a Boy Scout," she said. "An Eagle Scout, as a matter-of-fact. I'm sure you'll enjoy talking not only football but scouting with him."

As she expected, the food was delicious. Autumn had suggested to Nancy, who had placed the order with BBQ Bliss, to offer two desserts. One was peach cobbler and the other banana pudding. Both were hits.

After dinner, those outside went back inside to mingle. She found she enjoyed herself quite a bit, getting to know her colleagues in such a casual, comfortable setting. Everyone seemed to be having a good time and stayed on after Shorty and Marge packed up and left.

Around nine-thirty, Steven said, "If someone doesn't make a move to leave, we'll all need to break out sleeping bags and spend the night at Eli's. I'm usually in bed by nine, and I know most of you are the same."

Her gaze met that of Eli's, and they both smiled, knowing how he had slept in a sleeping bag until just a few days ago.

Goodnights were said, and guests went out the door. Autumn stayed behind, volunteering to help clean up.

"You don't have to do that," Eli protested. "Shorty and Marge took care of most everything. It's just going around and collecting drink glasses and napkins and washing those."

With a knowing look, she said, "Something tells me you're the kind of guy who won't be able to sleep until every-thing is clean and put away."

He laughed. "Guilty as charged."

Working as a team, it only took them a few minutes to gather up the used glasses and wash them.

"Shorty said he would stop by tomorrow and pick up the glassware," Eli shared. "I don't have iced tea glasses, much less wine goblets and beer steins. I suppose I've got more shopping in my future."

He looked at her hopefully. "Maybe you could help me with that, Autumn. You know I never could've pulled off tonight if not for you. For the first time in my life, I was relaxed around colleagues. Instead of talking work, I began making personal connections with the people I've hired. I listened more than I talked because I don't always have a lot to say, but I really enjoyed myself tonight. That's thanks to you."

Autumn took a step toward him, placing her palm against his chest, which was hard to the touch. She felt his heart speed up beneath her fingertips and gazed up at him. Eli looked back at her, seemingly baffled. With a boldness she never knew she possessed, Autumn slipped her hand around his nape and pulled him closer, until their lips met.

CHAPTER

Ten

E li had never kissed a woman.

But he had dreamed of kissing Autumn Sutherland for weeks now.

He had Googled how to kiss, finding a how-to site on Wiki, never dreaming he would actually have the opportunity to kiss Autumn. He knew he was supposed to stay relaxed. Keep his lips soft and not tense up. No smacking or smashing. Keep it easy and gentle. But her vanilla scent was swirling about him. The heat of her body near him had his heart pumping wildly. Eli decided to quit thinking about the kissing website.

And simply go with the flow.

Autumn's hand felt warm on the back of his neck. He liked her touch there. His hands came up and framed her face as their lips pressed together. She broke the kiss, her lips hovering near his, and then kissed him again. They traded a series of those light kisses, each one becoming longer than the previous one. His pulse began pounding, and he grew light-headed as this kiss lasted longer than all the ones before put together.

She had stepped into him, and their bodies touched. Her breasts pressed against his chest, and he had the urge to touch them. To kiss them, the way he was kissing her mouth. He couldn't do that, though. That seemed way out of line. Instead, he cradled her cheek with one palm and wrapped his arm around her, drawing her even closer. She made a little sound that caused his heart to skip a beat.

Again, she broke the kiss, and he felt the absence of her lips against his. He moved in, his mouth touching hers, thinking there was no place he'd rather be than kissing Autumn Sutherland.

Eli couldn't say how long they stayed that way, kissing, their bodies pressed together, heat enveloping him. His fingers pushed into her long, auburn locks, reveling in its silky feel. His heart raced, his breathing heavy. Instinct told him to end things now. Not to push too hard or too fast. So, he broke the kiss, his lips still so close to hers, his forehead resting against hers simply because he didn't want to break this intimacy between them.

"Thank you," he whispered. "I've wanted to do that for a long time."

He sensed her surprise. "Really?"

Lifting his head, he gazed into her eyes, ones which had mesmerized him from the first time they had met.

"Really."

"I've wanted to kiss you. I've been desperate to kiss you," Autumn admitted. "But too much was holding me back."

He slid his other arm around her. "You were very upfront and told me you had no intentions of getting involved with anyone. I know ending your marriage wasn't something you did lightly. That's why I didn't try to kiss you before now."

"My head told me to keep away from you, but my heart told me to go for it," she admitted. "You're right. I had no desire to be in a relationship." She made a face. "Especially one with my boss." She swallowed. "Not that this is a relationship. We kissed. That's all."

"Do you want to kiss some more?" he asked, hearing his voice was low and unlike it usually sounded. "Or is this the end of it?"

Her luminous eyes grew large. "I want more. But only if you do."

Eli smiled gently. "How could I *not* want more?" He hesitated. "But if I do kiss you again, I will need more."

"I'm not ready to have sex, Eli," she said, her voice tight.

"No, I'm not talking about that. I would never push you or rush you, Autumn. I know you're emotionally fragile now. What I mean is that if we kiss again, I'll become invested. In you. In us. I would want to see where this might go."

"I'm afraid," she whispered. "Not of you. Never of you. But what could happen if I let go. My heart is pretty damaged, Eli. You're a wonderful man. Thoughtful. Caring. Dedicated. I guess I'm afraid if I become invested and it's ripped away from me again, I might not survive it. Ending my marriage to Flint was the hardest thing I've ever gone through. I don't know if I'm ready to open up and try again."

Disappointment filled him, but he could understand her hesitation. He lightly kissed her brow.

"Then I think we should stop. For now, at least."

He relaxed, letting his arms fall away from her, feeling lonely without her heat next to him.

Autumn put a hand on his forearm, squeezing it. "Thank you for being such a gentleman. I'm never that forward. I mean, *I* kissed *you*. I've never made the first move. Ever."

He smoothed her hair. "I'm glad you did. Because I never would have done that."

She studied him carefully. "Because you're my boss?"

"Exactly that. I've worked too hard to treat my position lightly. I didn't want to do anything untoward and make you feel uncomfortable. I'm keenly aware of the fact that, as medical director at Triple H, I'm in a position of authority over you. I'm your evaluator. I didn't want you to feel pressured if I showed any interest in you."

She smiled ruefully. "Maybe we should quit now before things grow serious."

His gut tightened. Autumn was right. Becoming involved was a terrible idea. But now that he had kissed her, he didn't know if he could stay away from her.

"Whatever you decide, I'll abide by," he told her, his throat thick with emotion.

"Could you give me a little time to think about it?" she asked.

Eli held on to the tiniest glimmer of hope. "You can take all the time you need. I'm a fair man. I would never allow anything you said or did to influence how I view you as a professional."

"What is the policy regarding workers in a relationship?"

"I'll have to check with HR. Honestly, the thought never occurred to me. I have hired a couple of people who are married, and I know there's no rule forbidding that." He hesitated. "Do you want me to check with corporate?"

She took a long moment before replying. "Yes. I'd like to know. To be prepared."

Letting out a long breath, he said, "Okay. I'll do that and get back to you."

Autumn reached out and took his hand. His fingers wrapped around hers, feeling as if they belonged there.

"Thank you. I know you could have hired someone with more experience than I have to head up your nursing program. I also know that you could tell me just to forget about what just happened between us. I appreciate you showing patience with me and letting me get my head on straight before we agree to move forward or maintain our friendship."

"I want to be your friend, Autumn," Eli said. "Your friendship is very important to me, both at work and outside of it. Take all the time you need. Share what you feel when you're ready to do so. I'm in a no judgment zone."

Squeezing his fingers, she pulled her hand away. "You're a very special man, Eli. Thank you for giving me space." She grinned. "And not freaking out when I kissed you."

"It was a really nice kiss, Autumn," he said from his heart, hoping there would be many more of them to come. "Let me walk you to your car."

She collected her purse and then bent to where Atticus slept in his doggy bed. Autumn stroked the dog, who let out a sigh in his sleep.

"He must be dreaming of brisket," she said, grinning at the dog and then Eli.

He escorted her to her car, opening the door for her. Autumn stood looking at him, and it took everything Eli had not to wrap his arms around her and kiss her until they were both breathless.

"I think your first party was a resounding success," she told him. "It was nice to get to know people outside of work. Steven is always all-business, all the time. I saw a different side of him tonight."

"Who knew he liked to garden?" Eli joked.

"It was a great start to what you're building at Triple H. Relationships with co-workers are important. We need to know and respect one another. Trust each other. Tonight went a long way in making that happen."

"I'm glad you were able to come tonight," he said.

"Me, too."

Autumn leaned up on tiptoe and kissed his cheek. "See you Monday, Eli."

He watched her get into her car and start it. She gave a wave, and he returned it. Eli went back into his house, wondering if this had been the start of something with Autumn.

Or if he would remain in the friend zone with her.

CHAPTER

Eleven

A utumn saved the file she was working on and leaned back in her chair. Everything had gone extremely well the past two days. The entire staff of Triple H had reported, being greeted by Eli and all department heads. They had gone over the necessary training from human resources and headed to their various departments and positions. She had met with the entire nursing staff separately, laying out her expectations and those of Hogan Health.

She also spoke to those nurses as a Hawthorne native, telling them just how grateful the community was to have this medical facility in their town.

Though they weren't officially open for business yet and were simply going through dry runs of various situations, a few people had seen the lights on and stopped by the ER. One child had broken his foot at soccer practice. Another senior citizen had fallen while out walking her dog, becoming entangled in the leash and breaking her wrist. A third man had fallen off a ladder while changing lightbulbs, breaking his elbow. These patients were seen and tended to, but Triple H would officially begin seeing patients tomorrow.

First, however, they needed to get through tonight's opening reception.

Eli had asked Autumn to sit in on a Zoom meeting he had with Dr. Peter Richards, a VP of personnel for the corporate office, as well as his assistant Nancy Nichols. Dr. Richards had wanted a grand affair, but Autumn convinced him that was not the Hawthorne way, sharing that dressing up for most people in town meant church clothes for women and the newest, cleanest boots a man possessed. She explained that she knew what she was talking about, having come from the world of a prestigious Houston hospital and having attended several galas held there.

This grand opening reception would be held at six this evening, less than an hour from now. People would most like stop by on their way home from work and take a tour with a staff member, becoming familiar with the offerings Triple H possessed. The food would be simple, again thanks to Autumn's intervention, consisting of cookies and cupcakes provided by Luscious Layers, accompanied by what the town called Firecracker Punch. It was a mixture of cranberry and pineapple juice, with ginger ale and almond flavoring, and had been the go-to beverage to serve from everything to wedding receptions to school functions for as long as Autumn could remember.

Her cell rang, and she saw Summer's name and photo light up the screen. Picking it up, she said, "Hey, you."

"Hey, yourself."

"How is the world of publishing?" she asked her twin.

"It's still here. I'm still here. I spent two hours today at war with an author over some changes which need to be made to his manuscript. Granted, he is a bestseller. He's published five books, and the last two have graced *The New York Times* bestseller list. Still, he doesn't know everything, and I did my best to try and convince him to make the necessary changes so the plot would flow better."

"You can be stubborn when you dig in your heels. If he's going to work with you, he'll need to realize that."

"The thing is, I'm a new editor to him. His previous one recently left our publishing house and went freelance. I'm sure he would have followed her if he had the choice, but he still owes us this current book, plus one more. But enough about me. I'm calling to hear how things are going with you, especially with the hospital's reception tonight."

"We've had the entire staff present the past two days," she shared. "I've met with my nursing staff as a whole, then the charge nurses as a group, talking about scheduling needs, trying to balance people's strengths and weaknesses with others on their team. At this point, every nurse has been placed with a unit, and we'll see how they perform in that assigned area. It'll take some tinkering to get things right, though. It always does."

"And how is the elusive medical director?" Summer asked.

"Eli's not elusive," she said defensively. "He's merely reserved. Like me." She hesitated. "I kissed him."

"You did what? Way to bury the lead, Twinnie. Spill. Now. I want all the details."

Even though this was her twin, Autumn felt odd talking about the situation. Then again, her sister knew her better than anyone. It would be good to get Summer's opinion.

"Eli had a barbeque for department heads and administrators this past weekend," she began. "It went really well. I like the group he's pulled together to run Triple H."

"Quit stalling," her sister ordered.

"Okay. Anyway, I volunteered to help clean up after everyone left. We did so. And then ... I ... kissed him."

"Interesting. So, you made the first move. What kind of kiss was it?"

Autumn paused before answering, already having relived the kiss over and over.

"The kiss was really good. I wanted more of it. More of him," she admitted. "But we both kept our heads. I have to think really hard about this, Summer. He's my boss. My *boss*! If I get involved with him, tongues are going to wag. You know what a small town's gossip mill is like, and a hospital is like a small town, all unto itself. I don't want anyone to think Eli is showing any favoritism toward me. Besides, I haven't been divorced that long."

"Stop right there," her twin commanded. "We've talked about this. I know you. You're cautious by nature. How long do you believe you should wait after your divorce to date?"

"I don't know," she said defensively. "A year? Two?"

"See? That's what I'm talking about. In the meantime, life will just be passing you by as you cling to some stupid timeline, Autumn. Did Hot Doc seem interested in you after you initiated the kissing?"

She felt the blush flush her face. "He said he had been thinking about me but had respected the boundaries I had previously set up."

"I don't see what's stopping you," Summer declared. "You're two consenting adults who have a mutual interest in one another. You both are logical and won't do anything rash to jeopardize your careers. Don't twiddle your fingers, Twinnie. I know I leap before I look a lot of the time, but I'm advising you to look—and then leap. You're both wanting to get to know one another on a deeper level, beyond work. I think you need to give things with Eli a chance."

"What if it doesn't work out? Can you imagine how awkward that would be, coming into work and seeing Eli every day? Workplace romances which have ended put both people in a terrible position."

"Can you think how miserable you'll both be if you *don't* take this opportunity and give this relationship a chance? It might be something you'll regret the rest of your life. Nothing ventured, nothing gained. Except wallowing in unhappiness."

Autumn bit her lip. "I do really like him, Summer," she said softly. "He's intelligent. Thoughtful. Considerate."

"Oh, you mean everything Flint wasn't," Summer said sarcastically.

Ignoring that remark, she added, "He also is a little lonely. Eli was in foster care growing up. He never had a family adopt him."

"Oh, that's rough. No emotional support growing up? I couldn't have handled that. Mom and Dad were my rock. You and West, too. Family was everything to me."

"He's also off the charts. Like genius level. Skipped grades left and right. He was so much younger than his peers that he never really made friends with anyone."

Autumn swallowed. "We have become friends. I like him as a friend, but there's an undercurrent which is flowing between us."

"Then you owe it to yourself and Eli to pursue it. Give this a chance," Summer advised. "Don't start thinking it won't work out and how terrible it will be to work with him if it doesn't. Go into the relationship with a positive attitude. Be optimistic about it working out. I mean, come on, Autumn. You don't have to go on two dates and then marry the guy. Just test the waters. See if you're compatible. Then call me after you've kissed him again. I want to hear what kind of kisser he is since you've failed to elaborate on that topic now."

She laughed. If she were going to listen to anyone's advice, it would be her twin's.

"All right. I'll give this a chance. Go out with him. Even kiss him again and report back to you."

"It's not as if you'll be going out on a date with a total stranger. You said it yourself. That you've become friends. Hey, you even decorated part of his house and helped him with his new dog."

Autumn smiled. "It might be worth it to start seeing him just so I can be around Atticus. That dog is a little love."

"Keep me updated. Love you."

"I love you, too, Summer. Thanks for listening."

She set her cell phone back down on the desk, thinking about her twin's advice. She didn't want to be pessimistic about a relationship with Eli, yet she couldn't be overly optimistic. Hopefully, if they both went into this with their eyes open, neither would get carried away.

Glancing at her watch, she saw it was time to head downstairs and check on things. Autumn met Nancy in the foyer. Tables had been set up for the goodies from Luscious Layers. The charge nurse from women's services was stirring ginger ale into the punchbowl, and Autumn went to speak to the other woman now.

"How is the punch, Lucy?"

"I've sampled it. It's good." Lucy grinned. "It would be better with a little kick to it, but I know we're in the Bible Belt and not everyone is a drinker. I do plan to try Firecracker Punch whenever I give my next party. *With* a touch of vodka. Or even rum."

"I know you're settling in at Triple H, but where are you living?" she asked.

"The new apartment complex that's gone up a mile from here. A lot of the nurses have leased apartments there. It's me, my daughter, and our cat."

"Divorced?" she asked sympathetically.

"Going on two years now," Lucy revealed. "He was a lousy husband and an even lousier father. I didn't see the point of staying in Wichita Falls when he never made one single visitation to our daughter. When I heard through the grapevine about a new Hogan Health facility being built in Hawthorne, I decided this would be a place where my girl and I would have a clean slate. My daughter already loves her preschool teacher and has made a friend. I think I'll be happy here myself."

"I'm glad to know that," Autumn said sincerely. "As a member of the Divorced Club, I'm making a new start in Hawthorne myself."

"Didn't you say you were from here?"

"I grew up here. Finished nursing school at Baylor in Dallas. Then accepted a nursing position in a large hospital in Houston, where my husband had gotten into medical school after graduating from college. I was ready for the next chapter in my life after the divorce. So far, Triple H is everything I want."

Nancy joined them. "Everything looks great here. The staff is starting to assemble. I looked out into the parking lot and saw cars pulling in."

"Hawthorne people will be polite," she told the assistant. "The evite said six to eight, so no one will dare set foot inside the lobby until six on the dot."

Nancy shook her head. "Gotta love a small town."

As Autumn predicted, a stream of people poured in at six o'clock. They grabbed punch and a cookie and started chatting up the various staff members.

She made her way toward Eli, who excused himself.

"It's six-fifteen," she reminded him. "It's time for you to say a few words, then we can get the tours up and running."

He glanced around. "I don't see a microphone set up."

"Nancy has a lavalier mic for you," she told him, motioning the administrative assistant over.

Nancy clipped the mic onto Eli's lapel, and he slipped the rest of the unit inside his pocket.

"Go stand on the stairs so that everyone can see you better," Autumn suggested.

Eli nodded and moved through the crowd, going up a dozen stairs until he reached the first of three landings.

"If I can have everyone's attention for a moment?"

The buzz of conversations quieted, and all eyes were fixed upon him. Autumn stepped to where her parents were standing with West and Kelby. Mom slipped an arm around Autumn's waist.

"I'm Dr. Eli Carson, and I would like to welcome you to Hogan Health Hawthorne, or as we affectionately call it around here, Triple H."

The crowd chuckled, and Autumn knew Eli's nickname for the medical facility would stick.

"We are a proud part of the Hogan Health system, which has multiple healthcare facilities scattered throughout Texas and several surrounding states. They have built medical centers, along with professional medical buildings. As of now, Triple H sits on fifty acres, with room to expand, and ample parking. We are a full-service, acute care hospital, a Level III trauma center, and a primary stroke care facility. Triple H has one hundred and twenty-five beds at the moment, and a staff of almost four hundred and fifty employees. There's a finished medical building a quarter-mile to our south, and Hogan Health is building a second one next to it. All told, several hundred million dollars will be poured into Hawthorne with this hospital and the accompanying professional buildings."

Eli surveyed the crowd. "No one wants to get sick, but when you do? It's critical to have excellent healthcare in close proximity. There'll be no more driving to Decatur. Bowie. Gainesville. You can be treated right here in your hometown of Hawthorne. As Triple H's medical director, I have hired professionals in numerous areas, from women's services to oncology to cardiology and bone and joint care."

The crowd murmured approvingly.

"If you need surgery, the operation can take place here. The follow-up rehab, as well. If you're pregnant, all your checkups can take place in Hawthorne. You can deliver your baby in our state-of-the-art labor and delivery rooms. Any medical issue you have, from needing a triple bypass to placing a cast on a broken arm, Triple H is here for you. We will offer quick, efficient, professional care."

Autumn saw the satisfied looks on those who had turned out this evening. They would be glad to give up the inconvenience of driving thirty miles or more if they had a medical issue, and they would certainly take advantage of Triple H's ER if they experienced a medical crisis.

Eli paused a moment. "I'd like to introduce you to my various department heads, and then we're going to be offering tours of the hospital if you're interested. You'll be able to go inside the surgical suites. Radiology. Even the nursery for newborns." He looked to where his staff stood together. "So, give me a wave when you hear your name, folks."

He quickly ran through his department heads, not missing a one. She thought Eli was a good public speaker, despite his tendency to be reserved.

When he finished the introductions, he said, "I may be

the medical director for Triple H, but I'm going to turn it over to the real boss of this place, my assistant, Nancy Nichols. Nancy will get the tour groups started. Thank you all for coming tonight to both celebrate and support Hawthorne's new hospital."

The applause was enthusiastic, and Autumn felt pride swell within her, thrilled to be a part of a new hospital in her hometown, where she could make her mark and contribute to a place she loved.

Turning to her family, she said, "Thanks so much for coming tonight. I can't wait to show off everything about Triple H to you."

West grinned. "Does that mean we'll get an exclusive tour from the Director of Nursing?"

"Only if you promise to behave. I imagine Kelby can help keep you in line. Just don't let him touch anything," she teased.

Suddenly, she sensed a new presence and glanced to her left. Eli stood beside her.

"Just making the rounds, introducing myself," he said. Offering his hand to her father first, he said, "Eli Carson."

"Joe Sutherland. I'm the superintendent of schools here in Hawthorne. This is my better half. Meg is the head librarian at the public library."

Her mom shook Eli's hand. "Also known as Autumn's mom," she quipped. "We met briefly at the library several months ago."

"I do recognize the resemblance, Mrs. Sutherland. Both your hair and eye color give away that you're mother and daughter."

"Meg, please. No one in Hawthorne stands on ceremony."

Eli smiled gratefully. "Then please call me Eli."

Her brother offered his hand. "West Sutherland, Eli. I'm the head football coach at the high school and the district's athletic director. This is my lovely bride, Kelby. I know Hogan Health has its own PR and marketing department, but if you ever need anything on the local level, Kelby can help you out. She handles social media accounts, as well as creating everything from graphics to taglines."

Eli shook Kelby's hand. "Nice to meet you. Your husband is right in that Hogan Health does have an overall marketing department at their corporate headquarters, but I might be able to find some money in my budget for a local campaign."

Kelby produced her card and passed it to Eli. "Just in case you do find those funds. Holler at me anytime."

Eli looked around. "If you'll excuse me, I need to keep mingling. Nice meeting you folks."

"Let's come this way," she told her family, spying Coach Markham and his wife Georgia, and asking them to join their tour.

Chance, Kelby's brother, also fell in with them. "Mind if I tag along?"

"Of course."

Autumn took her group around the hospital, showing off the facility and then returning back to the ground floor lobby.

"I'm going to go and find Eli and talk about the hospital providing a doctor for athletic events," West said, taking Kelby's hand and setting off.

The others began moving away, beginning conversations with others. All except her mom. Meg Sutherland slipped her arm through Autumn's.

"You've talked about Eli quite a bit. I can see why. He's a very impressive man." Her mom's gaze bore into Autumn. "And something tells me that there's something going on—or about to go on—between the two of you."

CHAPTER
Twelve

Autumn's mouth grew dry, and she worried how to answer her mom, especially in a public place with so many people around them.

Mom squeezed her arm and said, "It's none of my business, though. It's yours. You've grown into a lovely, confident, impressive woman, Autumn. I want you to trust your own judgment." She paused. "But I do think Eli is someone special."

With a mischievous smile, Mom told her goodnight.

She collected her thoughts, which were racing. Was she giving off some kind of vibe that she liked Eli? Was he doing so for her? Or did Mom just know her so well that she picked up on the undercurrent sparking between Eli and her?

Mom and Summer were right. She was a grown woman who knew her own mind. She could be a professional at work and explore a potential relationship with Eli outside of the hospital. If it didn't work out between them, they could remain friends and colleagues. If it did, however, then she would be grateful that she didn't let some silly, pointless, made-up rule of not dating a man for a certain length of time wreck her life.

Confident in her decision now, Autumn circulated around the lobby. She saw people she hadn't seen since she'd graduated from high school and caught up on their news. In turn, they all showered praise on the hospital and Eli, saying he seemed to be the man to run things. Over and over, she assured everyone she came in contact with that Dr. Carson was an intelligent man with an extraordinary vision, and he would lead Triple H like no other.

Eight o'clock came, and the folks of Hawthorne magically disappeared. One minute, the lobby still had a good number of people milling about, munching on cookies and gossiping with neighbors. The next, the citizens of Hawthorne seemed to vanish, with only Triple H staff members present.

Eli looked around. "I don't see any non-hospital personnel here, so I'm going to say that I thought tonight was a tremendous success. Many leaders in the Hawthorne community came out, and all of you did a marvelous job, showing off our new hospital and answering their questions. I can't thank you enough for the investment you've made in Hogan Health Hawthorne."

"I agree," Steven Landry said. "The people of Hawthorne have been very welcoming of us, especially tonight. I'm eager to begin helping them with their medical needs."

"Everyone take home what's left of the cookies and cupcakes," Nancy said. "That way, we don't have to box any up and bring them to the staff break room."

Autumn didn't need to bring any sweets home. She left the lobby and returned to her office for her purse. She'd left it there so she didn't have to drag it around during the reception and subsequent tours. While there, she couldn't help but check her email. Then she took a call from her cousin, Darby, who was checking in to see how the reception had gone. They talked for about ten minutes, and then Autumn left her office. Going down the corridor, she saw Eli shutting off the light to his office. He fell into step with her as they stopped at the elevator.

"It went really well, Eli. I hope you're happy."

"Peter Richards is happy. I don't know if you saw, but he sneaked in during my welcome. Took a tour with one of your nurses and Paul Gentry. He found me afterward and said Hogan Health execs are pleased."

They stepped into the elevator. "That must be a relief for corporate to compliment you."

"He'll stop by tomorrow again. Wants to see how we operate with patients. From the surgical board, I know we have several minor procedures scheduled for tomorrow. You know how it is, though. Once a hospital opens for business, the doors never really close. Illness and emergencies don't recognize holidays or nights or weekends."

They stepped off the elevator and looked around. "This will be the last time we see ghost lighting like this," he said, speaking of how dimmed the lights were now. "Come tomorrow, lights will be on twenty-four seven. Where are you parked? I'll walk you out."

Knowing they were alone in the building, Autumn said, "Before you do, I'd like to talk if that's okay." She took in a breath and let it out slowly. "About us."

"Okay," he said carefully. "I did speak to the head of HR at corporate in Austin. She said Hogan Health had no rules in place for staff who chose to date. That it's left up to each medical director how to handle that situation. She said it wouldn't be good optics for a doctor to date a nurse assigned to his or her department. That a department head shouldn't see someone in their department since they would be evaluating that person. I agreed on those situations."

His gaze met hers. "That makes anything between us ... sticky. It's not as if I can hand off your eval to someone else. I'm in charge of assessing all my department heads and administrative staff. So, I guess that means we shouldn't start up anything."

Autumn heard the regret in his voice, as well as the yearning.

"But this HR head didn't forbid it outright, did she?"

Eli frowned. "What are you saying?"

She swallowed. "That I would like to see you outside the hospital. I believe we can be true professionals and maintain a collegial attitude at work. Away from work, we can—"

Before she could finish, Eli had grabbed her, his arms wrapping around her. His mouth found hers, and her pulse began beating at double its usual speed. She sensed the hunger in him.

And felt the same.

Slowly, he began to tease her lips apart, and she opened, ready to taste him. At first, it seemed slightly odd. He hesitated. Then it was almost as if he got a second wind, and they found their groove. His tongue swept along hers, and she stroked his in return. Their kisses became deeper. More fulfilling. Even drugging.

Her heart was still racing when he ended the kiss. His hands came up and framed her face.

"Thank you," he said huskily. "That was a kiss I'll never forget. I hope you won't, either. Forget—or regret it."

Autumn's fingers touched his wrists. "It was perfect."

Eli smiled. "Good. I thought so, too."

"I thought you were going to stop for a minute, and then you seemed to change your mind."

His thumbs caressed her cheeks. "I almost did. Because I didn't know what the hell I was doing. Then instinct just kicked in."

She frowned. "I'm not sure I understand."

Eli's hands fell away. She could see uncertainty in his eyes. He stepped away from her.

Something told her to go after him.

She closed the gap between them. "Eli, talk to me. If there's one thing I insist upon in a relationship, it's communication. I had very little of it in my marriage, and I see now how that led to making things pretty awful. I need transparency now if we're going to do this together."

His hand caught hers, and he brought it to his lips, brushing a tender kiss upon her fingers, making her belly flip-flop in a way it had never done before. She realized this one kiss with Eli had had more magic in it than any of the ones she had shared with Flint over the years.

Lowering her hand, he said, "You're the first person I've ever kissed, Autumn. The only one."

His words stunned her. Her mind raced, trying to comprehend what he had just told her.

He took both her hands in his and looked her straight in the eyes. "Foster kids don't have money to date. And remember, I graduated from high school when I was barely a teenager. I never had time or money to take a girl on a date. I did make pocket money, writing papers for other kids. Doing their homework. I tutored other students the entire time I was in college. My scholarships paid for tuition and fees and room and board, but I had nothing for clothes or incidentals. So I helped out others and made enough money to buy clothes I wasn't embarrassed to be seen in. To purchase my bike and a decent helmet."

Eli closed his eyes a moment, and she could feel the tension coiled within him.

"I want a different life than the one I've led since I became a doctor. I spent most of my waking hours in the ER, ministering to patients. Teaching interns and residents. Going home and doing a long run before crashing. Rinse and repeat."

Earnestness filled his voice. "ER medicine consumed me. I want my time in Hawthorne to be different. I want to have a social life. Develop some hobbies." He hesitated. "See you. That is, if you still want to after me revealing I've never kissed anyone before." He swallowed. "And you're bright enough to know that means I haven't had sex with anyone either. I'm pretty messed up, Autumn. The years in foster care damaged me more than I like to admit. I'm a lone wolf who finally realizes he wants more.

"I'd like to explore what *more* could be. With you."

His words touched Autumn's heart unlike anything she had ever heard. She reached up, her fingers entwining in his hair, and pulled him down so that their lips touched. She kissed him tenderly before breaking the kiss.

"I am honored to be the first woman you have ever kissed, Eli. And I want to do all kinds of things with you. Take you to a football game. Binge-watch one of my favorite series with you. Go hiking and waterskiing. Cook together."

She paused. "And when the time is right, make love with you."

This time, it was Eli who initiated the kiss. It was a lingering one, full of unspoken promises. He broke it and smiled at her.

"We'll work out the professional stuff. Hell, evaluations aren't even done for a year at Hogan Health. A lot can happen between now and then." He ran his fingers through her hair. "I love your hair. The color. The texture. The smell. I could play with it for hours."

Autumn grinned impishly. "Maybe I'll let you. This weekend. For now, we both need to go home and get a good night's sleep. Triple H opens at seven tomorrow morning, and I have a feeling we both want to be here when it does."

"Let me take you to your car." He smiled wolfishly. "And maybe steal a goodnight kiss."

She laughed. "You can try."

They went out a staff door and headed toward the employee parking lot, which was located next to the side of the building where the ER stood. As they reached her car, she saw headlights. A car came barreling up to ER, where only a dim light glowed since it was yet to be open. A man jumped out and ran up to the doors, knocking on the glass and shouting.

"Anyone in there? Please? Help! My wife is having a baby."

Without hesitation, Autumn and Eli broke out in a run, heading toward the car. By the time they reached it, the frantic man was returning and saw them.

"Can you help? Are you a doctor?'

"Doctor and nurse," Eli replied crisply. "Let's talk to your wife." He opened the passenger door, but it was empty.

Autumn heard a groan from the rear of the car and said, "Open the back of your SUV. What's your name?"

"Mike. Mike Anderson. My wife's Leah."

He hurried to the back and lifted the gate. She saw Leah Anderson lying on her side, moaning softly.

"I'll grab a gurney," Eli said, racing away.

"Hi, Leah. I'm Autumn. I'm a nurse at Triple H. Dr. Carson just went to get something to roll you inside. Can you tell me when you're due?"

"Not for another two weeks," the woman gasped, her face flushed. "Yesterday, I had those Braxton-Hicks contractions. Mike drove me to Gainesville, where my OB is. She said it was false contractions. That I would know the real ones when they came."

Leah panted as Eli returned with the gurney and instructed Mike to help him in lifting his wife onto it. Leah groaned as they transferred her.

Taking her hand, Autumn walked beside the gurney as the two men pushed it inside the ER.

"Have you had any children before, Leah?"

"No. This is our first." The last word came out garbled because Leah let out a shriek.

"Do you know how far apart your contractions are?" Autumn asked, glancing at her watch.

"No."

Mike raked his hands through his hair, looking helpless as Eli turned on lights. "The last time she yelled like that was just as we drove up to the ER."

"That's helpful, Mike," Autumn said soothingly. Glancing to Eli and back to Leah, she said, "We're going to take you upstairs to our labor and delivery rooms. Wash up quickly and check you out."

They began rolling the gurney, and Autumn realized Mike wasn't following. She glanced back. "Come on!" she urged. "Leah needs you now. You're a team, just as Dr. Carson and I are a team. It's going to take the four of us to get this baby out. We need to support one another."

Mike hurried and caught up to them just as the elevator arrived. As they rode up to the third floor, Autumn rolled up her sleeves, noticing Eli did the same. They took the mother-to-be into one of the labor rooms.

"Stay with Leah," Eli instructed. "We've got to wash carefully and get the instruments we'll need. Take her hand. Don't let go. Encourage her, Mike."

Leah began moaning again, and Autumn saw she had a death grip on her husband's hand.

Quickly, she and Eli threw on hospital gowns and washed their hands thoroughly before slipping on gloves.

"When's the last time you delivered a baby?" she asked.

"The day before I moved to Hawthorne. I had a lady come into my ER dilated to a nine. There was no time to get her anywhere. How about you?"

"I've worked the OB floor many times," she assured him. "We've got this."

They returned to the couple. Autumn helped Mike into a hospital gown while Eli examined Leah.

He looked to Autumn. "As close to a ten as I'll ever see." He glanced back to Leah. "It's time to push."

"Don't I get something to help with this pain?" she asked, crying out as another contraction seized her.

"It's too late for that, Leah," Autumn said calmly. "But we're all here. Dr. Carson and I have delivered countless babies. And Mike will be holding your hand, cheering you on."

"If I don't pass out," he said, his voice weak.

"Don't go fainting on me, Michael Anderson," warned Leah. "I've done the heavy lifting all these months, and I'll keep doing it until our little boy is out. But I need you here with me."

"Okay," Mike said, taking his wife's hand. "As long as I can stand up here and not down there." He looked at them. "I get queasy at the sight of blood."

Autumn told Leah how to push when the next contraction hit. As a team, they all praised Leah each time she bore down, her teeth gritted, pushing with all her might.

"The baby's crowning," Eli said. "You're doing a terrific job, Leah. Keep pushing when I tell you to."

"I'm getting tired."

"Only one or two more should do it," Autumn assured her, glancing to Mike, frowning at him.

He leaned down and kissed his wife's forehead. "You're doing amazing, honey. Scott is ready to meet you and me. Keep it up."

Her husband's encouragement seemed to give Leah new life, and her next push allowed the baby's head to come out, along with his shoulders. A final push, and little Scott Anderson had arrived in the world.

Glancing at the clock on the wall, Autumn said, "Time of birth is nine-thirty." She scooped up the newborn in a blanket she had collected. "I'll be back."

Moving across the room, she quickly assessed the infant's overall condition using the Apgar scoring method, which was done one minute after birth and again after five minutes. Between those exams, Autumn cleaned up Scott, who was fussing a bit by now. Premature and C-section babies often had a lower score, and Scott was a couple of weeks early.

Autumn quickly ran through the points of the scale, first checking for activity and muscle tone, where the baby's movement was active, earning him two points. His heart rate was slightly under one hundred beats per minute, scoring a one. When she suctioned his nose, looking for a response to stimulation, he began to cry, earning another two points. His color was mostly pink, though a few fingers were still blue. That meant one point. The final category was his respiration. Scott's was strong, and he received two points.

Swaddling him in a new blanket, she brought the baby to his parents, telling Eli, "Apgar was a six and then an eight."

He nodded. "Good for a baby who decided to make an early appearance. Afterbirth is handled."

She handed Scott to his mother. "You two bond for a bit. I'm going to see that a room is ready for you, and then we're going to clean you up, Leah."

Autumn didn't think either Leah or Mike heard her. They were too busy falling in love with their newborn.

After seeing that mother and baby would have all they needed, she rolled Leah and the baby to a room in the L&D area and saw that Leah was cleaned up. Eli had said no stitches would be necessary.

"We can put Scott in his cradle for now," she told the new mother.

"You're not leaving, are you?" Leah asked, suddenly in a panic.

"No. I'll be here with you all night. In about an hour, we'll let Scott try to nurse from you. I'll walk you through that."

"We've been to newborn classes," Leah told Autumn. "I listened carefully, but it's as if I can't remember anything right now."

She laughed. "It's called mom brain. Pretty much all you know right now is that you love this little guy fiercely. And Mike, too."

"You're right. I feel like a mama bear," Leah said sleepily.

"You take a nap, Mom. You'll have your work cut out for you soon enough."

Leah was already asleep.

She and Eli met with Mike, telling him everything had gone well and explaining that Leah would be in the hospital the next two days. They would meet with staff who would walk them through nursing, bathing, and swaddling, among other things.

"Can I see them?" he asked.

"Leah's sleeping now," Autumn cautioned. "Let her get some rest. But you can be in the room. Hold Scott if you want to."

"Oh, I want to," Mike said, a big grin on his face. "I was scared to become a father, but one look at my kid, and it was instant, pure love."

They got Mike settled with Scott, and Autumn told Eli to go home.

"I'd rather stay with you," he said.

"You've got a big day tomorrow. And the big Hogan Health guy is here."

"I've pulled all-nighters before."

Eli wound up staying. He was there by Autumn's side while she instructed the Andersons about how to care for their baby. He cheered Leah on as she learned how to nurse her child.

When six o'clock arrived and the day shift started arriving, they were discovered. Eli explained how the Andersons had come to the hospital needing a place to birth their baby.

"Scott Malcolm Anderson is our first official patient," Eli proclaimed. "We need to let corporate know. Maybe send out some kind of news release for the birth."

"You might want to go home and change clothes," she told Eli. "I'm going to do the same."

"I could use a shower to perk me up." He leaned in. "And maybe some more kisses tonight after work."

"I'll take that under consideration, Dr. Carson," Autumn said, smiling the entire way to her car.

CHAPTER
Thirteen

E li had always been able to compartmentalize, a skill he'd often used over the years. It had become particularly handy when he headed his own ER. He had directed medical personnel in several directions all at once, keeping all the patient traumas separate in his head. He could fire orders left and right, seeing in his mind what course of action would be needed to treat a patient. Many times, his swift thinking had saved lives.

This skill definitely helped him today with Peter Richards acting as his shadow. Eli forced himself to tuck all thoughts of Autumn away and focus on the Hogan Health official, who was here to see how Eli ran one of their hospitals.

He met Peter for breakfast at the diner, introducing him to Dizzy. During their meal, half a dozen people had come up to congratulate Eli on the opening of the hospital or ask him a question about it. One plumber even asked if they were still conducting tours since he'd been on an emergency call last night and hadn't gotten to attend the reception. Eli said they weren't at the moment, but he would consider doing so and took the plumber's card, promising to notify the man if the tours began up again.

"It wouldn't be a bad idea from a PR stance," Peter said. "Of course, visitors couldn't be taken everywhere in the hospital as they were able to do last night. The operating theaters would be off-limits. The morgue, as well. But you could show off many other parts of the hospital. Maybe run community tours once a month. That would allow groups such as Girl Scouts or a women's club to visit and see the facilities up close."

"I'll give it some thought and run it by a couple of my top staff members," he said.

"Be sure you get Autumn Sutherland's opinion on it," Peter suggested. "I'm very impressed with that hire, Eli. At first, I thought she might be too young and inexperienced to head up the entire nursing program. After meeting her last night, however, she impressed me. There's something special about her."

Eli couldn't agree more but couldn't gush about Autumn.

"She is well thought of. Of course, we're just beginning to gel as a staff, but Autumn is an integral part of operations at Triple H."

He moved Autumn to the back burner for now, asking Peter a few questions, and then they headed to the hospital.

"I want you to take me on a tour of the hospital now, Eli," Peter told him.

He frowned. "You did that last night. Why would you want to do it again?"

The VP smiled. "That was with no patients. I want to see what today is like as the staff is working."

Eli checked in with Nancy, telling her that Peter and he would be out and about in the hospital and to text him if anything important came up. They started in surgery, where half a dozen procedures were scheduled for today.

"All are elective surgeries at this point, unless someone comes through the door and needs immediate care." He glanced at the board. "Today, we've got a carpal tunnel. A mastectomy. A cataract operation. One for varicose veins. As our doctors see more patients, however, I know we'll add on everything from knee replacements to shoulder surgery."

He led Peter through each wing of the hospital, answered all the VP's questions with detailed responses.

"You really have a good handle on things," Peter noted. "I haven't been able to stump you once."

"It's my job to know everything as medical director," he replied. "I take it seriously."

They arrived in the labor and delivery section, and Lucy, the charge nurse, met them.

"We hear you are a real hero, Dr. Carson. You and Autumn. Mrs. Anderson can't quit singing your praises."

"I'd like to check on her and Scott," he said.

Lucy excused herself, and Peter asked, "What was she talking about?"

"After the reception last night, Autumn and I were leaving the hospital when a car came racing up. It stopped in front of the ER. A frantic man jumped out, needing assistance. His wife was in labor. Autumn and I brought the Andersons inside and delivered a healthy baby. Little Scott was two weeks early, but that kid has a healthy set of lungs on him."

"I'm surprised you didn't mention this before now," Peter said, frowning.

"To me, something like that is all in a day's work. I've had countless number of women in labor arrive in my ER in Houston. Many of them had never even seen a physician throughout their entire pregnancy. Some didn't even know they were pregnant. Leah Anderson did have an OB in Gainesville, but there was no way they could have made it that far with how close her contractions were. I was glad that we were able to help them bring their son into the world."

Eli went to Leah's room and tapped on the open door, seeing Leah look up and smile at him.

"Dr. Carson, come in."

They crossed the room, and he saw Scott sleeping in her arms.

Smiling down at her newborn, Leah said, "He just finished eating. The nurses say he'll be a good eater. I've also had several staff members in my room today, giving me instructions on how to care for him. I think everything you do at Triple H is first class."

Mike entered the room and greeted them, a coffee cup in hand. Eli introduced Peter to the couple.

Mike said, "This doctor opened up the hospital to us last night, sir. He and Autumn saved my wife's life. My baby's, too. There's no way we could've made it to Gainesville. She would've given birth in the car. With Scott coming early, I'm afraid we might have lost him." He glanced to his wife and smiled. "Leah, too."

"Triple H is here for the people of Hawthorne," Eli said. "And Scott had the honor of being the first baby born here."

Peter interjected, "I hope you don't mind if we do a little story about your family, Mr. and Mrs. Anderson. It would be terrific to put it on the hospital's website and let others know just how caring the physicians are at Hogan Health Hawthorne."

"We're happy to do anything," Mike said. "Dr. Carson and Autumn are the ones who deserve all the credit."

"Autumn came by this morning to check on us," Leah shared. "She also suggested a nipple cream for me to use. She's such a thoughtful nurse."

"We just wanted to stop by and check on you, Leah," Eli said. "Good to see that things are going well. If you have any questions before you're discharged, please let me know."

He gave Mike one of his cards and then guided Peter from the room.

"That's going to make for a fantastic story," Peter enthused.

"I hate that I don't know this detail, but who's in charge of our website? I know corporate set it up and it connects to the main Hogan Health website. We'll want to update things periodically from our end. How do we go about that?"

"Usually, your assistant would send information to our webmaster in Austin, but we've been opening hospitals left and right. It might be a good idea to hire local talent to update this hospital's website."

Thinking of Kelby Sutherland, Eli said, "Autumn's sister-in-law is a web designer and does graphics. She also handles social media accounts."

"Hmm." Peter thought a moment. "Our social media is handled at corporate. It's very generic, though. Why don't you schedule a meeting with her and have her create some social media accounts specifically for Hogan Health Hawthorne, as well as authorize her to do updates to your hospital's website? See what she can do with it. I'd like to sit in on the meeting with her if I could, but I'm driving north of Wichita Falls once I'm done here. I'm scouting land between there and Lawton, Oklahoma, trying to evaluate if it would be practical to build a hospital in that area."

"Let me give Kelby a call and see if we can work something out."

He pulled out the card Kelby had given him and dialed the number for Social Synergy Creations.

"It's Eli Carson, Kelby. I'm with one of the executives from the Hogan Health corporate office, and we'd like to schedule a meeting with you. Today, if possible."

"I could be at the hospital by one," she offered.

"That works for us. Thank you. I know this is last minute."

"I specialize in last minute, Dr. Carson. See you at one."

"She can meet with us at one this afternoon," Eli told Peter. "This pretty much wraps up your tour with me. Why don't we grab some lunch in the cafeteria and then head back to my office?"

On the way to the cafeteria, Eli told Peter about the cafeteria manager, who also served as the hospital's dietician, raving about the nutritious, delicious meals he had sampled.

"I've spent a good portion of my life eating hospital cafeteria food. At best, it was mediocre and not always nutritious. Veronica gives us a different take on what hospital food can be, both for visitors and patients."

They entered the cafeteria, and Eli saw it was about half full at the moment. Immediately, he spied Autumn at a table with several nurses in scrubs. It would be hard to keep thoughts of her on the back burner now with them being in the same room, but he doubled his focus and gave Peter all his attention.

"I like that you offer a salad bar," the VP said.

"We also have fresh bread which is baked at Luscious Layers, a spot in town. They'll also deliver a limited amount of sweets daily to us. Veronica says we should offer sweets, and she has some healthy ones on her menu, but there will always be people who want a slice of pie or cake with their meal."

He and Peter sat together, continuing to talk business. Eli deliberately seated himself so his back would be to Autumn.

When they finished eating, Peter said, "I see Autumn is about to leave. I want to see if she'll come chat with us a moment." He waved, apparently catching Autumn's eye, because she joined them moments later.

"Good to see you again, Peter. I hope that you're enjoying your time in Hawthorne and meeting the great staff and seeing firsthand the programs Dr. Carson has put together."

"Please join us," Peter encouraged, indicating a chair at their table, which Autumn took.

"I was telling Eli what a good hire you are," Peter said smoothly. "I was a little worried that you didn't have the experience necessary to manage a large group of nurses, but you've proved me wrong. Eli knew what he was doing when he hired you."

"I appreciate the opportunity Dr. Carson has given me," Autumn said. "I plan to take the Certified Director of Nursing exam once I have the required year of experience in this position."

"I heard that you helped deliver a baby last night after we all left."

Eli watched her face soften, and he thought she would be someone who took to motherhood with ease.

"I was happy to assist Dr. Carson with the delivery. Leah and Mike are first-time parents, and it was obvious how frightened they were. She had some Braxton-Hicks contractions the previous day, and she thought that her contractions last night were the same. By the time they figured out the baby was coming, it was too late to reach a hospital. I'm thankful we were here and able to bring Scott into the world."

They chatted a few more minutes before Autumn excused herself, saying, "Just like you, I'm making the rounds today in the different units. I'm trying to get to know my nurses, not only as professionals, but as people. I want to be out on the floor frequently and see them in action, as well."

After she left, they went to Eli's office. He informed Nancy that Kelby Sutherland would be arriving soon, and he wanted the meeting to occur in the conference room.

"I can have bottled waters and coffee ready for you, Dr. Carson," Nancy told him.

"Thank you, Nancy."

Kelby arrived a few minutes later, asking if she could give a brief overview of the services she offered, and they agreed to hear her pitch. She also showed them examples of her work and then asked what they might have in mind for Triple H.

Peter explained how everything from social media was of a generic nature, all under the Hogan Health banner, and how all webpage additions were made via the corporate office up until now, but he was willing to beta test using someone local who had their finger on the pulse of the community and could post to the Hogan Health Hawthorne website and social media outlets faster than corporate, as well as personalize the social media so that it reflected Hawthorne.

"I'd be happy to handle social media accounts for Triple H. I suggest we open separate ones for Triple H since I'll be tailoring those posts to this particular hospital. I'll always tag Hogan Health, however. I have various packages you can review and choose from. I would really enjoy placing human interest stories on the Triple H website. If your corporate office wants to maintain other areas, that's fine. I can also take over, however. I'm very flexible and want to do whatever you like."

Peter explained how Eli and Autumn had delivered a baby last night after the reception, and Kelby said it would be a wonderful social media story to kick off the opening of Triple H.

"I can email a contract now to Eli or you, Peter," she offered. "I use a local attorney, and he handles the legal end of things for me."

"What's his name?" Peter asked.

"Sawyer Montgomery. He's actually Autumn's cousin. If you'd like to meet with him, I can see if he's free this afternoon."

"Do that," Peter instructed. "I've got the authority to cut a deal such as this."

Kelby called the attorney, and he told them to come straight to his office. They did so and walked out half an hour later with a six-month agreement. Peter said he would be monitoring social media for the response, as well as reviewing the website weekly.

Kelby shook hands with both of them. "I'll head back to the hospital now. I want to get a few shots of the staff in action and talk with Leah Anderson before she is released. From what you've said, she'll be agreeable to me taking a few pictures and posting them to the new accounts I'll create for Triple H. Thank you again for your business, gentlemen."

Peter said, "Hogan Health couldn't be more pleased with how smoothly things are running, Eli. I think I'm going to go ahead and hit the road now. If you'll drop me at my car, I'll leave now."

They returned to the hospital and said goodbye. Eli went back to his office and took a moment to simply breathe.

Today had gone better than he had expected. He was

glad he was able to answer all of Peter's questions and believed Hogan Health was happy with his performance and that of his staff. He also looked forward to seeing what Kelby Sutherland could do to raise the new hospital's profile on social media. Of course, that meant he'd actually have to get on social media himself to see the progress. Maybe Autumn could help him with that.

He caught up on his emails and then decided to text Autumn. He asked how her day had gone and if she might want to grab some dinner with him after work. He didn't hear back from her immediately and figured she was busy.

Ten minutes later, though, Nancy buzzed him, saying that Autumn was here to see him.

"Send her in." His heart skipped a beat, and he tried to set aside instant nerves which sprouted inside him.

She came through the door, looking fresh as daisies blooming in springtime, despite the fact she'd been up all night with Baby Scott and his parents.

Closing the door behind her, she came and took a seat in front of his desk, asking, "How did everything go with Peter?"

"Really well. I wanted to share all that with you and hear about your day."

"I'm not quite ready for us to go public," Autumn told him. "I want to keep this between the two of us for just a little while if that's all right with you."

"I think that's a good idea," he agreed, wishing he could take her to a restaurant in Hawthorne and proclaim to the world that this amazing woman was interested in him. He understood what she was saying, though.

"What if we do takeout at your house instead?" she asked.

He smiled, relieved that she still wanted to be around him. "That sounds good to me. What would you like? I could stop at the diner if that sounds good. I do takeout from there a couple of nights a week, so that wouldn't raise any suspicions."

"Ordering two entrees wouldn't clue Dizzy in?" she asked teasingly.

Eli chucked. "Not at all. Sometimes, I order two at a time so I have a meal for the next night and don't have to stop. Of course, our cafeteria has pretty darn good food. I may try to eat my main meal of the day in the hospital at lunch and have something lighter at night in the future. What would you like me to order for you?"

"Anything but turnip greens," she declared, laughing. "It's probably the only food on the planet which I refuse to put in my mouth."

He glanced at his watch. "What time are you leaving?"

"I can leave now," she said. "I'll just go back to my office and grab my purse and turn off the lights. I'll meet you at your house."

"Sounds like a plan."

Autumn left, and Eli picked up his cell. Dizzy's diner was listed on his favorites since he called the number so often. Although he enjoyed eating in the diner, he had been putting in long days these last few weeks in the hospital, causing him to yearn for peace and quiet once his workday ended. He found it easier to stop by and pick up a meal and take it home and eat in silence, with Atticus for company.

Dizzy himself answered, and Eli said, "Got a takeout order for you, my friend. What's today's special?"

"Meatloaf, mashed potatoes, and green beans, Doc."

"I'll take one of that. Add to it a chicken fried steak, zucchini and tomatoes, and black-eyed peas."

"Rolls, cornbread, or both?" Dizzy asked.

Usually, he went for the cornbread, but he didn't know

Autumn's preferences, so he said, "Mix it up a little this time. I'll be there in about fifteen minutes."

"See you then, Doc."

Eli looked at his briefcase and decided it would stay here tonight.

Because he had other things he planned to do with Autumn.

CHAPTER
Fourteen

Autumn slung her purse over her shoulder and left her office, satisfied with how her workday had gone.

And very curious about what tonight would bring.

When Eli told her that he had never kissed a woman before her, she had to admit she was more than surprised. Actually, she had hidden her shock. He was an adult in his mid-thirties. The fact that he hadn't kissed a woman, much less that he was a virgin, was mindboggling in this day and age. Yet she found it incredibly sweet. She would never truly understand how out of step he had been his entire life. Simply growing up in foster care made his background far different from hers. Where Autumn had two loving parents and two siblings who would defend her and adored her, Eli had no one.

The fact that his intellect was vastly superior to everyone around him also made him an anomaly. As he skipped grades and went deeper into his academic career, he would have been considered everything from peculiar to abnormal to plain weird. While Autumn had not been as popular in school as Summer, who could make friends with a wall, she'd had her fair share of good friends. They had bonded over activities, from playing in the band to working on the newspaper and yearbook staffs. She had shared experiences with these friends, as well as her twin, and those friendships had been a part of the fabric of her life.

Eli had none of that. No home support. No friends. She knew he must have been respected at work since he'd led and managed a large ER in Houston for several years, but being the boss would have set him apart from the other doctors and nurses. Her heart ached, knowing he had never truly been close to anyone.

Until now.

From the moment they'd met, Autumn had sensed a kinship with Eli. She was grateful that he had hired her to work at Triple H, but she was eager to explore what there was to know about him beyond the intellectual professional he was at work. He did have one hobby. Running. And she loathed running. Walking was a different story. She could walk all day and enjoyed being out in nature. She hadn't really minded walking to work and giving Flint the use of the car, except for days when it rained.

Would Eli be interested in any of her hobbies? She hadn't pursued any of them since she'd become a nurse because she had no time working so many shifts and trying to maintain the apartment, with cooking and freezing meals and doing laundry in a Laundromat. She enjoyed watching old black and white films, especially film noir. She used to garden. Maybe he would want to do some of that with her in the local community gardens. She enjoyed reading, especially Jane Austen, an author Summer had gotten Autumn hooked on years ago. Though she'd never played any sports, she liked watching football and basketball. Maybe Eli would want to go to a game with her or at least watch a few on TV.

So many possibilities lay ahead. She wanted to explore everything with him.

And she definitely wanted to explore his body.

When she'd placed her palm against his chest, it had been as if she pressed it against a hard surface. Eli was lean, and she figured under his clothes, he had some nice muscles from the running. She didn't want to rush anything between them, especially something physically. No matter what Summer said, Autumn was just coming off a divorce. She didn't want to leap into bed with just anybody.

Then again, Eli wasn't just anybody. He was someone very special.

She reached her car and glanced to his assigned parking place. The rest of the staff parked wherever, but a slot was designated for the medical director of Triple H. It was empty now, so he had beat her out the door. Autumn drove straight to his house and parked at the curb. She took a moment to run a brush through her hair. Her makeup was intact. She found the small atomizer she carried in her purse and spritzed one wrist, rubbing the other one against it. Her racing heart told her how excited she was to spend more time with Eli.

Had she ever been this excited with Flint? It had been so long ago, it was hard to recall. She didn't want to compare the two men, but she couldn't help but do so. Flint was slightly taller and had a megawatt smile, which he had always used to his advantage. Eli rarely smiled, but when he did, his entire face lit up. Flint was self-centered, the kind of doctor who thought he was better than everyone around him. On the other hand, Eli showed more confidence but was also willing to listen and be more flexible.

Autumn told herself not to waste any more time thinking of her ex-husband. She was sure he hadn't given her a single thought since they had divorced. She didn't care what he was up to or what woman he was with. She would focus on her new job and her budding romance with Eli.

He pulled up less than five minutes later. Just seeing him get out of the car had her grinning like a fool. She joined him on the front porch.

"Smells good," she told him.

"You can smell that?" he asked, slipping the key into the lock.

"I have an excellent sense of smell," she informed him. "I should have been a perfumist. I saw a documentary about creating perfumes years ago. The people who create fragrances are called perfumists, but in the industry, they're referred to as a nose because of their keen sense of smell and how they can not only distinguish various smells but how they can create moods when they invent perfumes. It's innate."

She followed him into the kitchen, and he set the brown sack on the counter. He placed his hands on her shoulders.

"I'm glad you went into nursing. We never would have met otherwise. I don't wear cologne. I've never dated a woman, and so I've never perused perfumes."

Autumn liked the feel of his large hands and wished she could shed her jacket and blouse so that his fingers rested on bare skin. She told herself to show patience.

"My sense of smell can be a curse," she told him. "I can't stand to be near anyone who goes too heavy on the fragrance they're wearing. I once told a teacher that I needed another assigned seat because the girl next to me wore such a heavy musk perfume that I couldn't breathe sitting next to her. I couldn't even think to take notes."

"Did she oblige?" Eli asked, his hands sliding slowly down her arms, bringing a delightful shiver where they went.

"She did. She told me that she had stopped dating a guy in high school because he wouldn't lay off spraying cologne at his locker between classes."

By now, his fingers had entwined with hers. "Good that she was sympathetic." He leaned in and kissed her softly. "You smell good to me. You always do. It's not too heavy a scent. As Goldilocks would say, it's just right." He paused. "*You're* just right."

Eli kissed her again, his lips pressed against hers, his fingers tightening about hers. He broke the kiss.

"Let's eat while it's hot. Then see what we feel like doing."

Anticipation flittered through her.

Autumn unloaded the sack as Eli took Atticus out to pee. She noted paper plates and eating utensils had been included. She opened a smaller bag and said, "Oh, good. Rolls and cornbread. I love both," as man and dog returned.

Eli gave Atticus a scoop of food and some fresh water and said, "I'm glad I requested each. I usually just go with cornbread. It's not something I ever ate growing up. The cafeteria at med school made it once a week. They also served chili that day. When I think of chili, I automatically add cornbread to that mental image."

"You like chili?" she asked, opening the Styrofoam containers and seeing the two different entrees. "You have a preference?"

"Take what you want," he told her.

"We'll split," she said. "I love variety and tasting different things."

They sat at his new kitchen table, Atticus sitting atop her feet.

"Back to your question, I do like chili. My question is simple and might just be a relationship breaker." He studied her a moment. "Beans or no beans in it?"

"Definitely a no to the beans," she replied. "But I've heard that's mainly a Texas thing. What else do you like to eat?"

She found out he leaned toward Mexican and Italian food and thought the best dish in the world was a heated slice of apple pie with a scoop of vanilla ice cream accompanying it.

"I rarely ate desserts growing up. Again, the foster kid thing. As I told you before, most of the people who took me in also had four or five others fostering with them. Desserts were a luxury. When I got to college and found I could get dessert with every meal, I went a little overboard."

"That's where your running came in handy, I'll bet."

"I've always enjoyed running. I ran cross country in high school. The sport appealed to me because I was on my own. I was my full height of six feet by the time I turned eleven. Cross country athletes were cool. They didn't mess with me. No hazing like you see in other sports. We just all ran together. No talking. I stayed in my head and balanced chemical equations. Outlined essays. Thought about the kind of doctor I wanted to be."

"You knew that you wanted to be a doctor?"

"From the time I was young. Maybe seven or eight. One of my foster brothers fell off the top bunk and broke his elbow." Eli paused. "There might have been a little wrestling involved. He was younger than me. Cried like there was no tomorrow. He'd only been in the home a few days, but he stuck like glue to me. The foster dad, some guy who's name I don't even remember, said he'd take him to the emergency room. That was the first I'd heard of that. The kid wouldn't go unless I went along with them.

"That was my introduction to the ER and the world of medicine."

Eli talked about how kind all the medical professionals were that night. They were thorough but gentle. They allowed him to stay and watch the examination and the cast being placed on the younger boy's arm.

"I don't recall that kid's name. I was transferred to a different home not too long after that. But that night made an indelible impression upon me. From then on, I knew medicine would then be the trajectory I followed. What about you? When did the nursing bug bite you?"

"High school. Science courses came easy for me. So did math. I aced AP Bio and AP Chem. I wanted to do something in the sciences, but I thought research would be boring. I took some career tests, and the results came back with me scoring the highest in science as a subject and empathy as a trait. I've always been a nurturer. Looked after others before myself. I met with my counselor to discuss the results, and she said nursing would be a good fit for my interests and personality."

"Did you ever consider becoming a doctor?"

Autumn shook her head. "Not even for a minute. I looked into how long it would take, and I didn't want to be tied to school and all that training for that many years. I wanted to get out and do. Nursing has been something I enjoy. I also like what I'm doing now. I'm very organized, and I am blessed to not only see the big picture but be interested in the details going into that picture. I'm getting to use all my talents and skills in my current position."

She paused and took a bite of the mashed potatoes. "No

one does potatoes like Dizzy's Diner. I don't care if they're mashed or fried or plain or sweet. Dizzy's does things right."

They talked easily throughout the meal. Autumn learned that Eli had received a perfect score on his SAT and MCAT tests, a rare feat. He listened to jazz when he ran and liked to read a physical copy of newspapers.

"I know that sounds like I'm some Baby Boomer, but there's something about the feel of a news page that speaks to me. I've never subscribed to a newspaper, but I picked up stray sections in the locker room at the hospital to read. The funny thing is that I never watch the news on TV or scroll through news sites on my phone. I probably shouldn't admit this, but I rarely know what's going on in the world. Who's been elected to office or what sports team won the night before. I've been laser-focused on work. While I take my new job very seriously, I want to take my foot off the gas pedal and slow down a little. Maybe learn about a sport and watch a game on TV."

"I'm happy to do that with you," she told him. "I love watching sports on TV or in person. I'm not a runner, but if you walk Atticus, I'm happy to accompany you."

"Let's take him for a walk now," Eli said. "He's used to getting one after I've eaten dinner."

As they left the house, he took her hand in his. The simple gesture both comforted and excited Autumn. While they walked Atticus, who took his time sniffing everything along their path, she told him about what being a twin was like.

"I always had a playmate. Someone to talk to. A person who never judged me and would stick up for me. Summer was always more vocal, and I was more introverted, but we were a yin and yang. We worked together."

"Where is she now?"

"In New York. She's working for a publishing house in Manhattan, but what she would really like to do is write romance novels. She's almost ready to let me read her first one. I can't wait."

"You said before that you enjoy reading."

"It's one of my favorite things to do. Not that I've had much time for it lately."

"You'll have to give me a list of books I should read. And get me that TV watch list, too."

"I thought we'd start a binge together if you don't mind. I'm debating between a few different ones. We'll need to get you a couple of streaming services, though."

"Oh, Bill Bennett helped set me up. He insisted I get Netflix and Apple TV+. I've access to those. And I'm with some cable company for regular TV. They're also providing my internet."

They reached Eli's house again, and he let Atticus off the leash, watching him run to the door.

"He gets a couple of treats after every walk," he explained. "He knows the word treat, so don't ever say it."

They went into the house, and Atticus got his treats. Autumn went and sat in the middle of the large sectional. Eli joined her, resting his arm on the back of it.

"Thanks for coming over for dinner," he told her. "I know I can't always see you at work, so it's nice to have you here."

"I wanted to spend more time with you," she said.

His fingers took her chin in hand, and he gave her a long, slow, delicious kiss. Heat pooled in her belly as she opened to him. He accepted the invitation, his tongue sweeping inside her mouth as he took his time exploring her. She liked how his fingers pushed into her hair, holding her head in place. She liked his clean, masculine scent. And despite the fact that he'd only begun kissing, he was quickly becoming an expert at it.

They kissed for a long time, lost in one another. At one point, he scooped her up and placed her in his lap. Autumn liked being close to him, her arms entwined about his neck, his heat enveloping her.

Then his lips left hers, trailing down her neck. She shivered.

"You okay?" he asked.

"My neck is definitely an erogenous zone," she admitted, sensing her cheeks reddening.

Eli grinned. "Then let me do a little exploring and see what I can learn."

He learned plenty. He was a fast learner and wanted to give more than he took. His lips moved everywhere. Then his tongue began teasing her pulse point, causing her to suck in her breath. He began nibbling on her neck, his teeth grazing it, causing fire to shoot through her limbs.

Autumn returned the favor, saying, "Let me see what you might like."

She repeated what he had done to her, sensing when he liked something—and when he *really* liked something. She liked the tang of his skin as her tongue glided across it. She felt the shiver which ran through him. Her hands slid to his chest, kneaded it like a cat would.

Curling against him, she rested her cheek against his beating heart. They stayed in this position for a long time. The kissing had been incredible, but quietly sitting together seemed just as special.

"Was that too much?" she asked, raising her head and meeting his gaze. "I know this is all new for you." She paused. "It's new for me, too. Because it's you."

He kissed her lightly. "It is a new world to me. Touch. Scent. Taste. I'm just glad it's with you."

"Don't let me rush you," she cautioned. "I don't want us to go too fast."

"I'll follow your lead," he promised. "For now, we should call it a night. After all, neither of us got any sleep last night. Let me walk you to your car."

Atticus got out of his doggy bed, and Autumn knelt, rubbing the pup's head and giving him a kiss. "You be good. And keep your person in line for me."

He woofed softly in reply.

Eli took her hand and walked to her car with her. He pressed her back against the driver's door and leaned in for a long kiss. She wanted more but knew they had done enough for tonight.

"Thanks for dinner," she said. "Next time, it's on me, okay?"

"When is next time?" he asked huskily.

"Let's play it by ear," she said. "I'll see you tomorrow."

Autumn turned, but he caught her hand, bringing it to his lips and kissing it.

"Goodnight," he said softly.

"Goodnight," she echoed.

He opened her door, and she slid behind the wheel, waving to him as she drove off. For a moment, she wished she were Summer and could take a page out of her sister's play-book. If Summer had been here, she would have had sex with Eli tonight. Her twin wouldn't have been bound by how long she'd been divorced or what others might say or think. She would simply go for it.

In that moment, Autumn decided it was time to be more Summer and less Autumn where Eli was concerned.

CHAPTER
Fifteen

O n her way to work the next morning, Autumn decided to call West, knowing he was an early bird.

He answered on the first ring. "What's up, Fall?"

"Just wanted to touch base with you."

"I'm glad you did so. Kelby and I were really impressed with the new hospital you're working at. We talked about having you over to dinner soon, just to catch up."

"I'd like that," she said.

"I really like this Dr. Carson. Remember, I told you the other night I was going to talk to him about having a doctor from Triple H be at the football games this fall. Coach Markham told me it's been hard to get physicians to cover the games in the past, and we have to have one on duty before game play starts. Now, with the new facility in town, I thought it would be a little bit easier with so many doctors in the area. The thing is, he volunteered to do all the games himself. Said he was eager to become part of the community."

"He did? He didn't mention that to me."

West chuckled. "I assume your boss isn't required to run

every decision by you." He paused. "Wait a minute. Is some-thing going on between the two of you?"

"Yes. No. I mean, yes."

Her brother laughed. "Sounds like you're a bit confused, Autumn. Let me say one thing before you tell me anything else. I only was around Eli Carson for a few minutes the other night, but he is a vast improvement over Dr. Dickhead."

She knew West had never liked Flint. He had made no bones about it. Her brother had been courteous around Flint when they were at family holidays, but she knew he hadn't approved of her choice of husband.

"What did you like about Eli?" she asked, curious as to his opinion.

"In comparison to your ex? Or just in general?"

"Either. Both."

"Eli isn't cocky. He's confident. There's a difference. I saw it when I played football. There were guys who were talented and went out and did their job on the field. Then there were others who flapped and yapped to the press, stir-ring up a lot of trouble, letting people know how talented a player they were. I don't like cocky. I'm impressed by confi-dent, however. Eli is confident."

"He does have a quiet confidence about him," she agreed.

"He's smart. Likeable. Didn't seem as if he tried to grab a lot of glory or credit the other night, even though he has to be the man who's driving the machine in every aspect of Triple H. Most of all, he was smart enough to hire you. And not for a simple nursing position, Autumn. He saw potential in you, and he's never regretted placing you in the position he did. But enough of my opinion. I want to hear yours."

"This may sound odd, but from the first time we met, I felt a connection to him. I can't really put it into words. We just seemed to click. He surprised me by hiring me to be the

Director of Nursing. It wasn't some slick move on his part. We've worked together the past few months, and everything has been aboveboard. We have developed a friendship, though, and that seems to have changed in the last few days."

She pulled into the employee lot and into a parking space, cutting the engine.

"We finally admitted there's an attraction between us. I'm a little reluctant to go public, however. I'm also worried that it's too soon to become involved with someone. I haven't been divorced very long."

"Honey, Flint checked out of your marriage a long time ago," West said quietly. "From the little you've shared, you were like ships passing in the night. Never seeing one another. Never doing anything together. I noticed how cold he treated you when we were in New Orleans for the Super Bowl. Anytime you spoke to him, it seemed as if he was inconvenienced. So, I don't want you to think about the fact that on paper, you've only been divorced a short while. You were in a loveless marriage for a long time. Big brother's advice? Don't hold back because of some random timeline in your head."

She sighed. "Summer said the same thing. She thinks I should just go for it."

"I know the minute you're seen together in Hawthorne, the news will be out that you're seeing one another. Why don't the two of you come for dinner tonight? Or tomorrow night. It would give Kelby and me a chance to check out the good doc and see if he's worthy of my little sister."

"Oh, West, that would be great. I've been to his house a few times. It's not as if living with Mom and Dad means that I couldn't have him over. I'm sure they wouldn't mind, but it would just be weird."

"Talk with him and see if he'd like to come for dinner. Text Kelby and me when."

"I'll do that. Thank you, West."

She hung up and headed inside the hospital, remembering how West used to check out any guy who asked Summer or her out. It seemed almost comical all these years later for him to be doing the same thing. Her family was important to her, though, and she did want to see how Eli interacted with West and Kelby.

Once she was in her office, she texted Eli, telling him that her brother had invited them for dinner and asking if tonight or tomorrow night would work for him.

He replied immediately.

Make it tonight. That way I get to see you again and not have to wait.

Her heart fluttered reading his response, and she answered him, saying she would send him the details once she knew the time they were supposed to arrive. She then texted West and Kelby that tonight would be good. West simply sent a thumbs up.

Then her phone rang, and she saw it was Kelby.

"Hi, Kelby. I'm sure my brother has already talked to you."

"He called me right after the two of you got off the phone. I think Eli is a good fit for you, Autumn. We'd be happy to see you for dinner this evening. Would six o'clock be too early?"

She laughed. "The nights I'm home with Mom and Dad, we eat earlier than that. Six would be perfect. See you then."

Autumn sent Eli another text, telling him that they could leave the hospital at a quarter to six and easily make dinner, then she got busy with her day.

* * *

Eli sent his last email of the day and then picked up the phone, dialing Autumn's extension. She answered quickly.

"Hey. You about ready?"

"Yes. Should we meet in the parking lot and go together?"

"I don't want to leave my car here. Why don't you follow me?"

"See you in a few minutes."

He knew Autumn was close to her family. It was only natural for her to seek her brother's approval of their budding relationship. Eli had liked the affable West Sutherland, who had asked him about lining up a physician for each home game the Hawthorne Hawks played this fall. West had indicated there would be six games and said he wasn't opposed to having a different doctor at each game. Eli had spontaneously offered his own services, thinking it would be good to attend the high school games and be out and about in the community.

He reached his car and waited as he saw Autumn coming out the staff entrance. She came toward him.

"I'll text you their address in case we get separated for some reason, but it's not far from here."

"Should we stop and get something for dinner? I know people invited to dinner do that kind of thing."

"It's not necessary."

He looked at her longingly, wanting to kiss her. Doing so in a public place—especially the hospital employee's parking lot—was not the place it should happen, though.

"I'll see you there," he said.

They drove to a nearby neighborhood in Hawthorne. The house was unpretentious. He got out of his car and escorted Autumn to the front door, lacing his fingers through hers. He had never demonstrated any kind of affection to another soul since there hadn't been anyone, but every time he took Autumn's hand, a calmness filled him.

He rang the doorbell, and West Sutherland opened the door.

"Hey, guys. Come on in."

The house was small inside, and they stepped directly into the living room. He could see Kelby Sutherland in the kitchen, which adjoined the room.

She called out, "Be with you in a minute."

Autumn set down her purse, and West invited them to take a seat. They sat on a sofa which had seen better days. West sat to their left.

Kelby joined them, and Eli shot to his feet again.

"Sit," Kelby said. "We have a few minutes until dinner's ready. Can I get either of you anything to drink?"

Eli didn't know what custom dictated, and so he deferred to Autumn.

"I can wait until dinner," she said.

"Same," he added, thinking this was the first time he had been invited to dinner by someone who wasn't a colleague. Even those times had been few and far between.

"We're having King Ranch casserole. It's a recipe Tilda passed down to me." Kelby looked to Eli. "My mom had a stroke giving birth to me. We lost her two days later. Tilda was her closest friend. She came to the ranch to help out with Chance and me and never left. Tilda became like a mom to us. The ranch's housekeeper and cook. We couldn't have made it without Tilda in our lives. She was the only one who could stand up to my dad and get him to listen. Tilda is gentle but firm."

They chatted a few minutes about the opening of the hospital, and then a ding sounded from a timer.

"Time to eat," Kelby declared.

Dinner was a relaxed affair. Eli opened up more than he usually did but he also learned things about the town of Hawthorne and Autumn. At one point, West called her Fall, and Eli must have looked puzzled.

"Fall is my nickname for my baby sister," West said. "Summer was born a couple of minutes before midnight on the last day of summer, while Autumn made her appearance a few minutes after midnight. I like to tease her and call her Fall."

Kelby asked if Eli had seen any of her social media posts for Triple H, and he admitted that he hadn't.

"I don't get on social media. I need to learn what to do so I can follow what you're doing for Triple H."

Kelby laughed. "You and my brother are exactly the same. Chance has an email, simply because he needs it for business. He doesn't care about anything like TikTok or Instagram. He only carries a cell phone so the ranch hands can text him if they need anything. You should have an account, though, Eli. Even just if you follow the hospital's account. The Instastory about the Andersons has gotten a lot of traction. It's also been reposted on Threads more than a hundred times."

"Let Autumn and me clean up, hon," West said. "You go get Eli set up in the twenty-first century."

Kelby walked Eli through a couple of platforms and created accounts for him on three of them. She asked if he had any recent pictures on his phone that she might use for his profile.

He shook his head. He couldn't think of the last time he'd had someone take his picture.

"I don't want to use the formal one of you that's on the website. Let me take a few candids right now." She pulled out her cell phone. "Give me a smile, Eli. Not a big cheesy one. A relaxed one."

She took a few and asked which one he'd like to use.

"I'll let you choose. It isn't really something I know a lot about."

"I'll use a different one for your three accounts."

By the time she finished teaching him how to log in and scroll through his feed, plus how to search and make an account a favorite so following would be easy, Autumn and West had rejoined them. They talked easily for another half-hour. It struck him that these were two people he would like to be friends with, beyond his new work relationship with Kelby.

Autumn said, "I think it's time for us to head out. Hospital people are not night owls. Thanks for having us for dinner."

She hugged her brother and Kelby, while he shook hands with West and added to Kelby,

"Dinner was great. I think King Ranch Casserole is my new favorite meal. I would return the favor and have you two over, but I don't know how to cook."

"That's what takeout is for," Kelby told him. "Nothing wrong with that."

"I did host the top staff at Triple H last weekend. BBQ Bliss catered it. Maybe you'd like to come over sometime for barbeque."

"We'd enjoy doing that, Eli," West assured him.

The couple accompanied them out to their cars. Kelby walked with Autumn to hers, while West went with Eli. He sensed something was coming.

As they reached his car, West said, "Autumn told me that you're involved. I like you, Eli. I think you'll be good for Autumn. That she'll be good for you."

"She's been a little reluctant to begin seeing me. Or having others see us together. I know it's because of her recent divorce."

"Her ex-husband was an ass. One of those doctors with a God complex. Flint never was a loving husband or good partner to her. Autumn is way better off without him." West's gaze connected with Eli's. "Treat her right."

"I intend to do that very thing," he promised.

CHAPTER
Sixteen

Autumn went downstairs for breakfast, glad that both her parents were seated at the table. She poured herself a cup of coffee and got the creamer from the fridge, adding a splash of it and a dash of sugar. Taking her mug to the table, she placed it down and took a seat.

"We need to have a conversation," she began.

"Uh-oh," Dad said. "Sounds ominous."

"Honey, don't listen to your father. You know he's teasing," Mom said.

"I've already talked with Summer and West about this, but I wanted the two of you to be in the loop as well. First of all, I can't thank you enough for letting me come back to live with you. Housing is at a premium right now in Hawthorne, and it would have been hard for me to find somewhere to live."

"This will always be your home, Autumn," Dad assured her. "We love having you here."

"And I love being here. Eventually, I will want to find my own place, but that's not what I want to discuss now."

She took a sip of her coffee, letting the jolt of caffeine flow through her.

"I want to let you know that I have started seeing Eli Carson. We're in the early stages. We have built a firm friendship the last couple of months, and there's an obvious attraction between the two of us. We want to see where it goes. West and Kelby had us over last night for dinner."

Mom reached and took Autumn's hand. "We will support you in whatever, Autumn. You know that. It must be hard, getting back on the horse which has thrown you. Divorce is never easy. You must think a great deal of Eli if you're willing to open up and try to have a relationship with him."

"I really like him, Mom. I don't like comparing him to Flint, but he's pretty much the exact opposite. We're going to take it slowly. I just wanted to let you know." She took a deep breath. "Because there may be times when I don't come home for the night. I may be spending it with Eli."

Autumn glanced to her father, who had a concerned look on his face.

"I think Eli is a good man and has done a fine job getting the hospital up and running. The only thing I'm anxious about, though, is you dating a man who is your boss, Autumn. Does Hogan Health have a policy in place regarding that?"

"Eli checked on it. There is no policy forbidding it. Since we've decided to move forward, he will report it to HR at the corporate office in Austin. Evaluations for the level of my position won't occur until next spring. We aren't going to rush things. We'll see where we are by that time next year."

Dad smiled gently. "We're just concerned about your welfare, baby. You have a professional reputation to maintain, as well as your personal one. There will be gossip at the hospital once people realize you're seeing one another."

"We're prepared for that," she replied. "Eli's background is very different from mine. He grew up in foster care and didn't have the kind of love and support which was taken for granted in our family. He has so much potential within him, however. I'm eager to see what happens between us. How we'll both grow. I just wanted to give you two a heads up about the situation."

Mom squeezed Autumn's hand and then released it. "I'm glad you talked this over with Summer and West. That was sweet that West and Kelby had the two of you over for dinner."

"It was good for Eli, being around people other than those who work at Triple H. I think he and West might become friends. I'm so glad West has come back to Hawthorne. Kelby is perfect for him. Did you know that she's doing some work for Triple H?"

Autumn explained how Kelby was involved in beta testing a program for Hogan Health, creating separate social media accounts for Triple H, apart from the general ones run by Hogan Health for all their facilities.

"I saw on Instagram about the baby you helped deliver," Mom enthused. "You didn't even tell us about that! The couple seemed so sweet and grateful to you and Eli."

"Just don't move too fast," Dad cautioned. "You're coming out of a marriage of several years. It's going to take time to heal emotionally."

"I understand that, but I'm a lot more emotionally stable than you think. My marriage was over years ago. I just never acknowledged that. I haven't told you anything about why we divorced, but Flint was cheating on me. I caught him in the act, and I learned it wasn't the first time he'd strayed."

Dad let a few expletives fly, causing Autumn to chuckle.

"You don't have to worry about killing him, Dad," she

teased. "He's not worth it. I came to the realization that Flint merely used me. I put him through med school so he had no debt when he graduated. I did his laundry. I was the good wife who stood by him at any social function held by the hospital. But I don't think he ever really loved me. We had grown apart over the years and barely saw one another. I thought once he finished his residency that things would finally change. Now, I think he would've been the one to initiate a divorce once he had finished his medical training."

With confidence, she added, "I'm going to be open with Eli. Communication and transparency are my two catch words going forward in any relationship."

"It's hard working with someone on a daily basis when you're in a relationship," her dad warned. "It gets more difficult if there's a breakup."

"Summer encouraged me to stay optimistic and to not worry about what ifs, Dad. I'm going to take her advice to heart and not think of this relationship as doomed before it ever gets off the ground. Eli and I are level-headed adults, dedicated to our jobs. We will continue to behave with discretion, whether we are dating or simply decide to remain friends."

She took the last sip of her coffee. "Since it's Saturday, I'm going to spend the entire day with Eli. He doesn't know how to boil water, so one of the things we're going to do is have a cooking lesson. Something easy."

"How about spaghetti and meat sauce?" Mom suggested. "That's hard to mess up."

"That's a great idea. I'll see you later."

"Have a good time, sweetheart," Mom said.

She knew her mother would be more onboard than her dad. Mom was a romantic, while Dad was a pragmatist. Autumn was walking into this relationship with Eli with both eyes open. If anything gave her pause or caused doubt to form, she would give him a chance to clear it up. If she were satisfied with his answer, they could move forward. If she weren't, she would cut the line and step away.

Immediately.

Autumn texted Eli to let him know she was on her way. When she arrived, he and Atticus were sitting on his large front porch. The dog wore no leash, and she braced herself for him to run and greet her. Instead, he remained patiently by Eli's side.

As she approached, she heard Eli softly saying, "Stay. Stay," his hand held out.

She smiled, first at the man, and then turned her attention to the dog. "Good dog, Atticus."

She knelt and ruffled the pup's coat. He gave her a happy lick, causing her to laugh.

As she continued to stroke him, she said to Eli, "That's incredible that he stayed. Most dogs would have bowled me over at his age."

"I've been on YouTube," he admitted. "Dr. Watterman from ER told me he found some pretty useful videos there to help train the dog he adopted a few years ago. Atticus and I are working on things."

She lifted Atticus' paw. "How is this doing?"

"He's good. We had a follow-up at the vet's an hour ago. Everything's okay. Want to come inside? It's getting a little warm out here."

The three of them went into the house, and Atticus went immediately to his bowl, lapping water.

"I'm glad you agreed to spend today with me, Autumn. I haven't planned anything, though."

She chuckled. "That's because you are used to flying by the seat of your pants, managing an ER. There is something to say for making plans and being organized, though. And yes, I have some ideas for us. First, we're going to spend an obscene amount of money at Walmart."

"Buying what?" he asked.

"One of the things we're going to do today is have a cooking lesson. You've got to get some kitchen basics, Eli, else that's going to be impossible."

"Buy whatever you need. I'll reimburse you. Atticus and I will work on our training while you're gone."

Her gaze met his. "I want you to come shopping with me."

His lips parted in surprise. "Are you sure, Autumn? It's a Saturday. Half of Hawthorne will be at Walmart."

She took his hands in hers. "I want to be seen with you. Because we're dating now. If you haven't done it already, I want you to notify HR right now and let them know that we're seeing one another. Exclusively. That is, if that's what you want."

He grinned. "I definitely want that." He leaned in and kissed her lightly. "Give me two minutes to fire off an email. I want it officially on the record before any gossip starts up. As much as I like the staff we've put together at Triple H, there are bound to be a few gossips. I wouldn't put it past someone to send an email to corporate once they find out about us."

"Do you think you should also put something out to the Triple H staff?" she asked. "Or would it be better to let people find out by word of mouth?"

"We've got the usual Monday morning team meeting. That includes department heads and administrators. I think I'll mention something then. It'll be up to them whether they wish to inform their staffs or not."

"Okay. Go send your email."

While Eli was doing that, Autumn texted Summer.

Eli & I had dinner w West & Kelby last night.
Also told M&D we're seeing each other.
Spending all today together. Who knows
what tonight will bring???

Moments later, her phone dinged. Summer had replied with a scorching fire emoji and five exclamation marks. Autumn smiled to herself and slipped her phone back into her pocket.

"Ready to go?" Eli asked.

They went to the garage. As they backed out, she said, "Your yard could use a good mowing. I'll bet you don't have a mower or edger, do you?"

"What I do have is a lawn service," he informed her. "As of yesterday. I'd already been given the name of a pool service. The owner also has a landscaping company. When he serviced my pool yesterday, he asked if I might need lawn maintenance. I agreed. They should be here sometime today."

"I'm glad to hear that. You're in a small town now, Eli. You'll be judged on all kinds of things, big and small. One is if you keep a neat yard."

"Duly noted."

They entered Walmart and headed straight for the house wares section. Autumn began filling the basket quickly. She chose a boxed cookware set of aluminum, nonstick pots and pans, which had a good variety for a reasonable price. She picked up items such as a colander, corkscrew, and measuring cups. By the time she was finished, the cart was nearly full.

"Do you have any groceries in the house?" she asked.

He shook his head sheepishly. "Other than coffee, no."

"Go get another cart and meet me by the produce."

He did so, and she traded baskets with him, taking on the empty cart, placing items she would need for dinner tonight, as well as things she knew he would need immediately. Some were staples which would last a long time, such as sugar and flour, while others were perishables.

"Do you like spaghetti?" she asked.

"Love it."

"It's one of the easiest meals to cook, so that's what we'll make together for dinner tonight. Spaghetti and meat sauce. We'll move up to meatballs in another lesson."

Autumn made certain she had everything for tonight's meal, including a big tub of spinach salad and a couple of bottled dressings.

They paid for their purchases and took them to his car.

"You weren't kidding. That was a dent in my credit card," he joked.

"You won't spend that much every week. I would suggest shopping for groceries at the new HEB. They'll have more variety than Walmart. We can do a trip there another time to stock your pantry, fridge, and freezer."

They brought bag after bag into his kitchen, putting away everything.

"Okay. That wasn't the most fun," she said. "But we've got better things to do now."

Eli wrapped his arms around her. "Any time I spend with you is fun, Autumn." He kissed her lightly. "But I'm ready for round two."

"Grab a ballcap. I already have sunscreen and a small ice chest with bottled waters in my car. We're off to Gainesville now. Have you been up to it before?"

"Nope. I've heard it takes about the same amount of time to get there as it does Decatur. That's the extent of my Gainesville knowledge."

"It's a cute little town. Close to the Oklahoma border. One high school, just like Hawthorne. That's how we judge the size of a town, by how many high schools it has," she told him.

"Filing away that fun fact," he teased.

Autumn told him she would drive, and she liked that he didn't protest. Anytime she and Flint had gotten into the car, it was assumed because he was the man, he'd do the driving. She liked how Eli was easygoing and didn't throw his weight around, either at work or away from it.

They talked a little about work on the way, and then he asked about West returning to Hawthorne.

"I gather your brother is a big deal. Everyone seems happy he's back in town and ready to coach. He recently quit playing himself?"

She had to remember that Eli didn't follow sports and answered, "He was a star player here in high school. Won a scholarship to Texas A&M and then was drafted by the Dallas Cowboys. He played wide receiver for the Cowboys the past ten years. So, yes, he's retired now, with a few Super Bowl rings, but his heart is with kids."

Autumn explained how Coach Markham had previously coached the Hawks, going back to West's days as a player and even before that.

"He hired West to be on his staff next year, and then West became the head coach when Coach Markham decided to retire after he suffered a heart attack this spring. West may be worth millions of dollars, but he's a small-town boy at heart. I think he'll wind up enjoying coaching the Hawks more than he did his own playing days in the NFL."

They drew close to Gainesville, and she told him she was going to make a stop at something unusual. When he asked what, she told him to wait and see.

They left their farm-to-market road and connected with I-35.

"Gainesville has several wineries surrounding it. On another day, we might want to tour one of those. On the square, they have a place which is a coffee shop early in the day, and it becomes a wine bar in the evening. Oh, wait. There it is."

Eli turned and looked out the windshield. "What on earth?"

Autumn laughed. "Welcome to the giant brick statues, one of the quirkiest road attractions in Texas."

She exited the highway and drove toward the two brick pieces, pulling off the service road and turning off the car.

"Let's go see them."

They got out of the vehicle and headed toward the stacked bricks.

"They're at the entrance to a private ranch," she explained, looking up at the giant brick sculpture of a chess knight. "The artist of this fine horse made out of bricks was a bricklayer from Canada by the name of John Groves. The other sculpture is a fortress tower. West always said it was a rook that accompanied the horse."

Autumn watched Eli walk the entire circle of the horse head, seeing the awe in his eyes.

"He must be thirty feet tall."

"He is," she confirmed. "From what I recall, it took about eight thousand antique bricks to build it. The artist salvaged them from a fire which occurred in Chicago. He also wove in steel I-beams to support the structure. Groves was friends with Ernie Chrustawka, who owns the ranch. Supposedly, Ernie wanted something grand to mark the entrance to his ranch, and this is what the two of them came up with, with Groves creating the art."

They moved to the giant brick castle, and Eli said, "This does mimic a pawn and rook in a chess game. It's fascinating."

"I thought you'd like it." Autumn paused. "Are you ready to go full-on Instagram?"

Eli looked at her as if she were speaking gibberish. "Come again?"

"I'd like us to take a selfie and post it on Instagram. The minute we do, it means we've gone public with our romance."

He slipped an arm around her. "Selfie away."

She reversed her camera angle so she could capture them both and then gave him her phone.

"Your arms are longer. You can get a better angle than I can. Be sure to get as much of the horse as you can."

He snapped a few pictures and let her see them, then she took a couple of him in front of both brick sculptures. Eli returned the favor.

"Okay, ready to post," Autumn said, choosing two shots of them, one in front of each structure, and then one of Eli by himself. She typed a quick line and then added a few hashtags, her heart beating quickly. Tapping to post, she let out a breath. "We're up."

He slipped his arms about her waist. "This was a neat idea. I've never really been exposed to art. Never been to a museum. These unusual sculptures are a fun way to kick off my art education."

His stomach grumbled loudly, and she laughed. "I'm hungry, too. We'll head into town now. There are a few restaurants and shops along the square. We'll find something we both like."

Eli's gaze held hers. "I've already found exactly what I like."

His mouth touched hers, the contact sending electricity racing along her spine. He kept the kiss fairly chaste, but Autumn knew they were both ready to explore the banked fires within them.

Breaking the kiss, she said, "We'll do a lot of more that tonight. Right now, I want to introduce you to Gainesville."

She knew the rest of their day would lead up to what they were both eager to do.

Make love ...

CHAPTER
Seventeen

E li hadn't been on a date in almost six years.

But he was savoring every minute of this one with Autumn.

She had a quiet effervescence about her that was welcoming. Calming. Interesting. It was as if they were the last two pieces in a thousand-piece puzzle which he had been trying to put together for years. Suddenly down to the last two, they fit together perfectly, completing the picture for him. He could see a future with Autumn Sutherland, but he knew she had to be skittish after coming off a miserable marriage. He would go as slowly as she wanted to move, enjoying their time together.

Hoping that it would be forever.

She drove him around Gainesville briefly. It was obvious she was familiar with the small town. They parked on the square and went into a restaurant she thought he would enjoy. Starving, he went for a Swiss mushroom burger and fries, while she ordered a fajita chicken salad. She warned him not to order dessert.

"I have something else in mind."

His thoughts immediately went to *her* being dessert, but he knew she meant something else. Still, the thought of being more intimate with Autumn was something that he couldn't entirely dismiss.

After they'd eaten, she took him around the square. They went into several of the shops to browse. In one of them, she instantly went to the counter and picked up two items.

"This is the dessert I was talking about," she told him. "They're famous around here. It's an Arbuckle Mountain fried pie."

He'd never eaten a fried pie before, but if Autumn was excited about this find, he would be, too.

She paid for them, and they went outside, finding a bench to sit on.

"Actually, this is an Oklahoma food item, but they sell them across the border. It's like something fried you'd get at the State Fair of Texas, only better. They have both sweet and savory, but you can only buy the savory ones in Oklahoma. My favorite is the Polish sausage and potato one. Summer likes the spinach, mushroom, and potato one. And West eats anything you put in front of him."

Handing him one of the two fried pies, she said, "I bought two kinds, peach and pecan. Try the pecan first, then if you want, we can switch halfway through."

Eli unwrapped the fried pie and sank his teeth into it.

Instant bliss.

He chewed and swallowed. "This is really tasty."

"Wait until you try peach."

They did trade mid-pie, and he found the peach one even better.

"Which sweet one do you like best?" he asked, wanting to know everything about her.

"Blueberry. Or cherry. I like any kind of berry in anything. Fried pies. Gelato. Mousse."

He filed that fact away, hoping he could surprise her someday soon.

As they ate, she told him, "If you like to gamble, WinStar Casino is only about fifteen minutes from Gainesville."

"I've never gambled," he admitted. "Some of the ER staff had a football weekly pot on games, but since I didn't watch sports, I didn't participate."

"Maybe we should drive up and play the slots sometime. Or better, go to a concert. They've got a great venue to listen to music, and you can have dinner in one of the many restaurants spread throughout the casino." She chuckled. "I had a few friends go to OU, and one of the first things they were warned about in orientation was not to gamble." She laughed. "I didn't have that problem, going to Baylor. They didn't even allow dancing on campus. Not that I'm a big dancer, but I thought that was a little over the top."

"I thought their nursing program was in Dallas."

"It is. I went to school in Waco for two years, and then I transferred to the Dallas campus. It was interesting living in Dallas. It's such a big city. West would give me a pair of tickets for every home game. He's two years older than I am, so when I moved to Dallas, that was his first year with the Cowboys."

"You really like sports? You've mentioned watching games."

"I love watching sports, especially my brother. Watching West catch a pass was like poetry in motion. He was so graceful. So fluid. And so damn fast. If he wasn't tackled immediately after catching the ball, he would take off like a gazelle down the field."

"I need to learn more about football."

"I can teach you. I heard you've volunteered to be on the sidelines for home games for the high school this fall."

"Your brother needed a physician. I thought it would be good for me to get out in the community. I'm the face of Triple H, like it or not, and I want the citizens of Hawthorne to be able to ask me any question at any time."

They finished eating their fried pies, and he said, "That was really good, but it would've been better with a scoop of vanilla ice cream."

Autumn coyly batted her eyelashes at him. "You are talking my love language, Dr. Carson."

She stood, holding her hand out. He took it and rose, asking, "Where to now?"

"You'll see."

They returned to her car, and she gave each of them one of the bottled waters. Eli twisted off the cap and downed half of it.

"Glad you brought these."

After they left Gainesville, she said, "It'll be another fifteen minutes or so. We're going to Lavender Ridge Farms. A hundred years ago, the family who owned it raised strawberries and melons on the property. That changed near the beginning of this century. The owners planted a crop of lavender on a slope near a wooded edge of the property. The lavender just exploded. Nowadays, they have several gardens throughout the property and a garden center where you can buy plants. They operate a café, where they have amazing lavender cheesecake and lavender ice cream. They also have a gift shop with all kinds of products featuring lavender and other herbs in essential oils and candles."

"Sounds interesting."

"It really is. I think you'll enjoy it. Put on your ball cap. It's sunny today."

They arrived and parked. Autumn had them first visit an area with adopted and rescued farm animals. While you couldn't feed them, you could pet them, and he loved seeing the delighted look on her face as she did so.

"We're going to pick some fresh lavender now," she told him. "You can pick lavender from early June through usually the end of July."

They donned gloves provided and accepted sharpened pruners.

"You want to pick the swollen flower buds or the ones just beginning to open," she explained when they got to the field where they could harvest. "Stay away from small, droopy buds. They won't have as strong a scent."

Autumn taught him how to gather a bundle, which she called a bunch. Eli quickly caught on.

"We'll dry these when we get home. Outside in the sun, it'll only take a few days. If you dry them inside, it could take a couple of weeks. The main thing will be to keep Atticus from eating the lavender."

Curious, he asked, "What do you do with dried lavender?"

"Oh, you can put the dried stems in vases and place them around your house. They'll give off a light, sweet smell. You can use some of the buds in cooking, but only in small amounts. A little goes a long way. Lavender is really potent."

When they finished picking, they returned their gloves and pruners and he said, "I'm thirsty. Want to grab something at the café?"

"Let's ask for to-go cups," she suggested. "There are so many large oak trees scattered about. I'd loved to sit in the shade and lean against a trunk and just chill."

They walked to the café, where he ordered a lavender iced tea and Autumn chose a lavender lemonade. Finding an out-of-the-way oak, they settled on the ground. Eli leaned his broad back against the tree's trunk, and Autumn nestled between his legs. He wrapped an arm possessively around her waist, and she leaned against his chest. He could smell her vanilla scent mingling with that of lavender as they sipped their drinks.

"I'm so content right now," she said, breaking the silence. "I wasn't looking for a relationship when I took the job at Triple H and moved back to Hawthorne." She glanced up at him. "You've been a nice surprise, Eli Carson."

"Ditto. I was burning out fast after all those years in the ER. Too many hours blended into days and weeks and months and years. I was ready for a fresh start. I've gotten that at Triple H. Finding you was the icing on the cake. Hmm. I'll bet a lavender cake would be really tasty."

She laughed, and he found he'd grown addicted to that sound. He wanted to always hear it.

Eli wanted Autumn as his wife. As the mother of his children. Hell, he'd never even thought about having kids, but it seemed a given with Autumn. He didn't know how to have a family, much be a part of one, but she was the one woman he wanted to teach him these things.

They sipped their drinks, enjoying the serenity and shade for half an hour. He wished they could have stayed at Lavender Ridge Farms forever.

Finally, she stirred. "Let's stop by the gift shop. I can't visit here without doing so."

She picked out lavender coffee and an infused honey for her mother and chose a scented candle for Kelby.

"Summer needs some of the handmade soaps," she declared. "They'll remind her of home."

"Is she homesick?"

"She would never say that aloud, but I can tell," Autumn

said confidently. "Twins have that twin thing going on. We know when the other is hurt. Down. Joyful. Stressed. Summer thrives in a place like Manhattan. It's a beehive, and she's a buzzing bee, zipping around everywhere. But I get the feeling she would move back to Hawthorne in a heartbeat if she could."

"I want to meet her. She's important to you. Does she come home for Thanksgiving or Christmas?"

"Usually one of those holidays each year. Of course, we could both play hooky and fly up to New York some long weekend. She tells me it's beautiful there in the fall, starting around the week before Thanksgiving."

"Already a bad influence on your boss," he teased. "Trying to get me to play hooky."

He insisted on paying for her purchases, and she thanked him. He hadn't had money for so many years. Now that he did, he wanted to spend it on someone he loved.

Someone he loved …

The thought had come naturally to him. It wasn't something that he could pinpoint. Eli simply knew that he was in love with Autumn. A warm glow filled him, something he had never experienced before. He had received scholarships. Accolades. Awards. Nothing had given him the feeling he now felt inside. He wanted to share it, but it was far too soon to do so. If he did, he might frighten Autumn away and lose everything.

For now, he would keep quiet. And try to figure out when the time was right to speak.

He carried the sack of goodies back to her car. She pulled out two more bottled waters, saying, "I know we had the tea and lemonade, but it's hot today. We should stay hydrated."

"You don't have to convince me."

On the way back to Hawthorne, they didn't say a word. It

was a companionable silence, one he had never been a part of, but it seemed perfectly natural. He liked that they didn't need to have a constant, running conversation between them. Silence was nice.

When they got back to his house, Atticus greeted them enthusiastically. Eli attached the dog's leash to his collar, and he and Autumn took the pup for a walk. After they got home, he felt a little tired but very, very happy. He couldn't recall a more pleasant day in his entire life, and he wanted plenty more of them in the future.

With Autumn.

They both removed their shoes, and he said, "I suppose it's time for that cooking lesson."

Autumn looked at him, a look that caused his heart to slam against his ribs.

"I could really use a shower," she told him. "I'm sticky all over."

Swallowing, he said, "Sure. I'll grab you a towel and—"

"Eli, I want you to join me."

CHAPTER
Eighteen

Autumn couldn't believe she had just invited Eli to shower with her. It was so totally out of character for her.

But it sounded like it could be fun.

Her gaze held his. "What do you say?" she flirted, seeing the heat sizzle in his eyes.

A slow smile formed. "I say I'm all in."

Before she could say anything else, he swept her off her feet as if she weighed nothing. Autumn wrapped her arms about his neck, feeling the beating of his heart quickening as he carried her toward his bedroom. Her own heart began beating in harmony, anticipating what was to come. She knew he was inexperienced, but the sparks between them would see them through.

He stopped once he reached the bedroom and kissed her. Autumn's fingers tangled in his hair as they devoured one another hungrily. Eli gently set her down, the kiss still electric, his hands roaming her back, cupping her buttocks, bringing her flush against him. Between kisses, they slowly began undressing one another. He unbuttoned her shirt, kissing the flesh revealed each time, causing heat to flood her. He pushed the shirt from her shoulders, grazing one with his teeth, sending a delicious chill up her spine.

She returned the favor, lifting his T-shirt and kissing his rock-hard abs, seeing him quiver beneath her touch. He jerked the shirt over his head and tossed it aside, kissing her again, hard and long. Her breasts began to swell, aching for his touch. She slipped her hands behind her back and undid the clasp of her bra, allowing him to pull it away, the barrier now gone. His hands cupped her breasts, his thumb stroking back and forth, teasing her swollen nipples.

"Can I kiss you here?" he asked hoarsely.

"You can kiss me anywhere," she said breathlessly, anticipating the feel of his mouth.

He was tentative at first, his lips grazing her breasts. Knowing he needed a little push, she told him to use his tongue and teeth.

"You don't mind?" he asked.

"I want you to."

When he did, it rocked her to her core. He kneaded one breast as he sucked on the other, licking, nipping, and sucking again. She felt the tightness in her core and whimpered, knowing she was about to come.

She moaned low, and he stopped, looking at her worriedly. "Are you all right?"

"Better than all right," she managed to get out. "Don't. Stop. Doing. That."

He grinned sheepishly. "Okay."

When he slipped his mouth around her breast again, the pressure within her began building. His teeth toyed with her nipple, causing her to whimper loudly.

And then she exploded.

The orgasm came hard and fast, causing her to cry out loudly. She clung to him, and he kept doing what he was doing, making it go on and on until she was spent and weak.

He kissed his way back to her mouth and asked, "Was that a good thing?"

"That was a fantastic thing," she corrected, her hands framing his face, pulling him down to her.

The kiss was wild and delicious and the absolute best of her life. A humming raced through her body unlike ever before.

She broke the kiss. "I've never come that way," she panted. "It's because of you. You are ... incredible, Eli."

"And we're still half-dressed," he quipped. "I suppose it gets better?"

Autumn smiled at him. "Let's keep going and find out."

He unbuttoned the button on her denim shorts and slowly pulled down the zipper, working the shorts over her hips. She stepped out of them and allowed him to pull her panties down. She shed those and turned, hurrying to the bathroom.

Looking over her shoulder, she said, "Come on!"

As she opened the shower door and turned the nozzles on full blast, she knew he was ridding himself of the cargo shorts he'd worn. She closed the shower door and looked through the open doorway, seeing him standing in boxer-briefs, his long legs muscular and tanned from his years of running.

Their gazes met and he hesitated a moment before lowering his underwear and throwing it to the side. With deliberation, their gazes still connected, Eli came toward her, both admiration and hunger in his eyes.

For her ...

Before he even touched her, she had never felt so desired. She realized sex with Flint had been just that. Sex. Perfunctory. Quick. No cuddling after. Already, Eli had made her feel cherished. Wanted.

And loved.

Autumn ignored the fact that it was too soon. That she shouldn't be feeling such strong emotions for a man she'd only known for such a short time. All she knew was that a good man was looking at her with love in his eyes—and she wanted to make love with him.

Holding out her hand, Eli stepped forward, taking it. She turned, opening the door to the shower again, feeling the cascade of water and quickly adjusting the temperature. Then she stepped inside, leading Eli with her.

And the magic began.

It helped that his shower was large and had four nozzles, plus a rain shower head above them. Everywhere they went, they were embraced by the warm water. They clung to one another, kissing, their mouths hungry for the taste of the other. She didn't think. She just moved. Did. Accepted. Took. Gave. Her married sex life had revolved around what made Flint happy. She had been an afterthought. But Eli put her first in every way.

And she reveled in it.

Their bodies slick with water, their hands glided easily, as did their tongues, as they explored one another, marveling in what they found. He pinned her to the wall with his larger body, then kissed his way up and down her. She gently guided him, using both her hands and voice, showing him what felt good to her. Learning the same about him.

They lathered one another's bodies, and she found joy in touching his sleek muscles, seeing them quiver under her fingers. He worked shampoo into her hair, his fingers massaging her scalp lovingly. All her tension washed away beneath the tenderness of his touch.

The water began to grow cool, and she said, "Let's finish this in bed."

She caught the mischievous glint in his eyes as they quickly rinsed away any remaining soap. He turned off the faucet. As Eli retrieved two towels, she squeezed the excess water from her hair.

He toweled off quickly, wrapping it around his waist, and then opened the second towel for her. She stepped into it. Into his arms. He enveloped her in it, kissing her neck, that delightful shiver rushing through her again. Then he got down to work, drying her limbs and torso and rubbing the towel against her hair before wrapping it around her and bringing her next to him.

"I wanted to make love to you in the shower," he said huskily. "I'm sorry we ran out of time."

She kissed him lightly. "We can try again later. I think our first time together in bed will be nice."

He dropped a kiss upon her brow. "Thank you for guiding me along."

"You're a fast learner," she purred.

"Then let me go learn a little more."

Sweeping her off her feet again, he carried her to the bed and gently placed her on her feet, tossing aside throw pillows and pulling back the comforter she had purchased for him. Autumn discarded the towel, allowing his eyes to roam her body.

"You are so beautiful," he said softly, moving to her and wrapping her in an embrace. "I can't believe you're mine."

"Ditto," she said, knowing he wouldn't have seen *Ghost* and known how Patrick Swayze and Demi Moore used the phrase. It could be one of many things they did together in the future she saw for them.

Boldly, she slipped her fingers beneath the towel he wore,

peeling it away and dropping it on the floor. Autumn wrapped her arms around his waist and began kissing his chest, something he had enjoyed in the shower. She flicked her tongue against his nipple, hearing his groan.

"I can feel your smile," he said, sounding very satisfied as his arms came about her.

They fell onto the mattress, and the need which had been building within her pushed her to kiss him wildly. She had never lost control of her body or feelings, but this man caused a maelstrom to stir inside her. His kisses became deeper, his hands stroking her body until she felt afire. She took hold of his cock firmly, her thumb rubbing the smooth head seductively. He sighed into her mouth.

"That feels so good," he murmured. "I want to make you feel the same. Tell me how."

"Just like in the shower," she said, releasing him and taking his hand, guiding him. "Use your middle finger. Ease it into me."

He did as she said, stroking her deeply.

"Oh, yes," she said, leaning into him.

"Deeper?"

"Yes."

He caressed her, and she felt herself trembling. She had him add a second finger, guiding his hand until he found the perfect spot. It was empowering. Fulfilling. And openly sharing such intimate things together would strengthen their already strong bond.

She whimpered, and he said, "I'm recognizing that's a good sound when you make it."

By now, she was meeting his hand, ready to orgasm at any moment. She could only nod, speech impossible. Then it consumed her, and she rode his hand, calling his name, clinging to him as it went on and on.

When the orgasm ended, she forced her eyelids open and smiled up at him. "That was amazing. I've never felt like that." Tenderly, she reached up and caressed his cheek. "You know how to take care of me. You *want* to take care of me. That means everything, Eli. But now let me return the favor."

She thought it would be easiest to introduce him to the missionary position because it would give him control as he learned. Quietly, she explained to him what they would do together, and he began kissing her, his hands stroking her body. The curve of her hip. She took him in her hand, gripping him firmly, moving and encouraging, feeling him swell.

"You're going to enter me now," she told him, their gazes locked. "I'll help you find your way."

He hovered over her, his hands on either side of her head, as she brought him to what she now thought of as home.

"Here. Push. You won't hurt me. I promise."

"Okay."

Suddenly, he filled her with one thrust. Really filled her. In a way she'd never experienced before. It excited her. She moved against him, seeing his eyes widen.

"It's almost like dancing," she said. "We'll find a rhythm together and go with it."

They experimented a little, the heat and hunger building between them. Then she forgot all about instructing him and simply went with the flow again, their bodies responding to one another, knowing what to do. Her hands gripped his shoulders, his thrusts hard and demanding now, and she felt the climax about to happen just as he tensed. They reached their release together, with Eli pumping enthusiastically into her, joy on his face.

When he finished, he collapsed atop her. She inhaled deeply, smelling clean man and the shower gel they'd used.

"I need to get off you," he murmured into her ear.

"Just roll to your side," she said. "Don't leave me yet."

He moved, bringing her with him. His roll caused him to turn onto his back, however, and Autumn found herself sprawled atop him.

Eli wrapped his arms about her, one hand softly stroking her lower back. "I could get used to this."

"Me, too," she said happily.

They lay together in contented silence, her ear next to his beating heart, their fingers entwined. She'd never cuddled like this. Flint had always gotten up the minute he was done, heading to the bathroom to take a quick shower, as if he wanted to wash all traces of Autumn away.

With his free hand, Eli began finger combing her damp hair absently. His touch was gentle. He was everything she had always dreamed of. Hoped for.

"I don't think I deserve you," he told her.

Her head snapped up. "Why would you say that?"

He sighed. "I think a part of me will always be that lonely foster kid. The one no one wanted. It's like I wore some invisible sign, telling everyone how inadequate I was."

A fierce wave of love for him washed over her. "You never have to think that again, Eli. You have me. You'll *always* have me."

His brows arched. "What are you saying?"

Autumn swallowed, knowing she couldn't hold back. "I'm breaking every rule I've ever had for myself, but sometimes, rules have to be tossed out." She smiled tenderly at him. "I love you, Eli Carson."

His eyes widened. "You do? Oh, I've loved you and was afraid to tell you, Autumn. Afraid you would turn and run the other direction as fast as you could."

"We're both damaged souls," she admitted. "But we've found one another. We've been helping each other to heal, even as we fell in love. I feel stronger and more confident than I ever have in my life, and it's because of you, Eli. You believe in me. That's caused me to believe in myself. Not just professionally. Personally, too. I wasn't sure if I could ever trust my gut again when it came to a man because it had led me so far astray with Flint. But Flint is a distant memory. All I see is you. All I want is you."

He cradled her cheek. "You have given me a purpose I never knew existed within me. I want to be the best doctor I can be. The best medical director I can be. The best man I can be. It's all due to you, Autumn. I want to continue growing and becoming a better man, and I want you by my side. I feel I can achieve anything with you in my corner."

Eli kissed her tenderly. "Let's take the next step. Move in with me."

Could she even contemplate something like that? They hadn't known one another for that long. And yet it was as if they had always known one another, even before time began.

"Yes," Autumn said. "I want to take things to the next level."

Suddenly, Atticus leaped onto the bed and began licking her and then Eli.

"I think he's showing his approval," Eli told her.

"Or else he's hungry," she teased.

The minute she said that, both their stomachs growled noisily, causing them to laugh.

"I think we're going to laugh together a lot, Autumn," Eli said. "And they say laughter is the best medicine."

"Right now, food is what we need," she replied. "Let's throw on some clothes, and I'll walk you through how to make spaghetti."

He cocked his head. "Do we have to get dressed?"

"Nakedness and cooking do not go together," she

declared. "You better get dressed before I'm all over you again, devouring you and not the pasta."

Eli climbed from the bed and reached out a hand, pulling her to her feet and into his arms. He kissed her first and then said, "Food first. Then dessert later." He waggled his eyebrows, causing her to laugh.

"Well, I *did* buy some whipped cream," she said flirtatiously. "It was meant for strawberry shortcake, but ..." Her voice trailed off.

The heat in his eyes took her by surprise. "I'll empty the can on your body and lick every inch off you."

Autumn roared with laughter. "The man's had sex one time, and already he's addicted. I feel a bit like Dr. Frankenstein. What creature have I created?"

Eli gazed at her longingly. "One which will never get enough of you." He nuzzled her neck a moment and then released her. "Let's go get dinner out of the way so I can concentrate on dessert."

CHAPTER
Nineteen

E li awoke, blanketed by warm woman. He lay on his back, Autumn nestled firmly against his side. Her head rested on his shoulder, and her arm was slung over him possessively, just as his held her body to his.

Yesterday had been a day of revelations, culminating in them making love again after they had cooked dinner together. He had kept to what he'd promised her, using the can of whipped cream, squirting it strategically across her satin skin and lapping it up, along with her. His appetite for her was voracious. Though sex was a new experience for him, he realized he would not have appreciated it as much before if it had occurred with any partner but Autumn.

She was the difference.

He hoped she did not regret the words of love which had been exchanged between them. He certainly didn't, but he knew he was coming from a headspace much different than she was.

She began to stir, and he marveled at every curve of her body.

Glancing up sleepily, she said, "Good morning."

Smiling lazily down at her, he said, "Good morning, yourself." He paused a moment and then added, "Thank you for yesterday. Not just teaching me how to make love to a woman, but the entire day together. It was the best day of my life, Autumn. Because I spent it with you."

The back of her fingers brushed his cheek. "It was my favorite day, too. You're an amazing man, Eli Carson. I can't believe no one has snatched you up before now."

He captured her fingers and brought them to his lips for a tender kiss. "I've been waiting my whole life for you, Autumn Sutherland. I just didn't know it."

They made love slowly, taking their time, learning new things about one another with each touch. Each kiss. Each sigh. He liked that she wasn't shy about asking for what she wanted from him and found himself doing the same. He realized communication between them would always be key, something she hadn't experienced in her marriage. Eli would be certain to make that a priority.

They lay together in the afterglow, their limbs entwined, basking in one another's company. They talked for a good hour, the conversation drifting from topic to topic. She told him more about her life growing up in Hawthorne and being one half of twins. He recognized how deeply family ties ran within her, and for a moment, he was slightly envious, having no experience close to that.

Then Eli decided it was time to fully open up to Autumn.

"I have a brother."

She startled beside him. "What? You have a brother? Eli! Why didn't you tell me about him?"

He shrugged. "There's nothing for me to tell."

Autumn seemed to sense how difficult speaking had

suddenly become for him, and she snuggled closer, her palm over his heart. He placed his hand over hers, working up his courage to tell her.

"He's younger than I am," Eli began. "From what I can recall, I was five and he was maybe three when they took us away. Mom used to be gone all kinds of hours, leaving us alone, sometimes for days. Telling me that I was in charge. I remember making us peanut butter sandwiches. If there wasn't any bread, I would spread peanut butter on crackers for us for dinner. I'd wet a cloth and wipe his face, trying to keep him clean. Combing his hair and then mine. Making sure I put shoes and socks on him."

"Were you placed in the same foster home?" Autumn asked quietly.

He shook his head. "They came to get us. The lady from the state agency told me I was going with her. Another worker was there and scooped up my brother. We headed to one car, and they headed to another."

He paused, the memory of that moment emblazoned. "We broke away and ran toward one another. Hugged. Cried. As they pulled us apart, I told him to be good."

Eli swallowed down the pain, seeing his little brother crying, his arms reaching out as he called Eli's name as they were separated and placed in different cars.

"That's the last I ever saw of him. I'm hoping he got adopted. Being younger than I was made that a stronger possibility."

"You need to find him, Eli," she urged. "I'm sure he would love to see you. What's his name?"

Tears flooded his eyes as guilt overwhelmed him. He made a strangled sound. Suddenly, a sob escaped, and he was crying. Autumn wrapped herself around him, stroking his hair, trying to comfort him. She didn't ask him anymore questions and merely let him cry it out. When his tears finally ceased, he felt physically and emotionally drained.

Meeting her gaze, he said, "I'm ashamed to tell you this, but I don't know my own brother's name. I know he had to have had one, but I don't know it."

He raked his fingers through his hair in frustration. "When Mom left, she always told me to take care of my little buddy. She even called him Buddy. That's all I think of. And I never cried about losing him. Until now." He smiled at her. "It's because I feel safe sharing everything with you."

"You weren't ready to look for him before now, were you?" she asked.

"No. I pushed everything about my past as far away as I could. The more the years went by, the dimmer my early memories have become. I know I loved him. I took care of him. He probably doesn't even remember those first few years, though. Three is awfully young. Think about it. What do you remember from the time you were three?"

"Not much," she admitted. "What I do remember is more from having seen pictures of when Summer and I were that age. I know I had a favorite Disney Princess dress I wore all the time because I've seen me wearing it in pictures. When we were three, Summer and I took swimming lessons. Then again, I have those pictures to refer back to. As for actual memories? No, not so many. More just impressions. The way my mom smelled. Her wrapping me in a bath towel. Dad cuddling with me, telling me a story."

She hesitated. "Do you think he remembers anything about you?"

"I doubt it. Especially if he found a new family soon after we were separated. That family would have become his own. He would've had no ties to the past. We didn't even have a favorite toy or blanket to take with us when we left. We came from nothing, Autumn."

"You may not have had the time or inclination before now, but I'm encouraging you to think about looking for Buddy, Eli. He may feel as if a part of him is missing and not even understand why. I know not all parents tell their children if they're adopted. It's more common to do so nowadays than when your brother had a chance of going to a new family. My gut tells me, though, that Buddy does carry some memory of you and would love to meet you."

"I don't have a clue where to begin a search, Autumn. How do I look for someone whose real name I don't even know?" he asked, frustrated.

"You hire an expert to do that. Before we do so, there are some things we can do. Look for any information about your mom that we can find online. Find your birth certificate and hopefully your brother's, using her name to search. Contact the State of Texas and Child Protective Services. Assemble whatever information we can, then hire someone to look into it for us."

He smoothed her hair. "You keep saying *we*." He grinned. "I like the sound of that. I like being part of a *we*." Eli hesitated. "I hope you don't regret what's passed between us. What we've said to one another. I'm not much of a prize. You could easily do better."

Autumn kissed him softly. "Your past is your past, Eli. I don't judge you on it. I don't regret a single thing. I love you. I know I had some weird idea in my head about how my life should proceed after my divorce from Flint was finalized. That I would focus solely on my career for a year or two. Enjoy time with family and friends. Then I might think about dating."

She cupped his cheek. "But why put off the rest of my

life when it's right here in front of me? Yes, most people will think I'm foolish to jump back into another, serious relationship so quickly, but my feelings are real. True. Deeper and stronger than anything I ever felt for Flint. Don't think I'm constantly comparing the two of you. I'm not. I only know that in my heart I don't just feel this is right. I *know* it is. I only hope you aren't having second thoughts. That I'm not enough for you."

"Never," he told her. "I was attracted to you long before I said anything. I was afraid to speak up because I didn't want to mess up our working relationship or the friendship growing between us. I've hired two different couples who are working at Triple H in leadership positions. The workplace is a common place where people do wind up meeting and getting together. I don't think the Bennetts or the Gentrys are doing any less of a job simply because they're in love and married and working at the same hospital."

"I'm glad you're going to tell people at Triple H about us," Autumn said. "And I hope you weren't speaking too impulsively when you asked if I want to move in with you."

"If you think it's too soon, I respect that. But the door to my house—and my heart—is open to you, Autumn."

"Let's give it a week," she suggested. "Give us time to get used to our new relationship. If we still feel confident, I'll move my things over next weekend. That move is something I don't want to announce to the world, however. Where we live is our business. A small town loves to gossip about its residents. I don't mind Hawthorne knowing we're in a relationship with one another, but I'd like to let our living arrangements stay private."

"How do you think your parents will react? Or West and Summer?" he asked.

"My brother and sister will know I've followed my heart.

Mom, too. They will understand. Mom is a romantic and already likes you. Not that Dad doesn't, but I am one of his little girls, one who's been hurt pretty badly. It's going to take a little more for you to win Joe Sutherland over, I'm afraid."

"Then let's commence Operation Win Dad today," he declared. "How about I take your parents out to lunch?"

"That would be sweet." She glanced at the clock on the nightstand. "They'll be at church now. I think I'll go home and shower and change and then see if they'd like to eat with us. If they can't, I'll come back over here." She smiled. "Because I want to spend all of Sunday with you, Eli."

Reluctantly, he let her leave the bed and saw her to her car. He took Atticus for a quick walk and then fed the pup before jumping into the shower. He dressed in slacks and a sports shirt, per Autumn's request. As he was combing his hair, a text came in. He picked up his phone.

> We're a go for lunch. I made reservations at the Hawthorne Inn for one o'clock. Come to my parents' house at noon. We can visit a little and then go from here."

He texted her a thumbs up, knowing he wanted to make a good impression on Joe and Meg today. Yes, he'd already met them in a professional capacity, but this was different. Eli put himself in Dr. Sutherland's shoes, thinking if he had a daughter, he would want the best for her. He wouldn't want any man rushing her or taking advantage of her. He needed to make certain Autumn's parents knew his feelings were authentic and lasting.

Another text came in.

> Asked West and Kelby to meet us at the inn. Think that might help smooth the way.

Eli liked Autumn's brother and hoped they would become friends. Kelby Sutherland was also bright and personable. The couple would help keep the conversation moving if any lulls occurred.

He arrived at the Sutherlands' house, anxiety filling him. He'd always been confident, thanks to his high IQ, sailing through classes and medical training without thought. Where his fellow interns and residents had fretted over surgical procedures, he had thrived under pressure. It was what had made him so successful in managing a large ER.

Meeting his girlfriend's parents as her boyfriend was definitely a different thing altogether.

Knocking on the door, his heart began racing. When it opened, Joe Sutherland stood on the other side. He stepped out onto the porch, joining Eli.

His face serious, the school superintendent said, "I made the mistake of not asking the last man who showed an interest in Autumn what his intentions were. And I still want to kill the sumbitch for what he did to her."

"You don't have to ask," Eli replied, confident in his feelings regarding Autumn. "I'm happy to tell you that your daughter is a remarkable woman. One of the smartest, most capable individuals I've ever met. She knows medicine. She knows people. And she's claimed my heart, sir. I will never hurt her. I will do my best to protect her and love her."

The older man studied Eli. "Love her? It's already at that point?"

"Most definitely. I felt something for Autumn the first time we met." Quickly, he added, "I did not let that influence my decision in regard to hiring her. You can ask anyone at Triple H. Autumn is terrific at her job. And I was smart enough to keep my feelings to myself and simply be her friend." Eli paused. "But we both want more than friendship."

"You said love," Sutherland repeated. "You mean it?"

"With my entire heart," he said fervently. "I plan to stay at Triple H many years. I want Autumn by my side, both professionally and personally. I want to raise our family in Hawthorne and be a part of this community."

Joe Sutherland shook his head. "I guess when you know, you know. Right?"

"You absolutely know. Your heart. Your gut. Your every breath tells you. Autumn is the one for me."

Joe thrust out a hand, and Eli took it.

"West told me you two were an item. I can see you're more than an item."

"I would marry Autumn tomorrow, but I don't want to rush her," he admitted. "She's suffered a lot of heartbreak. I want her to be sure about us."

Joe chuckled. "Summer was the one who always flitted about. Autumn was the solemn one who knew her mind. If she's made up her mind about you—and it sounds as if she has—then who am I to stand in the way of true love? Come inside, Eli. And welcome to the family."

CHAPTER
Twenty

Autumn accepted Eli's sweet kiss as she stood on her parents' porch.

"I wish you were coming home with me," he said, his voice low, his lips grazing her ear, causing a shiver to run through her.

"I know. But we spent all day together. And it was good."

"It was," he agreed. "You're a lucky woman, Autumn Sutherland, and not just because you have me." Eli grinned cheekily. "You have an amazing family."

"I do. They already adore you. But not as much as I do." She kissed him again, lingeringly, before pulling away. "You better go. I'll see you at the meeting tomorrow morning."

"I hope I dream of you."

"Ditto."

She watched Eli move gracefully down the sidewalk, admiring his lean, fit, runner's body. She knew every part of it now and hungered for it.

He reached his car and waved to her. She returned the wave and entered the house. It was almost ten o'clock.

Someone had left a light on in the foyer for her. Turning it off, Autumn moved quietly up the stairs. She entered her bedroom and closed the door, hoping that Summer might still be awake on the East Coast, where it was almost eleven.

This call deserved a FaceTime, and she tapped the icon. Summer answered immediately, wearing an oversized T-shirt and what looked like a mud masque.

"Two mih-uts," Summer said, holding up two fingers, then ending the connection.

Autumn used the time to slip out of her own clothes and into a cotton gown that struck her mid-thigh. Then her phone rang.

"Hey, Twinnie," she said. "I see your face is looking better."

"It was time to wash off the mask. I'd put it on twenty minutes earlier, and it dried so hard. I couldn't talk. And I was afraid if I didn't wash it off when it said to, it would stick to my face and freeze my features. Thanks for showing patience."

Showing patience had been their mother's code word for the twins to calm down and take a deep breath when they were little. Autumn and Summer had continued to use it throughout the years, a little inside joke they still got a kick out of.

"I'm ready to report in about my weekend with Eli," she told her twin.

"No detail is too small. Don't leave anything out. And I already know you had him meet the fam for lunch today. I've been texting West like crazy, so I'd be in the loop."

Autumn laughed. "Then you know more than I thought you did."

"I want to know everything," her twin declared.

She sighed. "The past two days have been the best of my

life, Sum. Just being with Eli centers me. I feel a calmness when I'm with him, and yet my heart is beating madly, wanting him to kiss me."

"Go on," Summer encouraged.

Autumn told her sister about all she and Eli had done together. How they connected on every level. How they could talk about anything or nothing and feel natural around one another.

"And the sex?" her sister urged. "I know you had it. He's too hot for you not to have. I've Googled him like crazy. I probably know more about him than he knows. Or you," Summer teased.

"Off the charts." She would keep to herself that Eli had been a virgin at the start of this past weekend. "And I've turned into a brazen hussy."

"Oh, how very Austen of you," Summer drawled. "What *have* you been up to, you vixen?"

She felt a blush rise in her cheeks. "I tell him what I like. I ask him what he likes. Honestly, Summer, I've never been so dang bold in my entire life. I see now how my passive nature carried over to my sex life. Not that I think it would've changed anything with Flint if I would have spoken up more. But Eli and I communicate really well. I've found my professional voice, thanks to him placing me in a leadership role. Now, I'm finding my personal voice."

"Do you talk dirty?"

"Summer! No!" She paused, thinking back to coupling with Eli. "But I'm not shy in letting him know when he's doing something I like. The way he touches me or a certain kind of kiss."

Her twin beamed at her. "I am so happy to hear this, Autumn. It sounds as if you can really be yourself around Eli. I can't wait to meet him."

"He's dying to meet you, too. He knows how important you are to me."

"Then you'll have to come to New York. I've been trying to get you here forever. I want to show you so many things. Let you eat the best bagel in the world and stroll along the High Line. Walk across the Brooklyn Bridge and grab a slice of amazing pizza. See world-class museums."

"It sounds like we'd need more than a weekend there. Maybe we could come for a week next summer when we'll both get vacation time."

"I can't wait that long to meet him," Summer said, frowning. "Maybe I should come to Hawthorne instead."

Excitement filled her. "Would you? That would be so great. But wait. You were just here in the spring for West's wedding."

"I have some days coming. Let me see what I can work out with Dragon Lady's assistant."

"I'd still have to work," she said quickly. "I wouldn't be able to take any time off. We could do lunch, though. And if you were here over a weekend, we'd have lots of time together."

"I'll massage things from my end and see about what days I might be able to slip away. Technically, I could work at home on a day I was traveling. As early as you have to get to the airport, I could get a ton done while waiting on my flight, not to mention working the three hours on the plane."

"Just let me know. I'll do whatever I can to work around your schedule." She teared up. "Thank you for coming, Summer. I want you to meet Eli." She paused. "Because I'm in love with him."

"Get out! Have you told him?"

She nodded. "We've said it to each other. Do you think I'm crazy?"

"Maybe crazy in love, but never crazy. Autumn, you're one of the most rational people I know. If you love this guy, then you love him. And the fact he loves you? It just proves to me how smart Dr. Eli Carson is."

Summer hugged herself. "Oh, this is really good news."

"You don't think it's too soon?"

"What if I said I did?" her twin countered.

And Autumn realized it didn't matter.

"I would note your concern, but I don't care. I love him. I *love* him, Summer. And he loves me. I've never felt more sure of something in my life."

Her sister teared up. "I'm so happy for you, Autumn. You and Eli are lucky to have one another. I'll also be getting another brother. This is terrific news."

They said their goodbyes, and Autumn placed her cell phone on the charger. Summer had been right. Listening to her heart had led her to knock down the invisible walls she'd constructed around herself. She'd let Eli in—and look how happy she was now.

* * *

AUTUMN SAT through the early Monday morning meeting for administrators and department heads. She tamped down her nerves, knowing that Eli would be announcing at some point they were seeing one another. He ran through the agenda items quickly. She had learned he wasn't much for lengthy meetings and preferred to talk to others one-on-one regarding their concerns.

He finished elaborating on the final item and then said, "Before we dismiss, I'd like to mention something on a personal note."

All shuffling stopped. Eli had proved to be pretty

tightlipped about anything personal, and hospital people were no different from anyone else. They were curious about their boss.

He cleared his throat. "I've made it a point to emphasize transparency, and that's what I'm doing now. I want everyone here to know that I am in a relationship with Autumn. HR in Austin has already been notified, but I wanted our staff at Triple H to know, as well. Feel free to share this with your departments." He paused. "Just know that Autumn will have to wait in line for budget items and signatures just like all the rest of you."

"Then what's the point of dating the boss if you can't leap the line?" Barbara Bennett teased.

Everyone laughed, and Eli said, "Have a good day." He quickly picked up his tablet and said, "Steven, if you have a moment, I'd like to see you in my office regarding the new Holter monitor contract."

"Lead the way," the head of cardiology replied.

Others gathered their belongings, but Barbara and Tilda took their time doing so, making certain they were the last to be ready to leave.

"When did this start?" Tilda asked Autumn. "Were you two together the night of the barbeque at Eli's house?"

"No," she said, feeling her cheeks fill with heat. "We were just friends then."

Barbara said. "Friendship is the best way to start a relationship. Bill and I were in a study group in med school together. We went from being friendly competitors to red-hot lovers."

She and Tilda laughed, with Tilda saying, "Paul and I were good friends and colleagues until it came time to name the chief resident. We both wanted it so badly we could taste it. And then neither of us were elevated to that position. It went to a guy who knew all the answers and had zero people skills. We bonded as we commiserated on losing out. One thing led to another, and here we are, happily married. At least, I tell him all the time we are, and he's smart enough to say, 'Yes, dear.'"

"Seriously, I'm happy for you and Eli," Barbara said. "He seemed very lone-wolfish when I interviewed with him. Gradually, I've seen him coming out of his shell. I'm sure that's got a lot to do with you, Autumn."

"Maybe. Working in the ER for so many years, Eli was used to barking out orders," she said. "He's learning to build relationships in a different way as Triple H's medical director."

"Well, I think you two are great together. You'll balance him, Autumn," Tilda said.

"He's been good for me, too," she told the pair. "I was married before. To a doctor. I didn't think I would ever date another doctor, much less be in a relationship with one, but Eli's special."

"I hope you're ready for the deluge of gossip," Tilda cautioned. "You know this news will spread like a Southern California wildfire."

"I know. I encouraged Eli to get ahead of it and let others know before someone saw us together and started rumors," she said.

"It was smart to notify HR," Barbara added. "Cover your ass. Lunch today?"

"I'm meeting with my charge nurses at lunch," Autumn told her. "Maybe tomorrow. Text me when, and I can work my schedule around it."

"Will do," Barbara said.

Autumn returned to her office, knowing the news about her and Eli would be the hot topic at the hospital today. From the hospital, it would make its way through town. Already, they had seen a few people at the inn yesterday who probably had noticed they were together and had already fired up the phone lines. She wasn't expecting any nasty feedback. Then again, it didn't hurt to be prepared.

Her day passed quickly, with her lunchtime meeting with the charge nurses on the day shift going smoothly. She would hang around and meet with the night shift half an hour before they came on duty tonight. Autumn also was busy with observations and paperwork, causing the day to pass quickly.

When her phone rang late in the afternoon, she picked it up. "Autumn Sutherland, Director of Nursing. How may I help you?"

"How the hell are you a director of anything, Autumn? And you're seeing another doctor? Our divorce just happened, and you've already started fucking someone?"

Her gut lurched at the accusations from the familiar voice. "It's none of your business, Flint. *I'm* none of your business. You have your life. I have mine. Please don't call me again."

Shaking, Autumn hung up the phone. She let the next call and the one after that go to her voicemail as she sat, trying to get herself under control.

Why on earth did Flint even care what she was doing for a living or who she was seeing? *He* was the one who had broken their marriage. And who at Triple H even knew she had been married to Flint, much less had the gall to let him know anything about what Autumn was doing now?

She waited, the phone silent. Finally, she listened to both messages. The first was hospital business, and she relaxed, making a note of what she needed to take care of. The second, however, was from her ex-husband. The content was similar to what he'd said before, only a little more profanity-laced this time since she hadn't picked up. Though she was tempted to delete it, Autumn kept the voicemail, thinking if things escalated between them, she would want to document any contact Flint had made with her. She had previously blocked him from her cell phone, but that wouldn't be possible to do here at Triple H.

Her mood somber now, she tried to pull herself together, gathering the notes she would need for the meeting with her night shift in a few minutes.

She would not tell Eli about this call. He had enough on his plate as it was. Besides, Autumn doubted Flint would call again. He was merely blowing off steam, upset that she had decided to go on with her life and not be at his beck and call.

Casting aside her worries, Autumn left for her meeting.

CHAPTER
Twenty-One

As the end of August drew near, Eli couldn't feel more content. He and Autumn had settled into a routine, both at home and at work. She had continued teaching him how to cook, and he often took on dinner for them these days. Cooking had a soothing effect on him, and he was finding he had a talent for it. They'd had West and Kelby over a few times for dinner, along with Autumn's cousin. Eli had met Sawyer Montgomery through Kelby, and the attorney was a pleasure to be around. They'd also hosted Joe and Meg Sutherland for dinner, and Eli had grown more relaxed in their company, as well.

Today, Autumn was taking him to a Texas Rangers baseball game in Arlington. They had already watched a few games together on TV, with her explaining each position and the structure of an inning. West had also taken him in hand and explained the game of football. While it seemed simple, with four tries to make it ten yards in order to earn a first down, Eli knew there was much more to it, else football wouldn't be so popular across America and a billion-dollar business. He'd gone to a couple of practices at the high school at West's invitation and was getting to know the coaching staff and players. Next Friday would be the first home game for the Hawthorne Hawks, and Eli would be on the sidelines, ready if either team needed medical attention. He was already impressed with the team's athletic trainer and his student assistants and would defer to them whenever possible.

He dressed in his new Rangers jersey. Autumn had gotten him one for every professional sport team in the area and said she would take him to games at each venue. He looked forward to seeing hockey with the Dallas Stars and basketball with the Dallas Mavericks. Since those seasons didn't start for a couple of months, he still had time to bone up on the basics. West had guaranteed them tickets to any Cowboys game they wanted to attend, and Eli had left it up to Autumn and Kelby as to which one the four of them would attend together. West said while they could sit in a suite, it wasn't the same as being in the stands. Eli didn't care where they sat. He simply enjoyed being with Autumn and her family and deepening the new friendships he was making.

As he finished tying his tennis shoe, she entered the bedroom.

"Ready for some ballpark hot dogs and nachos? Don't ask me why, but a hot dog always tastes better at a game than ones you grill at home. They must have some super-secret special something they add at a stadium."

"A hot dog sounds great, but Scott Watterman warned me off the nachos. He said they were like eating cardboard with fake cheese sauce poured on top."

"When did Dr. Watterman become a nacho expert?"

"He said he had season tickets to the games in Kansas City when he lived there."

"Each ballpark does its own spin on nachos. You at least have to try some today. And peanuts." Autumn sighed. "I do love to sit and shell peanuts while watching a game. At least we can actually attend a day game now without broiling in the sun. Building an indoor stadium was the smartest thing the Rangers and Cowboys ever did. Not only does it take weather out of the game as a factor, but it makes it ever so comfortable for the fans to watch in person and cheer."

Knowing today was still going to be in triple digits, with the heat index adding another four or five degrees, Eli was thrilled they would watch the game in an air-conditioned stadium.

Autumn drove since she was familiar with the route and traffic.

On the way, she said, "We're actually making a stop before the game. To talk to the PI."

"What was his name again?"

"Mort Salinger. He's got an office in Grand Prairie. That's right next door to where we're going."

"Did he say if he'd found anything?" Eli asked casually, trying not to get his hopes up.

"No. He said we'd talk in person."

They'd hired the investigator three weeks ago, giving him very little to go on regarding the identity of his brother after hours of scouring the internet. A certain amount of shame still filled him, not knowing the name of the younger brother he had cared for. Dressed. Fed. Played with.

And even hid.

Eli had been thinking more about his early years ever since he had shared with Autumn that he had a brother. Too many fleeting images occurred, coming to him at odd moments, and he was trying to make more sense of his past. He had even dreamed of those days twice, awakening with a scream stuck in his throat. He could recall the slap of his mother's hand on his face. Her punch to his gut. Stepping in front of Buddy so that Eli took the brunt of her drunken anger. They had learned not to sleep anywhere in sight, hiding in the closet or even the bathtub to escape her wrath. Yet through it all, Buddy's true name never came to him.

Autumn took his hands in hers. "We go. We listen. We process whatever Salinger says. Then you can decide if you want to continue to pursue things."

"There may not be anything to pursue," he said, pessimism filling him.

"True. But don't get ahead of yourself."

They reached the investigator's office, located in a strip center. Autumn gave their name to the receptionist, who told them Mr. Salinger was expecting them. She led them down a narrow hallway to an office.

Salinger rose. "Come in. Thank you for stopping by."

"We were headed this way," Autumn said. "I hope you have some good news for us."

"I'm afraid not," the older man said. "Please. Have a seat."

Glumly, Eli took a chair next to Autumn and turned his attention to the investigator.

"I started with your mother's death records and worked backward. Found the court case where her parental rights were stripped. Spoke with people at DFPS, the Department of Family and Protection Services. CPS—Child Protective Services—is a branch of that."

Salinger shook his head. "Everything there is bound by legal red tape. Even if I have your permission to discuss your particular case, you nor I have the ability to access records related to any of your relatives, including your unnamed brother. A sympathetic social worker told me the only avenue to go down would be to hunt through birth records. Those are a part of vital records, and that can be done online. Most vital records websites won't let a person view an actual birth certificate, but she gave me a list of a few where you could at least see a person's name, date of birth, and either the city or county in which the birth occurred."

"But we don't have Buddy's real name," Autumn said, sounding discouraged.

"I know," Salinger said. He handed a list to them. "The one I highlighted in yellow lets you browse by location or by time period. I know it's the proverbial needle in a haystack, though. You can search based on name, location, relationship, or life events. I found your birth certificate, Dr. Carson. You were born in Harris County." He paused. "Do you have any idea if your brother was also born there? If he was also listed as a Carson?"

Frustration filled him. "I couldn't say. We moved around a lot. I understand now my mother was trying to stay ahead of the landlord and prevent eviction. Whether or not it was all in Harris County or not, I don't know. I was too young to understand much of anything back then. When I was older, I did ask to see my placement file at CPS. Every foster home I was placed in was in the Greater Houston area. I would assume Buddy also went to a home in that area."

"I'm afraid you can't assume anything," the investigator said. "With Harris County being the largest county in Texas, it would take months to comb through all birth records during a two-year or so period. Even then, if your little brother was adopted, many times the actual birth record is expunged, with a new one being created which reflects the names of the adoptee's new mother and father. So, in effect, it's a crap-shoot. We could look and find nothing because the original record may not even exist anymore."

Eli saw empathy in the older man's eyes. "I wish I had better news for you, Dr. Carson. My best advice to you is to join a few of those genealogy companies. Ancestry or 23andMe. Register and complete the kit. Get your DNA in their databases. See if any matches come up. If they don't, try and be patient. Maybe your brother will enroll in one of those programs someday. Right now, I can't take any more of your money or use any more of my time. It's not productive for either of us."

"I understand." Eli came to his feet. "Thank you, Mr. Salinger. For trying. I know I gave you next to nothing to go on."

"Memory is a tricky thing," the investigator said. "It changes as we age. Our perception of events does, as well, with maturity and experience. I hope you find your little brother, Dr. Carson."

They shook hands, and Eli and Autumn left the office, returning to her car. She stopped him before he opened the passenger's door.

"I'm sorry, Eli. I wish you'd received better news."

He shrugged. "It was always a shot in the dark. I will register with one of those services, though. Buddy could already have joined, looking for me. Or he may do so one day."

His words sounded optimistic, but Eli knew his little brother might have no memory of his older brother. He barely remembered Buddy, and he was probably two years older. He doubted a boy that young would have anything more than a hazy impression about the older sibling who'd spent so much time keeping him safe.

Seeing the distressed look on Autumn's face, he pulled her into his arms. "It's okay. I'm okay. I have you, and that's the greatest gift I have ever received. Let's go stuff ourselves with nachos and watch the Rangers blanket the Yankees."

Her lips turned up in a smile. "Blanket? It sounds as if West and Sawyer have been teaching you sports talk."

"Oh, even better. They have me listening to a sports radio station in Dallas. The Ticket. The guys talk way more than sports, but I've started listening to them every morning on my run. I am ready to dazzle you with my sports knowledge, Nurse Sutherland. I can even throw out a few pitcher stats today to impress you. Both starting pitchers today are vying to be the Cy Young winner this year.

She batted her lashes coyly. "My, a man who knows sports. You are my kinda guy, Dr. Carson."

He kissed her, his troubles melting away. He might never find Buddy.

But Eli had found lasting love.

CHAPTER
Twenty~Two

Autumn was looking forward to seeing Summer. Her twin had been swamped with work, including two uncooperative authors with looming deadlines, which had kept Summer in Manhattan. Finally, though, her sister promised she would be able to get away for a long Labor Day weekend. Summer was taking off tomorrow and Friday before the holiday and would fly in tonight, staying until the following Monday afternoon. Autumn couldn't wait for her twin to meet Eli in person. He had FaceTimed with Summer several times, and she thought the two of them got along well, but she still wanted to put them together in person.

She parked and entered the hospital. She and Eli took separate cars to work because they didn't want to inconvenience the other in case one of them had to stay late because of an emergency. Autumn had to admit her hours as Director of Nursing seemed cushy compared to when she was a floor or charge nurse. She still earned her salary, though, juggling half a dozen different balls at a time. She had a good handle on her job, though, and felt she was thriving professionally.

Peter Richards had visited with her and Eli last week in private, wanting to determine the status of their relationship. They shared they were committed to one another, and Eli said they would marry at some point. She had flushed with pleasure, surprised because they had not spoken about marriage. Still, they lived together. They loved one another. Marriage would be an eventual step. For now, she could wait on a ring and ceremony.

Because of what they had shared with the Hogan Health corporate VP, Peter had said that he would be handling Autumn's subsequent evaluations. It wouldn't be fair or have the right optics if Eli remained her sole supervisor and evaluator. Because of their relationship, she would still report to Eli so he would always be in the loop, with Peter being brought in on various occasions. Peter would visit Triple H a few times over the next several months in order to watch Autumn in action. He would also meet with some of her staff to discuss her supervision of various employees. Peter planned to review her budget, look over her hires and the evaluations she was doing for her nursing staff, and meet with various department heads to receive their input as to how Autumn was working with other administrators within the hospital. She had no concerns regarding Peter's supervision of her work. He had liked her from the beginning and was easy to talk with. They had brainstormed a few situations together and with others at Triple H, and she was confident that Peter had a good grasp of what she did and how well she performed.

As she reached her office, her cell rang.

"Hey, Mom," Autumn said cheerfully.

"Just wanted to check in and see if there's anything I can do with Summer coming in."

"The furniture for the guest bedroom arrived last weekend. I'd already purchased the bed linens and duvet. Eli thinks there are way too many throw pillows, but my philosophy is that you can never have enough of those."

"Taken straight from my decorating book," Mom quipped. "And you're still coming for supper tomorrow night?"

"Yes, we wouldn't miss it. Summer knows you're making all her favorites. She's not home often, so she's really looking forward to sinking her teeth into some chicken enchiladas and sipping Dad's margaritas."

"You're still doing the queso?"

"I am. And Eli made the dessert already. He's becoming quite the cook and even has tackled baking with a passion."

Mom sighed. "I wish your father knew how to cook. He made an omelet for me the first time he had me over. I was duly impressed." She laughed. "And that's the last thing he's ever made for me, other than reservations."

"In all fairness, Dad does the grilling," Autumn said.

"He does a mean hamburger and can really get those burn marks on a hot dog. You're right about that. You always remember the small details, Autumn."

'You deserve your fair share of credit, though, Mom. You're a terrific cook. Everything I'm teaching Eli how to make comes from the Meg Sutherland School of Cooking."

"I like to keep things simple. I'm no Julia Child, but I fed our family of five."

"And you did it well. Listen, I've got to go. I'll text when we've collected Summer at the airport and are on our way home."

"No, have her call us," Mom urged. "I'd rather talk to her. I'm so excited to see her again soon. It's been far too long since she came to Texas."

"Will do."

Autumn checked her email, answering pressing requests, and then responded to others. She worked through lunch, knowing she was going to leave the hospital an hour early today to drive down to DFW in order to pick up Summer. Eli said he would try and join her, but it would be up to any curves thrown into his schedule whether he could do so or not. At one point, Summer texted, saying she was on the plane and the doors were closing. Autumn sent back three smiley face emojis.

She finished up her last task of the day and walked down to Eli's office. Nancy greeted her.

"He's still in a meeting," the assistant said apologetically. "I don't think he'll be able to go with you. It's one of the board members. She always has a thousand questions at every board meeting and then makes an appointment with Eli to come in afterward and have him explain everything to her again, one-on-one. Personally, I think she's a bit lonely and likes the attention he gives her."

"Not a problem," Autumn said. "Just tell him we'll meet him at home."

"Is he cooking for you?" asked Nancy. "He brought in brownies for me the other day."

"He wanted to, but Summer is dying for barbeque. She says good barbeque simply does not exist anywhere in New York. I've already placed an order with Shorty. Eli will swing by and pick it up on his way home."

"Are you coming in tomorrow, with Summer being here?"

"I am. I've got a lot to do. Mom is taking off, though, and they're going to spend the day together. And my cousin Darby is flying in tomorrow. She'll go to West's football game with us Friday night."

"Go, Hawks," Nancy said, smiling.

"See you tomorrow."

Autumn returned to her office and removed her purse from her bottom desk drawer. She locked her office and headed to the elevator. It opened seconds later, and she waved to Nancy and stepped on, checking her phone to get an update on Summer's ETA. Only as the doors closed did she realize someone else was inside it. She glanced up to speak.

And saw her ex-husband.

Before she could utter a word, he pushed the emergency stop and turned. A loud bell started clanging, signaling the elevator was in distress.

Flint yelled over it, saying, "Listen, Autumn. I made a horrible mistake."

The old Autumn would have been apologetic. Uncomfortable. Maybe even terrified. The strong Autumn she had become ever since his betrayal reacted quite differently. Anger bubbled up, but she kept it under the surface. She wanted her ex to know she was mad and could still keep things professional.

"I don't have to listen to your bullshit anymore, Flint. Whatever you planned to say to me, I'm not interested in hearing your lies or apologies. Hit the button and get this elevator moving again. Now," she said firmly, proud of how her voice didn't waver once.

Tears welled in his eyes. She saw now that he'd always been a good actor with her, turning on whatever emotions he needed to convince her or persuade her or even gaslight her into doing whatever he wanted. Those days were far in her past.

"I need to apologize to you, Autumn. You were the best part of my life, and I blew it. Took you for granted. Didn't show you how much I loved you."

She snorted.

He looked shocked.

"I *was* the best part of your life, and you treated me abominably, Flint. You lied to me. Cheated on me multiple times. I put you through med school. Scrimped and saved. Did without, all for our future. I turned a blind eye and kept thinking if only I worked longer hours or tried harder, you'd come to appreciate me. Our entire marriage was a lie. You never loved me. You used me to make certain you had no debt once you finished your medical training. I'm sure your plan was to dump me once you did so, which makes me question why you're even here."

"I went to counseling, Autumn, Trying to understand why I treated you the way I did. Please. We have a history together. We were married a long time."

"We might have been married on paper, but we weren't marriage partners in any sense of the word." Autumn's fisted hands went to her waist. "I've grown up a lot since I shoved you out the door. I now know who I am and what I want. I'm a better person because of what I learned after all you put me through. And I would never, ever take you back under any circumstances."

She looked at him dismissively. "You're a world-class jerk, Flint. You might be smart and good-looking, but you have no morals. You only think of yourself. You're a narcissistic, cruel, pathetic excuse for a man. I pity any woman who would spend a minute of her time in your company."

The tears for show quickly disappeared. Flint's face set in stone. She knew how angry he was because of a tic in his cheek which kept jumping and his eyes which now glittered with hate.

He came toward her, and it took everything Autumn had not to allow him to back her into the elevator's corner. Instead, she stood her ground. He came so close their bodies touched. She could feel the hot air of his breath as he spoke to her.

"You're making the biggest mistake of your life, Autumn," he said, his jaw tightly clinched. "I came to give you a chance to come back. To give *us* another chance."

She looked at him coolly. "I have no interest in you, Flint. I have a wonderful life here in Hawthorne and the love of a good man. I finally understand what it means to truly be cherished. To have someone love me completely and thoroughly. I'm only sorry I wasted so many years on you."

The ringing finally stopped, and she felt the blood pounding in her ears as adrenaline surged through her.

Then a voice said, "You folks okay in there?"

Recognizing the voice of their chief engineer, she stepped around Flint and pushed the intercom button.

"It's Autumn, Ernie."

"I'm not seeing anything on my end to have caused the elevator to have stopped, Autumn. What can you tell me?"

She glanced at Flint, whose face was bright red. As she gazed at him, she said, "A visitor to the hospital deliberately pushed the emergency button. It's my ex-husband. Can you have security meet us on the ground floor? Tell me what to push to get the carriage started again, and I'll do it."

Ernie quickly told her what to do in order to override the elevator being locked in place. The entire time, Autumn never took her eyes off Flint. She did as the engineer told her, with Ernie telling her that it would take about sixty seconds for the system to kick in again. She calmly looked at Flint the entire time, showing no sign of weakness. Then the elevator jolted, throwing her for a moment, but it began descending slowly after that.

"If you don't want me to press charges, you'll leave quietly," she told her ex. "And never come back."

"Charges for what?" he sneered. Then he shook his head. "I was crazy to think we could make a go of things. You've changed, Autumn. And not for the better."

With no hesitation, she said, "I like who I've become. I'm never going back to who I was when I was with you."

The elevator arrived on the ground floor. The doors opened, and Flint rushed through them, pushing past those gathered in front of it. Autumn saw Ernie. The head of their security.

And Eli.

She stepped off the elevator and into his arms, wrapping hers tightly around him and giving him a kiss like they hadn't seen one another in a month of Sundays.

When she broke it, he asked, "Are you okay? Nancy saw you get on the elevator and then heard the alarm sounding immediately. She summoned me right away."

"I'm fine," she assured him. "More than fine. Because I'm with you."

Eli turned to glance in the direction Flint had stormed off and back to her. "He didn't hurt you? Scare you?"

"If anything, I put the fear of God into him," she replied. "I don't think we'll be seeing Flint Ferris ever again."

He looked to the others. "Everything's okay."

Once the small group dispersed, he pulled Autumn into a nearby alcove, obviously reluctant to let her go.

"I was worried when you told Ernie who you were with. I was standing right next to him, and I wanted to tear Ferris apart." He cupped her cheek. "But something tells me from the way he left that you took care of that."

"I stood up to him. Stood up for myself. And I let him know just how happy I was. You make me very happy, Eli. I love you more each day."

He beamed at her, and it was as if warm sunshine radiated through her. She would never be able to get enough of this man.

"What are we waiting for, Autumn? You've said it yourself. Why put our lives on hold when we know what we want? Let's not waste any more time. Let's get married while Summer's here." He paused. "Unless you want to plan a big wedding."

"No!" she said quickly, holding more tightly to him. "Not at all. Just family and a few friends is all I need. And my handsome, loving groom. My parents' backyard is lovely this time of year. Mom's green thumb has everything bursting with color. The zinnias. Marigolds. Pentas."

"I like the sound of that," he said, his voice low and raw. "We'll need a license. I've already researched how to get married in Texas. There's a seventy-two-hour waiting period before you can use the license, though."

She laughed, feeling freer than she ever had. "A judge can waive that for us. I'll get Dad to call Judge Stowe. They're golfing buddies. I'll bet he'd even agree to perform the ceremony."

Eli's mouth touched hers in a reverent kiss.

"Then we'll be at the county courthouse tomorrow morning when they open," he said.

"I need to leave now to get Summer," she said. "She's going to be thrilled about this news."

"I'm coming with you. I'll text Nancy and let her know. She can also drop Atticus off in the backyard."

"You sure?"

The look of love in his eyes caused her to melt. "Never more sure."

They went to his car, and he said, "Mine's larger. From what you've said, Summer will be bringing a ton of luggage, even though she's only supposed to be here for less than a week."

"That's Summer," Autumn said happily.

As Eli drove them to DFW, Autumn called her mom, filling in her mom, who was over the moon hearing they were getting married.

"Do you think you could have Dad talk to Judge Stowe? And could we use your backyard for the wedding?"

"Are you thinking Saturday or Sunday?"

"Either, Mom. Whatever works for you. It's good Darby's also coming into town. I'll text her and Sawyer and let them know. West and Kelby, too. Oh, Mom, I'm so excited!"

"Then let's go with Saturday afternoon. I'll start handling the small details, but you have to bring Summer here tonight because we have so much to talk about. A cake. Some flowers. What you'll wear. Oh, Autumn, I'm so happy for you. You have a good man in Eli."

Autumn glanced to the man she would spend the rest of her life with.

"Yes, I most certainly do."

Once they arrived at the airport, she consulted her app too see if Summer's plane was still on time and what baggage claim she would be at. They found a parking place close to where Summer would arrive. Going inside, Autumn couldn't help but be giddy. She kissed Eli spontaneously.

"I can't believe we're getting married this weekend."

He grinned. "I can't believe I get to spend the rest of my life with you, Autumn."

They were kissing again when a familiar voice said, "You must be Eli. I'm Summer."

Quickly, they pulled apart, having been oblivious to everything going on around them.

"Summer!" she cried, falling into her twin's arms.

They hugged tightly, and she pulled away. "We're getting married! This weekend!"

Her sister's radiant smile lit up her face. "Then I guess I'm glad I flew down for the wedding." Summer turned to Eli and hugged him. "Welcome to the family, Eli. Anytime you're ready to make me an aunty, I'm all for it."

"Summer!' she cried, but secretly, Autumn knew she wanted babies with Eli soon.

"Wedding first. Then babies." He looked to her and grinned. "Maybe three or four. Your sister and I will need to negotiate that. Let's grab your luggage, Summer, and then Autumn can tell you how kickass she was when she confronted her ex-husband today."

"What?" Summer asked, her jaw dropping.

"It's a long story," Autumn said. "But it has a very happy ending."

CHAPTER
Twenty-Three

E li finished the last bite of his burger and dabbed his mouth with a paper napkin. "I better head over to the field," he told Autumn.

"Okay," she said brightly, giving him a smile. "Will you be down on the track or in the stands?"

"I think West wants me close by. I'll let you know." He gave her a quick kiss and then looked at Summer and Darby. "See you later."

He tossed his empty plate in a nearby garbage can and strode from the pre-game tailgate in the parking lot next to Hawks Field, medical bag in hand. Talk around town said that the stadium might be renamed for Coach Markham, longtime coach of the high school's football team and West's predecessor. It was something the school board would take up at their next monthly session.

Slipping his lanyard from his pocket, he placed it around his neck and showed it to the person at the turnstile, who waved Eli through. Even though the weather was still warm in Texas this early September night, Autumn said it was officially football weather since the season had started. He caught the excitement in the air, as well as a whiff of popcorn coming from the concession stand being run by band parents.

Autumn had taken him to last week's away game, the first of the season, patiently explaining each play as it unfolded. Thanks to West and her tutoring him, Eli had a decent grasp of the game. At least he didn't think he would embarrass himself and cheer at the wrong time.

He entered the stands and went down the concrete steps to a gate. Opening it, he walked down a few more steps until he reached the bottom. The red track surrounded the lush green turf, and players from both teams had taken to the field, going through warmups. Eli joined West, who stood on the sidelines, watching his captains lead the team in group exercises.

"Ready for tonight?" West asked. "Anything can happen."

"I'm overprepared," he joked. "I got online and went down numerous rabbit holes, researching the usual types of injuries seen at a football game. I'm ready for everything from sprains, strains, and tears such as ACL and MCL knee injuries, to concussions. I've also met with your trainer and his student assistants. Those kids are sharp. They've asked me a million questions, all of them on point. Your athletes will be taken care of. How about you? First home game as the new head coach."

West nodded, his eyes still moving across the field. "Last week's win against the Panthers helped calm some of my jitters and those of the team. We've got a solid bunch of kids playing this season. I'm hoping I've created the culture I've wanted, from the locker room to on and off the playing field. I want these kids to care about one another. Play their hearts out. Learn from their mistakes and take joy in when they perform well."

"Is it odd being back here where you played all those Friday nights years ago?" he asked. "I ran cross country. No one ever came to our meets." He glanced into the stands. "This is way different. You can feel how charged the air is."

West smiled. "It's great to come home. To Hawthorne. This field. This job. I feel I was meant to coach." He looked over his shoulder and smiled. "Kelby's made all the difference in my life. But I guess you know something about that."

"I feel like I've finally become the person I was supposed to be. As if I were a butterfly who's emerged from its cocoon. I know my purpose. I see life sharper now. It's richer. And I'm a better person than I ever have been, all because of Autumn."

West chuckled. "I'd say you have it bad for my sister, Doc. Talk later."

Eli watched West trot out onto the field as players broke up into smaller groups, their group stretches complete now. He knew they were dividing up by position, based upon what he'd learned at practice. He watched the athletes run through a different kind of warmup now, related to their positions. The punter was taking snaps and kicking downfield as far as he could. Receivers were running quick routes, allowing the quarterback to warm up his arm. Others did short sprints down the field.

He let his gaze roam the stadium. Cheerleaders with pompoms and megaphones were setting up on the track. The band and drill team had taken their places in the stands. Fans were beginning to pour into the stadium. Eli walked the side-lines, talking to the student trainers, watching the action. He made his way to the other side, introducing himself to the head coach of the Warriors, tonight's opponent, and circling back around.

By now, the Hawks were leaving the field. He decided to join them to see West in action in the locker room, curious as to what he would say to his team before the start of tonight's game. The players gathered alongside the coaching staff, and West spoke from his heart, telling the young men they were prepared. Talented. Ready to play this game with both minds and hearts. He praised their work habits and told them now was their time to shine on the field.

Eli ran out with the team, which tore through a large banner held up by the cheerleaders. The band was on the field, playing the school fight song, with the drill team shaking their pompoms alongside them. It was a natural high, feeling the strong emotions. He'd seen a little of this last week, but a home game changed everything. No wonder they referred to home field advantage, because it was palpable.

He turned, skimming the crowd, finding Autumn and waving at her. She had Kelby on one side and Darby and Sawyer on the other. Her parents sat in front of her on the next row. It had worked out well, with Darby flying in from Kansas City this weekend for a quick visit before she attended meetings in Dallas right after Labor Day. The national cheer finals would be held in Dallas early next year, and Darby was meeting with the head of the venue where the competition would take place. Fortunately, her visit now coincided with their wedding.

He only wished Buddy could be here for it. Eli had requested kits from two different registries and sent off his DNA to be placed in their databases. The waiting game now began, with him hoping that Buddy either had already submitted his own DNA sample to one or both places or would in the near future. His gut told him his little brother was out there, and Eli would do whatever he could to reunite with him.

Suddenly, a chill came over him, the proverbial someone walking over your grave goose bumps. He looked around, puzzled by the odd feeling. It left as quickly as it had come upon him, and he shrugged it off, returning his focus to the game.

At the end of the first half, the score was tied, ten-all. Eli opted to stay on the sidelines and watch the halftime show put on by the band and drill team. He had seen one for the first time last week and been amazed at the level of talent and precision on display. The Hawthorne Hawks didn't let him down. The band performed a medley of Beach Boys' tunes, while the drill team did a disc routine to a song most of the crowd seemed to know because they were singing along. He had missed out on a lot of pop culture, but Autumn would help catch him up.

The second half started with the Hawks receiving the ball. The kick returner fielded the ball and ran it back for a touchdown, causing the fans to go wild. The extra point was good, and from that point on, Hawthorne couldn't seem to do anything wrong. By the end of the third quarter, the score was 31-10.

Eli, who now stood next to the high school's principal on the sidelines, said, "Fred is really looking good out there."

Her son was the starting quarterback for the Hawks, a senior who had a strong arm on him. West had said Fred was one of the most accurate passers he'd seen at any age, and Eli assumed that meant Fred Biggerstaff had a future playing football beyond the high school level.

"Fred lives for football," Blanche said, smiling. "And girls. I hear you and Autumn are taking the plunge this weekend."

"We are. Tomorrow afternoon. I couldn't be happier about it."

"The town thinks a lot of Joe and Meg Sutherland and their three children. You, too, Dr. Carson. We couldn't be more pleased to have Triple H here in Hawthorne."

His eyes returned to the field for the first play of the fourth quarter. Fred dropped back to pass, and Eli shouted at the teenager, who didn't see the defensive player barreling toward him from Fred's right. Just as Fred released the ball, he was hit hard, going down and hitting the ground.

He did not move.

Immediately, Eli sprinted onto the field, medical bag in hand, closely followed by the Hawks' athletic trainer and his cadre of student assistants. As Eli knelt at Fred's side, he heard the fans erupting in cheers, but he blocked out the noise, focusing solely on his patient.

"Can you hear me, Fred?"

The teenager opened his eyes and looked at Eli. "Did we score?" he asked.

"I have no idea. You've likely had a concussion, Fred. We need to get you off the field and talk to you and your parents about what happens next. First, let me ask. Do you have a headache?"

"A big one. I also feel like I'm going to barf."

"Barfing is allowed," Eli said good-naturedly. "A double vision? Ears ringing? Dizziness?"

Fred frowned, thinking. "A little bit of dizziness. I can see and hear fine, though."

"Did you lose consciousness?"

"I don't think so. I just went down hard. I closed my eyes. That's all. The lights feel kinda bright."

"That's good to know." Eli checked the teenager's eyes,

saying, "Follow my finger with both eyes, Fred." He was pleased to see that Fred did so without any problems.

"Any numbness or tingling?"

"I'm not numb. Still tingling a little in my back from the hit. Man, that lineman came out of nowhere."

"I agree. Can you tell me what today is?"

"Game day. Friday."

"And where we are?"

"Our stadium. In Hawthorne."

"Good. Spell *world* for me, but I want you to do it backward."

Frowning, the quarterback said, "D, L, O, W."

Fred had missed a letter, but Eli wasn't too worried. "Repeat these numbers back to me. Thirty-eight. Twelve. Two. Ninety-seven."

The athlete reversed the last two. Again, not uncommon with a mild concussion, which seemed to be what Fred had experienced.

"Good job, Fred. We're going to take you to the locker room now."

He signaled for the stretcher, and Fred was carted off the field. The stands, which had gone totally silent while he'd spoken with the quarterback, now sounded with applause from both sides. Autumn had told Eli this was the polite thing to do after an athlete had been injured and left the field, and he was glad the young man was receiving recognition for his efforts tonight.

Blanche and her husband accompanied them to the locker room, where Eli went over exactly what a concussion was.

"A person doesn't have to lose consciousness for it to be a concussion. Fred doesn't think he did. Has he ever suffered a concussion before?"

"Never," Blanche said. "And he's played football a good ten years now."

"That's good to know. His speech isn't slurred. He does have a headache and some nausea, though. I'd like to go ahead and send him to Triple H overnight for observation," he shared with the couple. "I've already administered a SAC test, which is a standard assessment of concussion. I'll let them know Fred's results."

"Do I have to go to the hospital?" Fred asked.

"If Dr. Carson thinks that's what needs to happen, then you're going," Mr. Biggerstaff said firmly. "Does he need to go by ambulance?"

"No, you can drive him to Triple H. No stops in-between, though." He smiled at Fred. "Unless you need to barf."

"Guess that means I'll miss tonight's dance," the teen said glumly.

"There'll be plenty of dances in your future," Eli assured the athlete. "Let me call ahead and give Triple H a heads up that you're coming in. Since it's late, go straight to the ER. They'll get you all taken care of. I'll stop by tomorrow morning to see you."

"Aren't you getting married tomorrow, Dr. Carson?" Mr. Biggerstaff asked.

"Not until late afternoon. Plenty of time for me to stop by and check on Fred. Right now, I need to get back to the game. You never know when I might be needed."

He left the locker room and returned to the stadium, calling the ER on his way to let them know the Biggerstaffs were on their way. He told them he didn't think Fred's concussion was severe since the boy had been speaking and making good sense, but it was purely a precaution on his part, wanting Fred to remain overnight for close observation. Eli had come to know a lot of these football players in the last few weeks. Giving them their physicals. Attending practices. Watching them play two games. He wanted all the boys to have the best care possible.

First, he found West on the sidelines and gave him a brief report, letting him know that Fred was doing fine and would be admitted overnight at Triple H to be on the safe side.

"I'll go see him first thing tomorrow morning," West said.

Eli turned, looking into the stands, his gaze connecting with Autumn's. He gave her a thumbs up and saw she visibly relaxed.

The Hawks scored twice more in the final minutes of the fourth quarter. One was a run from the six-yard-line. The other touchdown came on a scramble by the backup quarterback, David Jordan, who was known for his aggressive running.

West shook hands with Eli after the game, thanking him for being on duty and taking such good care of Fred Biggerstaff.

"No need to come to the locker room. I'll give the team the news about Fred."

He went into the stands, where Autumn and her family waited for him.

"Fred is going to be all right?" Meg Sutherland asked, her face full of concern.

"He will be. Thankfully, it's the first concussion he's ever suffered. He was talking fine and even walking in the locker room. His balance was good, but I had his parents take him to Triple H to stay overnight. I'd rather be safe than sorry when it comes to someone's health."

Eli shook his head. "I guess there was a little more excitement tonight than I thought would happen."

"You were out on that field before I could blink," Joe

Sutherland told him. "I think the whole town is impressed how quickly you moved to help Fred."

"All in a day's work," he said, slipping an arm around Autumn's shoulders.

They walked to his car together. He would drive her to her parents' house tonight to spend the night, tradition dictating the bride and groom not see one another the day of the ceremony.

"I assume you'll be going to the hospital tomorrow morning to check on Fred," she said.

"Part of the job." He kissed the tip of her nose. "That means *you* need to stay away from Triple H."

Before he could open the passenger door for her, her fingers clasped his nape and pulled him down to her for a long, slow kiss.

"It's going to be hard for me to keep away from you all day tomorrow," she teased.

"Not any harder than it's going to be for me to keep away from you. I'm addicted to you, Autumn Sutherland. To the curve of your breast and the scent of vanilla which always seems to cling to your skin. You're one habit I never want to kick."

"I wish it could already be tomorrow," she told him.

"Just think. This time tomorrow night, we'll already be man and wife. In bed and making love for maybe the third or fourth time."

She laughed. "You must have a lot of stamina, Dr. Carson."

He framed her face with his hands. "I'd go to the ends of the earth for you, Nurse Sutherland."

Eli kissed her—and thought about how he'd be a husband soon.

CHAPTER
Twenty-Four

E li awoke and stripped the bed of its sheets, replacing them with a fresh set. He left the bed turned back invitingly, the roses he had picked up yesterday sitting in a vase beside the bed. The buds were just starting to open, and the florist had assured him by tonight, when he and Autumn returned after their wedding ceremony, the flowers would be fully open and fragrant.

He brewed a quick cup of coffee and let Atticus out to pee, then fed the dog before snagging a bottle of water and driving to the hospital. He cut through the ER and spoke to one of the nurses on duty there about Fred. She checked the computer and gave him Fred's room number, and Eli proceeded to the stairs.

When he arrived at the teenager's room, Fred was sitting up, talking with not only his parents but two other players Eli recognized from the football team, along with a dark-haired girl.

"You look alert," Eli said. "How did last night go?"

Fred laughed. "It seems every time I went to sleep, some nurse would wake me up and ask me questions. Don't worry, Dr. Carson. I passed with flying colors. I know the day and date. Who's the president. Who won the last Super Bowl." He grinned at the girl. "My girlfriend's name. I'm firing on all pistons today."

"I'm glad to hear that," Eli said.

"When can I get out of here?" Fred asked. He glanced to his girlfriend. "I've got to make it up to Laurie since we missed the dance after the game last night."

"Let me look you over, then I'll review your chart and check with the charge nurse. You should be good to go."

Eli did a quick examination and then spoke to the charge nurse, who confirmed that Fred was showing no signs of trauma.

"Go ahead and have his discharge papers drawn up then."

"Will do, Dr. Carson," the nurse said.

He pulled a brochure from the nurse's station returned to his patient's room, giving him and his parents the good news.

"Thank you, Dr. Carson," Blanche said. "We're so grateful you were on the sidelines last night."

"You'll need to keep a close eye on him." Handing Blanche the brochure, he said, "Read this carefully. It's a guideline for Fred's recovery plan. He'll need to get some extra rest the next forty-eight hours but not too much. If he sleeps too much, it can extend his recovery period. I'll also make certain Coach Sutherland speaks to his staff and Fred's teachers and counselor regarding his concussion protocol."

"How soon until I can play again?" Fred demanded.

Eli turned his attention to his patient. "You'll also need to become familiar with the steps to recovery, Fred. You can't return to play Monday, no matter how good you think you feel."

Disappointment filled the teenager's face.

"It's a six-step process," Eli explained. "Each step takes at least twenty-four hours. You only moved to the next step if you don't show any symptoms of concussion at the step you're on. If you do, then you're pushing your body too hard and need to back off."

"Walk us through it, Dr. Carson," Mr. Biggerstaff said.

"I'm happy to do so."

He explained that after a weekend with lots of rest, returning to school on Monday would be the first step.

"You can go to football practice, but only do light aerobic activity, something that will increase your heart rate. The trainer will work with you. Riding the exercise bike would be a good start. No lifting, though. If that works well, you can pick up the pace on Tuesday. Jog. A brief run. More bike work. Add in some moderate weightlifting."

Eli let this soak in before continuing. "Wednesday, you can do some sprints and get back to your regular lifting routine. You can also participate in some drills. But absolutely no contact. From there, you can practice Thursday and have full contact. Then by Friday, Coach Sutherland and the athletic trainer will decide if you're at a hundred percent and ready for competition. They may think you are. They may hold you out a game because you could be a little rusty. Just don't rush things. When you return to the field, you want to be at your best, not half-best."

"Got it, Doc," Fred said enthusiastically. "Thanks again." He grinned. "And it *was* a touchdown after I got hit."

Eli laughed. "Let's hope you can play on Friday. I hear the Tigers are going to be much stiffer competition."

He left the hospital room, passing West who was on his way in to see Fred, and called Autumn.

When she answered, he said, "I hope it's okay that I called you. I know I'm not supposed to see you, but I missed you in our bed last night. So did Atticus."

"I missed you, too, Eli. I don't ever want us to be apart again. If you have a conference to attend, I'm coming with you. How is Fred feeling this morning?"

"I just left him and his parents. A few of his buddies and his girlfriend had also stopped by. West, too. He's in good spirits and itching to get back on the field again."

"He's a teenager. They think they're invincible. West has suffered a concussion before, so he'll be super careful with Fred. Changing subjects, I wish we hadn't set the wedding for late afternoon."

"Why?"

"Because that's an awfully long time to wait before I can see you."

He laughed, love for this woman pouring through his veins. "We'll make up for lost time later tonight," he promised.

"I'll hold you to that," Autumn said.

"Should I stop at the store and pick up another can of whipping cream?" he asked, causing her to laugh.

"There's already one waiting for us in the fridge," she informed him saucily. "Along with a squeeze bottle of honey in the pantry."

"Honey?" he asked. "That sounds intriguing."

"I can't wait to be married to you, Eli Carson."

"Ditto," he responded, having now watched the romantic movie *Ghost* with her. The word had become part of their conversations. "I love you madly and can't wait to make you Mrs. Carson. See you this afternoon."

He slipped his cell phone into the pocket of his shorts and stopped at his car, using it to stretch against. Then Eli set out for a long run. His thoughts wandered during it, but they always came back to Autumn and the future they would build together. They both wanted children, and he had told her there was no reason for them to put it off. She planned to finish up the packet of birth control pills next week and then stop using them. He couldn't wait to be a husband and a father. Though he'd never had a father himself, that wouldn't stop him from being the best dad he could be. Joe Sutherland would be a good dad for Eli to model himself after. Even though he and Autumn would make mistakes, they would learn from them and do the best they could for their children.

After his run, he returned to his car in the hospital parking lot and guzzled the bottle of water he'd brought with him. Once at home, he took Atticus on a walk. With time still on his hands, he took a long, hot shower and then shaved. Not wanting to wrinkle his clothes for the wedding, he donned shorts and a T-shirt. Going to his home office, he put in a couple of hours of work, eating a sandwich as he did so.

Returning to the bedroom, he dressed in a dark blue suit and crisp white dress shirt. He chose a tie of silver and blue and fastened it about his neck before running a comb through his hair a final time. Then he drove to Hawthorne's town square, entering the jewelry store he and Autumn had visited yesterday to pick out their wedding bands. Eli had insisted that she also choose an engagement ring, and she had been drawn to a simple solitaire. Autumn had asked if her two rings could be soldered together by the wedding, and the jewelry said he could do so.

The jeweler greeted him now. "Dr. Carson, let me get Autumn's ring for you."

The man disappeared and returned quickly. Handing Eli

a small black box, Eli opened it and saw the rings sitting against black velvet. He pulled the joined rings from the slot, thinking they would forever be nestled together, just as he and Autumn would be.

"Thank you for doing this so quickly," he said.

"Everyone in Hawthorne thinks a lot of the Sutherlands. The entire town is also thrilled you've brought Triple H to Hawthorne."

He chuckled. "It wasn't me. It was Hogan Health who decided to locate the hospital here. I'm just helping to run it."

"We're still happy you're here. Congratulations on your marriage, Doctor."

He returned to his car and drove to the Sutherlands' house, which sat on a corner lot. A few cars were parked in front of it, and he eased his vehicle to the curb.

As he got out, so did someone in a gray sports car across the street. Eli didn't recognize the man, who wore dark sunglasses. He closed the distance between them, coming to stand before Eli.

Suddenly, chills raced through his body.

The man removed his sunglasses, and Eli experienced a sense of déjà vu, saying, "I can't place you, but I feel as if we've met before."

Their gazes held, and a rush of emotion swept through him. "Buddy?" he asked hesitantly.

The stranger looked surprised and then broke out in a smile. "I'd forgotten that. That you used to call me that."

Eli shook his head. "I can't believe ... it's you."

They moved toward one another, wrapping their arms tightly about the other. He closed his eyes, the years swept away in an instant. It was as if he were embracing his little brother as he had that final time before they were permanently separated.

He pulled back, grasping his brother's elbows. "How did you find me, Buddy?"

"It's a long story, Eli. Or should I say E-wi?"

It struck him that his little brother had always had trouble saying L's, and he had called Eli *E-wi*. A lump formed in his throat, and he swallowed down the emotions.

"What's your name?" he asked. "Your real name. I'm ashamed to admit that I don't remember it. Mom always just told me to look after my little buddy, so I called you Buddy."

Tears filled his brother's eyes. "I ... don't know what my name was. My adopted name is Jason Tanner. I've always gone by Jace. My birth certificate reflects that name and that of the couple who adopted me. I don't know who I was before, Eli. Only who I've become. But I've missed you over the years. I always loved you. I knew you were out there somewhere, and I was determined to find you."

Eli threw his arms around Buddy again. No, Jace. He hugged him tightly but pulled away again.

"Jace. It suits you." He paused. "Were you at the football stadium last night?"

His brother nodded slowly. "I was."

"I sensed you."

"I saw you look into the crowd. You looked as if you were searching for someone. I was afraid to approach you. I left the game, not sure if I'd try to contact you. But I couldn't stay away. I had to make contact with you." Jace cleared his throat. "You've done well for yourself. A doctor. Running a hospital."

"What about you?"

"I'll tell you all about me sometime. I know you're about to get married. I just stopped by to wish you good luck. Give you my number. Maybe we can get together some time."

"You're not going anywhere," Eli proclaimed. "You're coming to my wedding."

"No," Jace protested. "I can't. I don't know anyone." He smiled ruefully. "I don't really even know you."

"You're my flesh and blood, and I've been looking for you, as well. I even registered and sent in my DNA to a few sites, hoping to connect with you that way. You need to meet Autumn and her family. And you'll be my family at this wedding."

They went to the Sutherlands' door, and Meg Sutherland answered it.

"Eli, don't you look handsome. And you've brought a friend." She cocked her head, studying them a moment. "No, this is something more."

With pride, Eli said, "Meg, I'd like you to meet my brother. This is Jace Tanner."

Not missing a beat, Meg embraced Jace. "We're so happy to have you with us today, Jace. Please, come in."

"Meg is Autumn's mother."

"You need to meet everyone else, Jace," Meg encouraged.

They went into the den, where West and Kelby sat, along with Sawyer and Darby. He assumed Summer was upstairs helping Autumn to finish dressing.

"Joe is out back with Judge Stowe," Meg explained. "Everyone, this is Jace Tanner, Eli's brother."

He saw the surprised looks on everyone's faces as they came to their feet. He introduced Jace to them.

"This is Autumn's older brother West and his wife Kelby. West is the football coach of the Hawthorne Hawks, and Kelby runs her own social media and branding business."

West beamed. "I already know Jace. He's been my sports agent for years."

Stunned, Eli looked from his brother to Autumn's brother. "What?"

Jace shrugged. "I guess you can say it's a small world. Good to see you again, West."

Recovering quickly, he turned to the other pair. "These are Autumn's cousins. Darby Montgomery and her brother Sawyer. Sawyer lives here in Hawthorne and has a law practice. Darby is in visiting from Kansas City."

Jace greeted all of them, and Joe and Judge Stowe stepped inside. More introductions were made, and then Meg said, "I think we need to introduce Jace to Autumn and Summer. Come upstairs with me, Jace. You stay down here, Eli. In fact, everyone should head outside. It's almost time for this wedding to begin."

Eli accompanied Judge Stowe and the others into the backyard, lush with colorful flowers. Meg returned and adjusted Eli's tie slightly, patting it, and then slipping a boutonniere into his lapel.

"I'm so happy for you, Eli," she told him. "I know you've been searching for your brother. It must mean a great deal to you to have found him."

"He's the one who found me," Eli revealed. "He was waiting outside when I got here. I have a thousand questions to ask him. I don't even know where he lives."

"You have the rest of your lives to learn about one another," she assured him.

Judge Stowe had Eli come and stand next to him. West, who was serving as Eli's best man, joined him.

"Are you going to give me the ring?" West asked.

He reached into his pocket and handed over the small ring box the jeweler had given to him. "Thanks for being my best man, West."

"I think it would be better if your brother stands with you today."

Surprise filled him. "You don't mind?"

West clasped Eli's shoulder. "I think having Jace serve as your best man would be perfect."

West returned the ring box to Eli and removed the boutonniere he wore, handing it to Eli. West went to stand next to Kelby, sliding an arm around her waist. Summer, clutching a bouquet, appeared with Jace. She smiled widely at Eli and moved toward him.

"Autumn will be here any moment now. She is thrilled about Jace."

Eli motioned to Jace, and his brother joined him.

"Would you do me the honor of serving as my best man?" he asked, his voice quivering with emotion.

Jace looked astonished but then smiled broadly. "I'd be happy to, Big Brother."

He took the boutonniere Eli offered and fastened it to his lapel. Eli handed over the ring box, and Jace slipped it into his coat's pocket.

Judge Stowe said, "Are we ready to begin?"

"Yes, sir," Eli said firmly.

Moments later, Autumn and her father rounded the corner. She was wearing a cream, tea-length dress and carrying a bouquet of yellow and white roses. Their gazes met and held as Joe escorted his daughter to Eli. She glanced over and saw Jace standing next to him, and her smile grew even more radiant.

Joe kissed his daughter's cheek. Taking her hand, he offered it to Eli. "Take care of my baby girl, Son."

His eyes misted with tears, knowing that Joe Sutherland really did think of him as a son and trusted him with Autumn.

His fingers entwined with hers now, and they looked at one another.

"I love you, Eli," she said, her eyes misty with tears.

"I love you, Autumn," he replied.

They turned to their officiant. "Ready when you are, Judge," he said.

Eli was ready to speak his vows and for a lifetime with Autumn by his side.

Epilogue

ONE YEAR LATER ...

Autumn stood at the door to the nursery. Kelby had helped her put the room together, using a palette of light pink and soft gray. Kelby had painted a mural of animals from Noah's ark on one wall. Above the crib was a mobile which also had some of Noah's animals. On the wall beside the crib, Kelby had stenciled *Sarah Elizabeth*. Those were the names of Autumn's two grandmothers. She had always loved both names and thought they sounded beautiful together. Eli had agreed, but she had insisted they check with Summer before going with the name. Her twin had encouraged Autumn to use the two names, agreeing both their grandmothers would have been touched to be honored in that manner.

Looking out over the room, she thought that she would soon be sitting in the rocking chair, rocking their newborn daughter to sleep before placing her in her crib. She brought her hands to her huge belly, rubbing it. Immediately, Sarah responded with a kick, causing Autumn to chuckle.

"What's so funny?" Eli asked, coming up behind her and

wrapping his arms around her. His hands stroked her belly, and then he said, "Oh!" since Sarah gave another kick. "I see she's awake."

"She was most of last night," Autumn informed him. "I didn't get much sleep. I'm a little bit tired today."

He kissed her temple. "You should be tired. You're due to give birth tomorrow. That is, if our daughter decides to cooperate and arrive on her due date. First babies do tend to be a little late, though."

"If she doesn't come on Labor Day tomorrow, I have an appointment with Barbara first thing Tuesday morning."

Eli turned her in his arms, kissing her lightly. "Do you even feel like going to the cookout today?"

West and Kelby had moved into their new home four months ago. The family was gathering there today, not only because it was a large house with an outdoor kitchen and eating space, but also because it would be convenient to put Kate down when it was time for her nap. Her niece had been born three months ago and already had stolen the hearts of everyone in the family. She was glad that she and Eli were having a girl and that the cousins would grow up together here in Hawthorne.

"Yes, I want to go and see everyone."

"Then we better get moving."

They stopped in the kitchen for the banana cream pie Eli had baked. Especially with Autumn so heavily pregnant and still working fulltime, Eli had taken over all the cooking. He said it relaxed him. Desserts had become a specialty of his. He liked how baking combined science and art.

They drove to West and Kelby's house, which was less than fifteen minutes away. West answered the door, Kate in his arms. He wore a navy T-shirt with *Girl Dad* in white script, surrounded by a pink heart.

"Come on in," he said. "How are you feeling, Fall?"

"Like a ton of bricks is sitting on my chest," she told him. "And I'm not kidding."

Kelby joined them, taking the pie from Eli. "Oh, I remember that feeling. That last month, I didn't get one deep breath. It felt like an elephant had parked on my chest." She smiled at her daughter, smoothing Kate's hair.

As they went into the kitchen, Eli teasingly asked, "Does West ever let you hold your daughter?

West answered for his wife. "I told Kelby she lugged Kate around for nine months. It's simply my time to return the favor."

"I think she's going to be a daddy's girl," Kelby said. "And I'm perfectly fine with that." She handed a gift bag to Eli. "For you."

Looking perplexed, he opened it, pulling out a shirt identical to the one West now wore. Her brother grinned. "Girl dads need to stick together."

"Thank you," Eli said. "I'll wear this with pride."

Sawyer came into the kitchen, greeting everyone. "Uncle Joe wants to know if it's time to light the grill."

"Darby just texted and said they're running late," Kelby said.

"Ooh, they must've had sex more than once this morning," West joked, looking down at Kate.

"West Sutherland!" their mom reprimanded. "Behave yourself."

"Well, it's true," West said. "They're crazy in love." He glanced around. "Just like all the married couples in our family."

"Way to make me feel left out, Cuz," Sawyer said, pretending to be offended. "I'll tell Uncle Joe to hold off for another ten minutes." He left the kitchen.

"Do you need to sit?" Eli asked her.

"Yes," she said, feeling weary. Her pregnancy had gone well, with very little morning sickness. She had gained the right amount of weight, and all her appointments had gone well. It was only in the last week that Autumn had been so fatigued.

She started toward the kitchen chair when an odd feeling came over here. Then a loud whoosh sounded, and she looked at the kitchen floor, water now puddled beneath her.

"Oh, your water's broken, Autumn," Mom said. "We need to get you to Triple H. I'll tell your father not to start the grill."

"Don't do that, Mom," she protested. "You know first babies take forever to come. All of you might as well enjoy some hamburgers and hot dogs. Eli can keep you posted on my progress."

"I don't want to miss the birth of this grandchild," Mom said indignantly.

"We'll call you in plenty of time, Meg." Eli laced his fingers through hers. "Let's go. Slowly."

They returned to his car, and her husband said, "I'll text Barbara and let her know."

"I hate to call her in on a holiday weekend," Autumn said.

"She needs to know what's happening," Eli insisted. "It'll be up to her when she arrives at the hospital. No matter what, you'll be in good hands."

He got Autumn settled in the passenger seat and then texted Barbara Bennett before setting his phone in the cupholder. Starting the car, he headed toward Triple H.

His phone dinged, and Autumn picked it up. "Barbara said she'll come in a few hours."

They reached the hospital, and Eli pulled up to the ER. Scott Watterman hurried out.

Eli told the physician, "Autumn's water broke ten minutes ago. Get a wheelchair so we can get her up to L&D."

"Be right back," Scott replied.

"I can walk."

"I insist you ride, and I'm the medical director. My word is final."

Autumn sat in the wheelchair Sam brought out to the car. She was actually glad because walking suddenly seemed beyond her. Her legs felt like quivering Jell-O.

A nurse rolled her into the elevator. By the time they reached L&D, Eli met them, a little out of breath.

"You must have taken the stairs after parking the car," she said.

He brushed the backs of his fingers along her cheek. "I wanted to be here to greet you. We're having a baby!" His love for her sparkled in his eyes.

The waiting game began. They turned on a baseball game and played cards for a while. Her contractions gradually began to grow stronger and closer together. When they were four minutes apart, Eli texted her parents, letting them know it was time to come to the hospital because their grand-daughter would be arriving soon.

Barbara Bennett sailed through the door. "How is our mom-to-be?" she asked, picking up Autumn's wrist and checking her pulse.

"A little tired. Ready to get this show on the road and meet Sarah."

"Let me examine you and see how dilated you are," Barbara said. After a moment, she said, "You're almost at ten, Autumn. After the next contraction, we'll begin pushing with the one which follows. Do you have any questions for me?"

"No. I've delivered enough babies. I know what's coming next."

Her friend laughed. "You think you know. Assisting in a birth and actually giving birth are two very different things. I've done it twice, so I know what I'm talking about."

The pushing soon began in earnest. Eli held Autumn's hand throughout as she grunted. Moaned. Even shrieked and shouted.

"Excellent work, Autumn," Barbara said. "The head has crowned. This next push, we should see all Sarah's head."

A new wave of pain hit, and she pushed as the OB instructed her.

"That's it," Barbara said encouragingly. "Oh, she's got a headful of hair."

"I had enough heartburn," Autumn said. "Everyone said it was an old wives' tale. That heartburn meant lots of hair."

"Bear down again," the doctor said briskly.

Eli squeezed her hand. "The shoulders are out. She looks beautiful, Autumn. Come on, honey. One more time. You can do this."

Autumn bore down as hard as she could, gritting her teeth, pushing with everything she had.

"Done!" Barbara declared, lifting the baby so Autumn could get a glimpse before a nurse whisked Sarah away.

"You know what comes next, Autumn," Barbara continued. "You'll deliver the afterbirth. Sarah will go through her Apgar test with her pediatrician and be cleaned up and returned to you in a jiffy."

In the next few minutes, Autumn finished the birthing process. Two nurses stepped in to help clean her up, and they transferred her to another bed with clean, cool sheets. One nurse gave her some cold water to drink, and she greedily guzzled it, handing back the empty glass.

She closed her eyes, feeling all her energy had been zapped from her. Eli spoke encouragingly to her, but she was too weary to even make out his words. Then she sensed a change in the room and opened her eyes. A nurse handed their baby to Eli. As long as Autumn lived, she would never forget the look of love which washed over his face as he looked down at their baby girl.

"She's absolutely perfect," Eli said, awe in his voice.

He turned and placed the newborn in her arms—and Autumn fell instantly in love with Sarah Elizabeth Carson.

Eli climbed into the bed with them, one arm going around Autumn, the other one lightly stroking his daughter's cheek.

"She's so tiny. And so perfect. Look at that little rosebud of a mouth."

"Not that tiny," her husband said. "She looked to be about eight pounds to me."

Barbara said, "Everything looks wonderful for both mother and daughter. The pediatrician said Sarah's Apgar score was a nine. We'll leave you three alone for a few minutes so you can bond together as a family."

"You did a good thing, Autumn. I can't believe the two of us produced this little miracle."

She gazed lovingly at her newborn and then up at her husband. Eli had proven to be a wonderful husband, a partner to her in every way imaginable. She knew he would also be an outstanding dad.

They contentedly watched Sarah, cooing to her and telling her how happy they were that she had finally arrived in the world.

His voice thick with emotion, Eli said, "I have everything I could possibly want. You've made all the difference in my life, Autumn. I love you and Sarah more than I ever thought possible."

He kissed her softly, and Autumn knew their new family of three would multiply over the years, each child wanted and welcomed.

"I know now might seem unusual to bring this up, but I want to talk about our other children," Autumn began. "I know we've only been parents a few minutes, but I want to grow our family not only through giving birth to our babies. I want us to adopt someday, Eli. An older child. One who has given up hope of ever finding a family."

She watched tears fill his eyes and spill down his cheeks.

"You really want to adopt?"

"I do. Maybe we can have a couple and adopt a couple. Four sounds like a great number to me."

Eli wiped away his tears on the sleeve of his shirt. "We can talk about it later. But that idea makes me truly happy, Autumn. As if everything will come full circle."

Love for him swelled within her. "I love you so much, Eli. My heart is bursting with love for you and Sarah. I look forward to all the rest of the days of our lives. With each other and the family we create."

Eli kissed her again, and Autumn felt enveloped in love.

Also by Alexa Aston

HEARTS IN HAWTHORNE

Heartstrings and Helmets

Heartbeat Harmony

Agent of the Heart

Hearts and Hooves

Hoops and Hearts

LOST CREEK, TEXAS HILL COUNTRY

The Perfect Blend

Painted Melodies

Script of Love

Love in Every Bite

Whispered Melodies

SUGAR SPRINGS

Shadows of the Past

Learning to Trust Again

A Perfect Match

A Fresh Start

Recipe for Love

MAPLE COVE

Another Chance at Love

A New Beginning

Coming Home

The Lyrics of Love

Finding Home

HOLLYWOOD NAME GAME

Hollywood Heartbreaker

Hollywood Flirt

Hollywood Player

Hollywood Double

Hollywood Enigma

LAWMEN OF THE WEST

Runaway Hearts

Blind Faith

Love and the Lawman

Ballad Beauty

SAGEBRUSH BRIDES

A Game of Chance

Written in the Cards

Outlaw Muse

KNIGHTS OF REDEMPTION

A Bit of Heaven on Earth

A Knight for Kallen

SUDDENLY A DUKE

Portrait of the Duke

Music for the Duke

Polishing the Duke

Designs on the Duke

Fashioning the Duke

Love Blooms with the Duke

Training the Duke

Investigating the Duke

SECOND SONS OF LONDON

Educated by the Earl

Debating with the Duke

Empowered by the Earl

Made for the Marquess

Dubious about the Duke

Valued by the Viscount

Meant for the Marquess

DUKES DONE WRONG

Discouraging the Duke

Deflecting the Duke

Disrupting the Duke

Delighting the Duke

Destiny with a Duke

DUKES OF DISTINCTION

Duke of Renown

Duke of Charm

Duke of Disrepute

Duke of Arrogance

Duke of Honor

SOLDIERS AND SOULMATES

To Heal an Earl

To Tame a Rogue

To Trust a Duke

To Save a Love

To Win a Widow

THE ST. CLAIRS

Devoted to the Duke

Midnight with the Marquess

Embracing the Earl

Defending the Duke

Suddenly a St. Clair

STANDALONE ROMANTIC THRILLERS

Leave Yesterday Behind

Illusions of Death

About the Author

USA Today and Amazon Top 100 bestselling author Alexa Aston lives with her husband in a Dallas suburb, where she eats her fair share of dark chocolate and plots out stories while she walks every morning. She enjoys travel, sports, and binge-watching—and never misses an episode of *Survivor*.

Alexa brings her characters to life in steamy historicals, contemporary romances, and romantic suspense novels that resonate with passion, intensity, and heart.

KEEP UP WITH ALEXA
Visit her website
Newsletter Sign-Up

MORE WAYS TO CONNECT WITH ALEXA